THE MARILIANS

Book Two of the Earth's Angels Trilogy

By Beth Worsdell

Beth Worsdell
Visit my website at www.bethworsdellauthor.com

Printed in the United States of America

First Printing: August 2019
Beth Worsdell Publishing

Dedicated

To my husband, kids, family and close friends, thank you for always believing in me.

Thank you to everyone who has purchased, read and reviewed Earth's Angels. Your support and encouragement have been marvelous and inspiring. I truly appreciate every single like, share and follow from you all. Telling your friends and family about my books helps me more that you know. I have been blown away with the reviews I have received on Amazon and Goodreads. It is always humbling to read your wonderful reviews, and they inspire me to keep promoting my work.

Keep chasing your dreams my angels and believe in yourselves.

"OUR PLANET IS THE GREATEST SHOW IN THE UNIVERSE, SHOWING US BEAUTY EVERY DAY, IF ONLY WE TOOK THE TIME TO NOTICE."

QUOTE BY BETH WORSDELL.

CHAPTER 1

"Mom…. mom, wake up," a very soft feminine voice said gently.

I could feel a soft hand stroking my upper forearm, as I started to come around. When I began to open my eyes, I heard the familiar soft voice speak again.

"Mom, wake up, please!" the voice pleaded.

It took me a few more minutes to realize that whoever it was, was speaking to me. My mind was quickly trying to bring me back to my senses and reality.

I opened my eyes fully and slowly turned my head to the soft voice. It was my daughter Holly, and she looked utterly distraught; her angel boyfriend, Nalik, was standing next to her holding her other hand. He appeared to be almost as distraught as my daughter.

"James!" I said, as I quickly tried to get myself up in a sudden panic, "Where's your dad?"

Holly and Nalik both moved quickly to help me sit up on the bed that I found myself on. Looking around, I quickly realized that we were back in our room, and I was laying on my own bed.

"James is in the medical room; he is being healed by Harrik and Zanika. Please do not worry Mel; they believe he will make a full recovery," Nalik assured me.

"I thought that woman had killed him; she tossed him over the banister...... as if he was nothing!" I sobbed.

Then I completely broke down as the memory of James being thrown and left for broken on the floor ran through my mind, and my heart broke all over again. Huge sobs escaped me as Holly wrapped her slender arms around my shaking shoulders, and within moments, Holly was sobbing too. I felt my whole body shaking as I cried out the emotional pain and the guilt I felt for not being able to stop my husband from getting hurt.

"James was badly injured, but we can heal him completely, Mel, do not worry. It will take time, but he will be back with you soon," Nalik said kindly.

Nalik waited patiently as I released all the emotions from my body and my soul. He only came forward when both of our sobs began to subside. I felt his feather-light hand touch my back, and a soothing calmness started to spread throughout my body.

Once I had my emotions back under control, Holly reluctantly released me. Nalik's other hand was resting on the side of her waist, and I knew she was probably just as grateful to him as I was for his soothing power.

I took her hand in mine, and I looked into her tear-stained, flushed and worried face.

"Thank you, my darling," I told her, as I wiped away the tears from her flushed pink cheeks, "Where are your brothers and sisters?"

She wiped the rest of her tears away with her hands while trying to compose herself.

"They're with dad, Harrik and Zanika. Do you feel up to going to the medical unit?" she asked, "The Angels have healed you already, but you may still feel a bit squiffy," she added.

"I'm ok; I want to go see him now," I told her earnestly, "I want to be there when your dad wakes up."

Every fiber in me needed to be with James. I had to see with my own eyes that he really was alive. All I could picture in my head was my husband being thrown off the walkway, his body crashing to the ground. Then the love of my life, lying still and broken on the floor of the Cruiser. I suddenly felt sick to my stomach.

Nalik moved towards me and put his hand onto my arm. As soon as I felt his touch; I felt the calmness spread through me again and all my anxiety and worry fading to nothing. I suddenly felt strong and determined.

"Thank you, Nalik; I needed that," I told him, feeling extremely grateful. I looked back to Holly, "Come on; let's go and see your dad."

When we walked into the white-walled medical unit, James was lying motionless on a bed. There were no other patients in the room and no hustle and bustle of a normal medical facility.

Zanika was stood at the top end of the bed with her hands on either side of James' head. I could see her white shimmering healing power flowing from her palms and gently soaking into James hair and skin. His face was still showing some bruising, but the bruises were green and yellow, indicating that they were old and gradually fading.

I ran my eyes along his body, which seemed to look a normal shape under the silvery sheet he was covered with. Harrik was stood at James' waist; one of his hands was hovering over James' chest area, and his other hand was over my husband's hips. Again, I could see Harrik's power flowing into James.

I actually felt quite comforted, seeing the angels' healing power and energy flowing into my husband. It meant that he was already on the road to recovery and that I would be getting my love back.

A movement to my right caught my attention, and when I turned to look; my heart broke again. There were our other kids, all draped over each other exhausted and fast asleep. They obviously didn't want to leave their dad, knowing he was so badly hurt. The angels had draped silvery sheets over them and had given them soft pillows to rest against. My kids all looked so drained but yet still very angelic.

Not wanting to wake the kids, I quietly walked towards the bed and my unconscious husband with Holly and Nalik following behind. I only had eyes for James. I could feel my heart pounding in my chest as I reached out to touch his hand, sliding it into my own. He felt warm and alive and relief flowed through me like a wave.

I watched his chest slowly rise and fall, covered in the glow from Harrik's power. Lifting my head, my eyes connected with Harrik's. It was as if he could feel every emotion that I was feeling. His peacock, sapphire blue eyes swirled with silver, reflecting the storm of relief, anger, guilt and frustration I felt inside me.

"There was nothing you could have done to stop this from happening, Mel," a strong but gentle female voice said from behind me.

Instantly, I knew who it was, and I could feel her power and emotions filling the room. When I turned to face Christik, she was gliding towards me in all her grace. I suddenly felt as vulnerable as a small child and when she reached for me; I walked into her open arms without hesitation.

Christik held and comforted me, just as I had comforted April when she'd learned that her girlfriend had died. It was only at that moment that I truly appreciated how much we all needed each other. Not only to heal from everything that had already happened but also to heal from the battle that we were all going to be recovering from soon.

I cried, letting everything out as Christik's power glowed around me. Her arms and wings were drawing me in and making me feel safe and protected. I don't know how long we stood there for. I don't know how long Christik held me, but I needed every second.

She sensed when I had received what I needed, slowly folding her wings behind her back. Moving her hands to the tops of my arms, she looked at me with love and compassion.

"You do know; you could not have stopped this, don't you, Mel?" Christik said as she looked deeply into my eyes.

It felt as though she were looking into my heart and soul. Her calming power flowed through my body, and I could feel it in every fiber of my being. Not only did I hear her words, but I could also feel them.

"Yes, I know I couldn't have stopped this," I replied, knowing in my heart it was true.

Christik moved her hands down to mine and held them. Her power was still glowing with the contact between our skin.

"If you had engaged the woman, you would have been possibly killed. Your baby may have been killed too, Mel," she said firmly, "I am sure that James would not have wanted either of you to be harmed in any way."

She was right; the last thing James would have wanted was for any of us to be hurt or killed, even if it was from trying to protect him.

"Be with your husband Mel," Christik told me softly.

I didn't need to be asked twice. I turned back to James and stood next to his bed. I stroked his bruised but handsome face, and my heart ached for him to wake up.

I was aware that Holly and Nalik had sat down with the kids, cuddling them while they slept. None of the kids moved, so they were clearly exhausted.

I looked up to Zanika, who was still sending her healing power through James; her eyes showed her effort and concentration.

"How long before he's fully healed, Zanika?" I asked her quietly.

She smiled at me with understanding and love.

"We hope that James will be healed completely in a few days, Mel. He has many injuries, but the worst injuries are to his spine and his brain. They take the longest to heal. We believe he may be able to hear you if you would all like to talk to him as we work."

"Thank you, thank you all," I said, as I looked at all three of the angels in turn.

Christik, Zanika and Harrik nodded their heads. My gaze moved back to my husband, his chest still rising and falling gently with each breath. I leaned forward until my lips brushed against his ear.

"You're going to be back with me soon, baby, my other half!" I whispered softly.

We spent a few hours with James; the kids had all woken up and had taken turns talking to him, telling him what had been going on and promising to look after the baby and me. All the kids were so protective that it made my heart swell with pride.

"You all need to get some rest and some food. I will stay and talk to James until you return," Nalik told us kindly.

I was so touched by Nalik's offer; how could I have possibly turned it down. I also knew that he was right. We really did need some rest and food. As I thought about food, my stomach growled loudly, and I felt the baby flutter.

"Thank you Nalik; we would appreciate that very much. I believe my stomach and the baby agree with you," I told him with a warm and humorous smile.

We left the medical room with Christik, with the kids walking closely together as if they wanted to continue to comfort each other. There were no conversations between them, and I knew that would probably change once they'd eaten and had some of their energy back.

I also knew our kids were probably not only in shock because of what had happened, but also because they probably realized that their dad wasn't the invincible father they thought he was. We were all guilty of believing that our parents were infallible and indestructible until something bad happens and, no matter our age, we all live in denial of our parent's immortality.

"Would you mind if I eat with you and the children?" Christik asked, breaking me from my thoughts.

"I would love for you to join us Christik. I think I need a friend right now," I told her honestly.

7

Christik had obviously requested our food because the moment we arrived at our rooms, we could smell the scent of fresh vegetables and fruit. Yet again, I felt the greatest need for lots and lots of bacon.

What was strange was that I'd never been a bacon type of person, always preferring granola and Croissants to the cooked breakfasts that James and the kids liked.

"I do not know what food you are thinking of Mel, but I do not think we can provide it for you," Christik said, with confusion on her beautiful face.

I smiled at her, knowing that she was picking up on my pregnancy craving.

"Part of being human and pregnant, Christik, is sometimes having to deal with strange cravings for food we wouldn't normally eat. For me right now it's bacon, which is a cured and cooked meat from pigs," I explained.

Suddenly, all the kid's ears picked up on my words, and they all looked around with looks on their faces that said, '*who said bacon.*' They were so much like James. He only heard me if I mentioned food, beer or football normally–typical male selective hearing.

"Don't worry Christik, even if you could produce a plate full of bacon, I don't think I could eat it anyway," I assured her.

"We could eat bacon!" Abigail and Harrison called over in unison, as they took seats at the small table.

"Yes, I'm sure you all could," I told them with a smirk.

I followed Christik as she glided to the table and chairs, taking seats next to the kids. They all looked so drained, even after having their sleep in the medical room. '*My poor babies*' I thought to myself as my heart ached from their emotional pain.

"Are you ok, Mom?" Anthony asked as he leaned across and put his hand on mine.

"I'm fine now I know your dad's going to be alright, darling," I told him, hoping he believed me.

I didn't want the kids worrying about their dad and me at the same time. I turned my attention to Christik. I felt curious about our current situation with Peter and his bitch of a wife who'd nearly killed my husband.

"What happened after I blacked out at the cruiser, Christik?" I asked.

"Ooh, we've been desperate to know too. No one has told us anything!" Holly stated bluntly.

Christik looked at all of us with compassion and understanding.

"We are very confused at the moment, and we find ourselves in a unique situation," she told us calmly, "I did not see what kind of magic your baby girl created to protect you, Mel. However, I did feel it, and it was very powerful."

"Woah!!" Abigail said in aww, "Our baby sister's powerful!"

I couldn't help but smile at Abigail's expression of sheer wonder.

"I heard you call 'Star of David' to me, Mel, so that is what we did. My angels and I already had Peter surrounded, so we used your technique, and we managed to trap him," she explained.

"Where is he now?" I asked, feeling my heart pound again at the memories.

Peter ripping off his ski goggles and revealing his fiery blood-red eyes seemed to be burned into my brain. I never thought, no, I hoped that I would never witness those evil eyes in a human in real life. I felt my body shudder from my head to my toes.

Christik picked up on my emotions straight away, and she leaned over to me, placing her hand on mine.

"Peter is secure in a holding room with his wife," Christik assured me, "I am afraid because he is as powerful now as the Marilian, we have had to contain him like the Marilian. He will not be harmed."

"And what about his wife?" I asked as anger started to simmer within me.

I instantly felt Christik's power flow into me through her hand contact and, when I looked down at our connected hands, I could see the ice white glow between them.

"I'm sorry, Christik. I'm trying to keep control, but every time I think of Peter's wife, I feel so much anger towards her for what she did to James," I explained.

Christik looked at me with compassion in her sapphire eyes.

"I understand how hard it is for you, Mel. You do not need to apologize for being human. Your protectiveness for your family and those you care about are one of your best human qualities," she said kindly, "I would like you to come with me after we have eaten to see Peter's wife. I know it is the last thing you would like to do Mel. However, I believe you healed her corruption. Or rather you and your baby healed her," Christik added.

The memory of walking up to the shimmering blue bubble my baby daughter and I created came back to me. I remembered watching the woman's eyes as they turned from fiery blood-red back to the human green eyes she'd been born with.

"Is she still inside the blue bubble the baby made?" I asked with a slightly shaky voice as I looked into Christik's face.

The kids weren't saying a word. They sat in silence with intrigue and confusion on their young faces, apart from Harrison who was watching and stuffing his face at the same time.

"That is why I need you to come with me, Mel. Kay is still inside the blue fluid bubble. So, we need to figure out how to get her out and find out if you and your baby can heal Peter too," Christik said.

I felt completely torn at her words. I still felt the anger trying to surface, but I also rationalized that this whole situation wasn't Peter and Kay's fault. They didn't ask to be corrupted by the Marilian, and I was positive that they had just wanted to live their new life, happy and hopeful like the rest of us. I suddenly felt another wave of guilt flow through me.

"You cannot allow yourself to feel guilty for others' actions, Mel. Your anger was normal, and now you are processing that anger. Helping Peter and Kay will soothe your soul, Mel."

As I looked into Christik's eyes again, I knew she was right.

"We all feel angry, Mom, we're in this together," Holly added.

Looking at my children's faces, I was again reminded how amazing they were. They were now so mature for their ages and so strong. Pride and love began to replace the anger, and it was a relief.

"Yes, we are in this together, darling," I told Holly.

I slipped my hand from Christik's, gave her a warm smile, and then I turned to face all my kids.

"So, I'd like you all to come with us," I said, "If that's ok with Christik."

The kids all looked at Christik with expectant and hopeful eyes.

"It will hopefully be good for them to see what their sister can do," Christik answered with a smile, "Afterwards, we need to travel back to the Gate of the Gods in Peru, as our elders are arriving today."

I think we'd all forgotten about the elders arriving, with everything else that had happened since Stonehenge. It was hard to believe that only two days before, we'd witnessed the Angels summoning them. It felt like a lifetime ago, and by the look of my kids' faces, they had definitely forgotten about it too.

As we ate our food, there seemed to be growing anticipation in the air, a growing excitement that was tangible. I wasn't looking forward to seeing Peter and Kay again, but I was really looking forward to meeting the elders. I wondered how Christik was feeling, considering it had been so long since she'd seen them. It was going to be interesting to see if the angels had the same paternal bonds as we humans had.

"Ok, are we all ready to see Peter and Kay?" I asked the kids, as I stood up and began to put the stone cups back on the tray before us.

"Born ready, Mom," Harrison said, giving me his dad's winning smile.

"This is going to be very interesting," Holly added, her voice showing her concern.

Holly was very much like me in that she always looked at all angles of situations, weighing up all the options and eventualities.

"It's going to be fine. Hopefully, we can have both Peter and Kay back to normal and with everyone else at the cruiser in next to no time," I told them.

I was trying to sound a lot more positive than I felt.

We made our way down to the holding room along the pearlescent corridor, Christik leading the way with her usual graceful glide. The kids were talking between themselves about the tasks they still had to do with the others in our group. I was so proud of how driven they all seemed to be and very impressed with their determination in defeating the Marilians. I couldn't help but smile again as I listened to them.

"You should be proud of your children, Mel," Christik said, startling me from my thoughts.

'Would I ever get used to the Angels being able to feel our emotions?' I very much doubted it. I gave Christik a responding smile.

"They are quite impressive, aren't they," I told her.

"Yes, they are Mel, and they are going to be a major part of rebuilding your world!" She said with conviction.

"We are here," Christik added as she indicated to an archway we were approaching.

It appeared to be the same as the other holding room entrances in size, and it had the hieroglyphs at the top, glowing against the background.

Just as we got close to the archway, two red-headed angels appeared next to us, making us all jump out of our skins.

13

"Bloody hell, you could have given us some warning, Christik, I nearly had a heart attack!" I exclaimed, as my heart hammered in my chest.

The kids all started laughing as Christik and the two angels all looked at me with wide eyes. Anthony leaned forward, placing his hands on his knees, taking long slow breaths.

"Looks like Anthony nearly had one too, Mom," Abigail added, as she reached forward and stroked his back.

He straightened himself up and pulled his shoulders back.

"I'm good," Anthony said as he held up a hand, "Cheers Abigail," he added, giving his baby sister a wink.

"My apologies everyone, I did not think to inform you that I had arranged support, in case the situation turns awry," Christik told us with sincerity; "I will try to be more understanding of your human needs. Shall we?" She asked as she glided towards the shimmering barrier that sealed the entrance.

The two angel guards dipped their heads to us all before one raised his arm, indicating for us to follow them. Just as my heart had started to slow back to a normal rate, it began to speed up again as my nervousness grew.

CHAPTER 2

As Christik reached the barrier, she raised her arm, her hand glowing bright white as she deactivated it. She passed through it with ease, and I followed suit with the kids and the angel guards following behind.

The room was plain and white, just like the holding room the Marilian was contained in. On the left side of the room was Kay. She was still floating peacefully inside the shimmering blue bubble, and in the corner, on the right side of the room, was her husband, Peter.

The evil rage coming from Peter as his eyes settled on Christik was so strong that my knees abruptly felt weak, and I honestly thought I was going to drop to the floor. Before my legs buckled, the two guards rushed forward, slipping their hands under my arms on either side of me, taking my weight.

"I'm ok, honestly, I'm alright," I quickly assured them, not wanting my kids to worry; "I just wasn't prepared for the rage Peter's giving off. It's much stronger than last time," I added.

"Yes, his rage is very strong Mel," Christik agreed, "It is strange, he is Marilian inside through and through. However, even with his corruption, he does still seem to feel protective towards his wife. Even though she has been healed."

I was sure my confusion showed on my face, just as it showed on Christik's.

"I don't think he can sense that she's been healed, Christik, I think the bubble is shielding her," I explained.

"I believe you may be correct, Mel. Let us try and free Kay, so we can deal with Peter," she replied.

After a few minutes, the guards released me, sensing that my strength was back to normal. I could still feel Peter's rage, but now, I was prepared. Instead of his rage bombarding my body and soul, it now felt as if it were flowing over me. When I turned to my kids, they were already over with Kay. They were surrounding the bubble that enclosed Kay's body, studying the weird sight before them. Abigail lifted her hand, and she ran it palm down over its surface.

The shimmering fluid shifted beneath her hand, and ripples began to form from the pressure of her touch. The tiny ripples created larger ripples and, like ocean currents, each set of new ripples were large and stronger. The kids all began to move away, their eyes becoming wide with surprise and uncertainty.

The ripples were becoming miniature waves, and they were moving towards Kay's feet, rapidly getting bigger as they created yet more waves. Within seconds the shimmering blue waves were moving over the end of the elongated bubble and were traveling underneath Kay's suspended form. Soon, the waves were looking more turbulent, and I could feel the worry emanating from my kids. Their worry and Peter's evil anger combined was just too much. I felt my baby girl's magic building within me, and I was sure she was sensing her siblings' growing unease. Neither of us liked it at all.

"Enough!" I declared, as I raised my palms towards the turbulent fluid, which was coming towards us once again. I walked forward with purpose, letting my instincts take over. As soon as I faced my palms towards Kay's fluid prison; my hands began to glow a bright blue. I was expecting the fluid to settle and stop; however, that didn't happen, and I was amazed that Kay's body wasn't moving, even with the turbulent motion around her. Not even her hair was moving; it was perfectly still around her head.

I looked over at Christik, hoping for help or words of guidance. Instead, I heard her voice in my head as she smiled reassuringly at me. *'You can do this, Mel, trust yourself and your baby daughter.'*

I turned back to face the growing blue waves that were crashing against each other with great force. Nervously, I moved closer, and with each step; I could feel the power building within me and increasing in my hands. As soon as I got within two feet of the shimmering turbulent bubble; the nearest waves reached for my outstretched palms.

I braced myself for the violent contact, expecting to be forcefully thrown backwards. My whole body tensed for the impact, and I closed my eyes in fear. As the blue fluid make contact; I felt a massive rush of energy flow through my hands and into my whole being. Opening my eyes in surprise, I looked before me. I was adsorbing the fluid from the bubble, and my whole body was glowing with the powerful energy.

The fluid surrounding Kay was lessoning by the second, and her body was slowly lowering to the ground as the energy around her reduced. Still, there wasn't any movement from her whatsoever.

My kids stared in awe with their mouths agape as they watched the scene before them. Their faces no longer showing panic or worry but more surprise and relief. Their eyes kept looking from me to Kay, watching the whole magical process happen.

My body felt so energized as the shimmering energy soaked back into me and my baby girl. It reminded me of how I felt when Christik and the angels reactivated Stonehenge. The flow was steady as my body took it all in, while the bubble became thinner and thinner around Kay.

Within moments, patches of Kay's body and clothing began to be clearly visible, and as her scent was released, Peter began to snarl loudly. The last of the shimmering blue fluid entered my palms in a trickle, and Kay's body made full contact with the floor.

Christik glided over to Kay instantly, her glowing palms moving over Kay's body as she checked her over. We all watched silently, all of us hoping that Kay was going to be alright. As Peter's snarls grew louder, I noticed that Kay's foot was starting to twitch and subconsciously, we all moved forward. Now that Kay was free from her containment, I assumed that Peter could sense and smell that she was healed and was no longer the same as him.

Christik looked up to me.

"She is fully healed, Mel, and she is waking," she said with a raised voice, over the noise of Peter's guttural snarls and growls. The evil coming from him was really starting to make my skin crawl. All I could sense from him was his murderous wrath.

"Should we remove her from the room, away from Peter?" I asked Christik.

I was concerned about Kay's reaction when she came around. We didn't know if she'd remember that her husband had been corrupted, and the last thing we needed was a hysterical or panic-stricken lady.

"If we remove her, it may make Peter harder to deal with," Christik replied, "My Angels can remove her instantly if we need too," she added.

"So, how are we going to heal him?" Anthony asked as he pointed at Peter behind him with his thumb.

"Your mother and baby sister are the only ones who can heal him," Christik explained to him, "Your sister has a unique gift, which she can channel through your mother."

"I really don't want to go near the bastard," I told them, being completely honest, "I know it's not his fault, Christik, but he really is bloody frightening."

"I don't want you to go anywhere near him either, Mom!" Abigail added, her eyes wide with uneasiness.

"I understand Mel. I am hoping that you can heal him while he is still restrained," Christik said.

Just as Christik began to rise from kneeling next to Kay's body, Kay abruptly flipped over. She scrambled to her hands and knees, her head turning quickly as she tried to scan the room to get her bearings. I could hear her quick breaths as her anxiety heightened. Kay was in fight or flight mode.

Christik straightened herself and backed away from Kay, giving her the space to adjust to her new surroundings. Raising her palms, showing she was no threat, Christik spoke to her softly as the rest of us followed suit and backed away.

"Kay, you are safe," Christik told her, "Do you remember me?"

I'm sure Kay heard Christik speak, but she carried on looking around the room wildly. Her eyes were darting from one person and angel to the next until her eyes landed on her husband.

"Peter, what the hell!" She shouted in panic.

Suddenly, she tried to rush forward on wobbly legs, desperately trying to reach him. I wasn't sure if she'd noticed that his eyes were blood red. As she tried to get to Peter, his snarls became louder and more aggressive, and just as the two angel guards rushed forward to stop her, she started to stagger backwards. Kay was staring at her husband's fiery eyes; her mouth was agape as the realization hit.

Kay turned, almost knocking one of the angel guards over in her rush to get away. Luckily, the angel was able to steady himself, and he grabbed her arm. Instantly, there was a bright white light emanating from the contact between them. She turned to look at the angel who had stopped her in her tracks. The angel was calm, and he looked at Kay with compassion. As her eyes connected with his and his power flowed through her, calming her down, he spoke gently.

"You are safe, Kay, please give yourself time to adjust. We will explain everything. Your husband will be fine," he told her, as her body started to relax.

"PPP Peter's eyes!" She stammered, "His eyes are red!"

The angel's hand glowed brighter as he tried to calm her rising panic.

"We are going to try to heal your husband, Kay. Please do not panic," Christik told her, as she glided forward to reach her.

Christik smiled kindly at Kay, and she raised her hand to point at me.

"Mel's new baby has a special gift, Kay. It was Mel and her baby daughter she is carrying who healed you," Christik explained.

Kay's eyes opened even wider and then her brows furrowed as she took in what Christik was saying.

"I was like that?" She asked as she looked and pointed at her husband again in horror.

"Yes, you were, Kay," Christik told her, "A Marilian managed to stow away on one of our crafts when we left their planet. Before we caught him, he was able to corrupt you and Peter. Do you not have any memory of that happening?" She asked her softly.

Kay looked at Christik with her brows furrowing even deeper as she strained to remember something, anything.

"No, I don't remember anything about a Marilian," Kay answered.

It sounded as if she was relieved to have no memory of being changed, and I didn't blame her. After what I saw in my dream, I wouldn't want to remember something like that either. Kay looked to the angel who was calming her, and she smiled at him sweetly.

"I think I'm ok now. Thank you for helping me," she told the angel with gratitude evident in her voice.

The angel smiled back at her, and he dipped his head to her in respect.

"You are welcome, Kay," the angel told her, as he released his hold on her arm.

"Are we going to fix my husband now? Kay asked as she looked at Christik again.

Christik looked to me and then back to Kay.

"Yes, we are," Christik told her, "Mel, are you ready?"

I have to be honest. I was nowhere near ready and just the thought of going anywhere Peter was again making my skin crawl. Also, I had no clue as to what I was supposed to do to heal him. With Kay, it was different because, at the time, my life and the life of my baby was in danger. Taking back the energy from Kay had felt easy too as if I was just taking back what was ours, or should I say, what was my baby's. I just wanted to get it over with.

Pulling my big girl pants on, I strutted over to Peter, and the kids instinctively followed me, standing behind me as if they were my back up. When I turned to look for Christik, she was smiling proudly at them.

"I am sorry children, but you need to give your mother some space. We do not know what is going to happen," she told them gently.

Their faces showed how put out they felt and who could blame them when their dad had been hurt so badly? Reluctantly, they moved away and stood next to Kay, giving Christik and the guards the room to flank me. I appreciated having the angels so close, as I knew they would step in within a split second. I turned to Christik.

"I don't know what to do," I told her; "It just happened last time, I think the baby did it to protect me, and I'm not feeling anything right now."

Christik looked very thoughtful for a moment, seemingly weighing up some options.

"The only definite way would be to release Peter, to recreate the dangerous situation and activate your baby's protective instinct," Christik explained, "However, I am not prepared to do that, Mel. Not only will I not willingly put you in danger, but I don't think James would ever forgive me, or your children," she added.

I looked to my kids, and they were positively glaring at Christik for even suggesting it. It made me smile to see how protective they were, just like their dad. He would have been very proud of them if he'd been with us.

"I agree, that definitely wouldn't be a good idea," I said with a smile, and then I became serious, "He's already making me feel scared, I think just getting really close to him may trigger something," I explained.

Christik nodded in agreement, and she lifted her hand, indicating that I could start. The kids looked so tense. I really didn't want them there, but I knew that I didn't have a hope in hells chance of getting them to leave.

I turned back to Peter, who hadn't stopped the snarling the whole time. In fact, every time he looked at his wife, he got worse, and he certainly didn't like the fact that the angels and I were getting closer. *'He's going to be seriously pissed in a minute,'* I thought to myself. At just the thought of getting closer to him; my heart began to race in my chest, and I could feel the anxiety coming off my kids and Kay filling the room.

I reluctantly started to take hesitant steps towards the Marilian's minion, and his eyes firstly widened in surprise, and then they narrowed as he let his hatred for me flow. His animosity was so strong that I was struggling to breathe under the weight of it, and my heart hammered, matching my racing pulse. I knew I had to keep going forward to get as close as possible.

Within moments, I was standing less than a foot away from Peter. I could feel his hot breath on my face, and it turned my stomach. My body began to tremble as my baby girl's protective instincts kicked in. She didn't want me anywhere near Peter. She could feel his evil soul and murderous instincts just as much as I could.

I knew that my hands were beginning to glow with her shimmering blue energy as I could feel it. My whole body was tingling, and I felt my baby's power building in my stomach. The energy was flowing through my body, moving down my arms and into my palms and fingers. As I moved my fingers; I could feel it building and building. '*We can do this baby girl,*' I told my daughter, knowing she would feel my sentiment or hear my words.

Instantly, I felt her energy peak, and I instinctively raised both of my palms towards Peter's restrained body. His eyes enlarged with shock and sudden fear. The blue power shot from my hands in an explosion of light, and this time, I kept my eyes open. My fear of Peter was gone as I accepted and relished the power flowing from my child and me.

The energy flowed quickly, hitting Peter's body, and then it began to swirl around him in the same way it reacted when Abigail touched it; when it encased Kay. Miniature waves crashed around his body as it covered him, and he was freaking out.

There was nothing he could do to escape what was happening, and he knew it. He strained against the silver vines that were wrapped around his body, and he strained his neck, trying to lift his face away from the blue energy that was now moving up his chest towards it. Peters snarls were now becoming more desperate as he realized that his efforts were useless.

Then abruptly, it was as if he just gave up. Peter stopped struggling against the silver vines, his body losing its tension and beginning to sag against his restraints. Slowly, his head lowered, and when his eyes connected with mine, I gasped. His blood-red fiery eyes were beginning to change as I watched in fascination. The fiery red was draining from his pupils like the color was being washed away. I could see his normal eye color, a lovely green beginning to come through, and as the red vanished, the blue energy swallowed his forehead and head completely.

Peter was completely cocooned inside a shimmering blue bubble just as Kay had been. Only this time, I was still awake, and I instinctively knew that I shouldn't bother lowering my hands. It felt like it wasn't over.

"What's going to happen now?" Kay asked, with shock and worry evident in her voice.

"Be patient Kay, and please do not worry; it is not over yet," Christik told her gently.

Christik could obviously sense the same thing as I could, that my baby was getting ready to take her healing energy back. Within seconds, the feeling in my body changed. It was as if a tide changed deep inside me and instead of the energy building and wanting to burst free, now it felt like a void, wanting and needing to be filled again.

As I stared at Peter's motionless body and his green eyes, the flow of blue energy turned. The current of shimmering blue waves changed direction, and the flow started to come back to me. It felt amazing as the flow returned and the fact that I could no longer feel the evil animosity coming from Peter was a massive relief. I think all of us were gradually relaxing now the whole atmosphere in the room had changed for the better. We could all sense that Peter was healed again.

While Peter's body began to gradually appear, his wife started to walk forward. I couldn't blame her for wanting to check for herself that he was back. I think I would have felt the same way if it was James. In fact, I know I would have been.

The blue fluid receded from Peter's head and face first, and as it ebbed away from his neck and chest, his eyes started to try and focus. He looked so confused, and I felt bad for him as his brain registered that he was restrained and unable to move. Kay realized what was happening too.

"Don't worry, Peter, it will be over soon; you're going to be fine," she assured her husband. I think that was going to be easier said than done. He was back to himself, but he was vulnerable, and he knew it.

Christik glided to my side with the two guards, and all three raised their hands to show they were of no threat.

"Trust us and your wife Peter; we are healing you. You will be alright in a moment and released as soon as it is over," Christik told him kindly.

Her eyes never left his as his brain still tried to rationalize the situation. Gradually, his body and face calmed. We could actually see him processing and relaxing at the same time. Why wouldn't he trust the words of his wife, and also the angels who we all knew wouldn't lie.

When the last of the healing energy entered my palms, I lowered my hands. I was so relieved for it to be over, and I was thrilled that it had actually worked. The guards glided to either side of him, dipping their heads in respect and showing Peter they were there for support while Christik raised her palms.

Instantly, Christik's hands began to glow with her white power, and the silver vines that were wrapped around Peter's body started to slither away. A silver pool began to form inside the gold disc that was underneath Peter's feet.

Minutes later, Peter was free, and the guards took him by the arms to help him down from his place of imprisonment. The gold disc that was above his head slowly descended until it met the disc that had been under Peter's feet, and then both were gently lowered to the floor. No sooner had his feet touched the ground, Kay rushed forward flinging herself into his arms; sobbing out of sheer relief.

"Woooo, whooo!" I heard behind me.

When I turned; I found my kids absolutely beaming. I think they were all just as relieved and thrilled as I was, that it was all over.

"What the hell happened?" I heard Peter say in a deep voice.

Kay was still wrapped around him, sobbing softly with her face buried in his neck. He was looking at Christik with confusion on his face. He must have realized that Kay wasn't in a fit state to explain anything, even if she had known what had happened.

Christik looked at Peter with understanding; she could sense not only his confusion but also the worry for his wife.

"You have both been through a lot, Peter, let us take you back to your cabin so we can explain everything," she told him gently.

Peter was too overwhelmed to say anything more, but he nodded in agreement.

"Mel, if you would like to rest with your children back at your rooms; I will come and get you later if that is ok with you?" Christik said.

"Yes, that's fine, I could do with chilling out for a bit," I told her honestly.

CHAPTER 3

Christik and the angel guards used their power to take Peter and Kay back to their cabin at the holding structure. Kay gave all of us huge hugs and thanks before leaving, and Peter shook hands. It was going to take Christik a while to explain to them what had happened, but at least she could reassure them that the Marilian responsible for what had happened was secure and couldn't attack and change anyone else.

When the kids and I got back to our rooms, we were all buzzing. I had every intention of chilling, but after releasing Kay and healing Peter, I still felt supercharged. The kids were also full of excitement, and it was all they could talk about. While they were talking among themselves, I took a moment to touch my com around my neck to check on James. '*Zanika, are you still with James?*' I asked. I didn't have to wait long for my angel friend to reply. '*Yes, Mel. Harrik and I are still with James,*' she answered. '*How is he doing?*' I asked, desperate to know of any changes.

I wanted to be there with my husband, but I knew that the kids needed me to spend time with them, even if they didn't know it. '*James is healing well, Mel,*' she said '*His head injuries are nearly healed completely. We believe he will be back with you all by tomorrow,'* she added. *'Thank you both, I owe you everything,'* I told her sincerely.

I knew she wouldn't be able to sense how grateful I was as we weren't close enough, so I wanted to tell her to make sure that she knew. *'You do not owe us anything, Mel. You and your family are a gift to us,'* she replied, *'If anything, we owe you. I will inform you as soon as James is awake.'*

It meant a lot to hear her words. I knew she would be true to her words and would let me know. I couldn't wait until he was awake. It would make him being ok real and not just a hope.

I told the kids how their dad was doing, and their relief was clearly evident. They had become so close to their dad while I'd been in my long sleep state, and it made my heart full of joy to see it. We all seemed to have a greater appreciation for family now as well as friendships.

Just as Anthony was asking another question about James, there was a tap on our archway entrance.

"Come in," I called, half expecting it to be Christik, although that would have been very quick.

Hulaz glided into our room with a stone tray of refreshments and behind her was a young lady I recognized straightway. April looked very shy and uncomfortable as she walked behind Hulaz and immediately, I wanted to give her another hug. After losing her girlfriend and now being alone, I felt very protective of her, and I'd been asking after her on a regular basis.

"I found April outside your rooms, and I convinced her to come in with me," Hulaz explained.

"Well I'm very glad you did, Hulaz," I told the angel with a smile on my face.

April looked up at me through her eyelashes, obviously feeling nervous and maybe regretting her decision to come over. I really didn't want her to feel like that. Standing up from my seat, I went over to April, and I wrapped my arms around her small shoulders. The moment my arms were around her, her arms encircled my waist, and she leaned into me with her head resting on my chest.

I couldn't hear her crying, but I could sense that she was. For someone so young, she'd been very brave since she'd woken up. Although she clearly hadn't been coping quite as well as I thought she had, suddenly I felt really guilty for not checking on her more thoroughly.

My kids were quiet and respectful as April let her built up emotions out, and it was a few more minutes before she released her hold from my waist. When she took a couple of steps back, her face was full of tears, and she attempted to quickly wipe them away; her face began to glow pink with her embarrassment.

"You don't need to feel embarrassed, April," I assured her, "Let me introduce you to the rest of your family," I told her with a warm smile.

As soon as I said the words, her eyes became wide with surprise, and her lips began to tremble. I stepped forward and gently wiped away the last of her tears.

"Come on, let's say our hellos," I told her, taking her hand in mine.

I led April over to the seating area where Hulaz and the kids were waiting patiently. My kids all gave her a lovely warm smile as her cheeks continued to glow bright pink. The moment we reached my kids, they all stood and moved towards her.

"Everyone, I'd like you to meet our new family member, April," I said, as I felt April's hand trembling in mine.

Holly was the first to throw her arms around her. I hoped they would get on well as they were so close in age.

"Welcome to the family, April," Holly told her gently, giving April a huge smile.

As soon as Holly released her, Harrison moved forward, also giving her a big friendly hug and saying welcome. By the time all four of my kids had welcomed her, she was positively beaming with happiness. Hulaz looked on with a big smile on her face. She was picking up on April's happy emotions the same as I was.

"So, what do you think, April, would you like to move in and be part of the family?" I asked her.

Her resounding smile spoke volumes.

"Yes please, if that's ok," she said, looking absolutely thrilled.

Holly and Abigail were also looking just as thrilled.

"This is so cool," Holly said to everyone, "Now we have two new sisters," she beamed.

Abigail was bouncing on her heels as her mind worked overtime.

"Us girls are so going to whoop your asses on the next games night," she stated to the boys with a huge grin on her face.

Anthony and Harrison responded with over-exaggerated eye rolls and laughter at her excitement.

"I will arrange for April's belongings to be moved here, and I will arrange another bed for the children's room," Hulaz said.

"Thank you, Hulaz," I said as I sat back down, "Come on kids, let's get eating."

The kids and I happily chatted with April while we drank and ate our snacks. She was very honest, explaining that she'd felt too embarrassed to say that she wasn't coping well and that she had felt very alone. The English lady, Joanne, had suggested that she come to see us, and I was so pleased that she had.

While the kids were telling April about what had happened to Kay and Peter, I heard Christik in my mind. *'Mel, are you and the children ready to greet the Elders with me?'* She asked.

Straight away, my heart began to race. I was really excited to see them arrive and meet them. I knew the kids were very excited too. *'Yes, we can't wait to meet them, Christik,'* I told her. *'We'll meet you at the craft.'*

"Right, kids, it's time to go back to Peru. April, would you like to come with us to greet the Angel elders?" I asked.

April beamed in sync with my kids at the mention of the elders.

"Yes, please!" She answered quickly.

"Awesome. Anthony and Holly, would you like to ask Christine and Nalik if they'd like to come also?" I asked as I rose from my seat; "they can meet us in the hanger."

Soon, we were all arriving at the small craft and greeting Christik, Livik and Jakiz with dipped heads and smiles. Christine was already there with Nalik. Both of their faces lit up at the sight of Anthony and Holly. In fact, Nalik's whole body lit up like a beacon. I could feel their bond becoming stronger, and I couldn't have been happier.

"Shall we board?" Christik asked.

"Yes, kids, you go first," I said, as I indicated for them to get on the craft.

I could feel a nervousness coming from Christik, which was a little unnerving as she was always so confident.

"Are you ok, Christik?" I asked.

Christik looked at me with hesitant eyes. She knew I could sense what she was feeling.

"I am feeling nervous about seeing my parents again," she said honestly, "It has been many of your lifetimes since I have seen them."

I couldn't imagine what it was like to be a being, with a whole different view of time, but I did know what it was like to be a parent. The angels didn't seem that different when it came to love and the value of family and friendship.

"I really don't think you need to be nervous, Christik," I told her truthfully, "I honestly think that you and your parents will reconnect exactly where you left off from the last time you saw them. We parents always see our children as our children, no matter how old they are or how much time passes," I added.

"Really?" She asked in surprise.

"Yes, really. Our love for our children doesn't lessen as they grow up and become independent," I explained, just as Anthony's head popped out of the small craft.

"Are you two coming or what?" He asked with a grin.

Christik smiled and led the way on board.

The rest of the kids were already in their seats, and I could feel their excitement in the cabin and see it in their young faces. Nalik was sat next to Holly, watching her adoringly, and April was sat next to Abigail. It was lovely to see the two girls chatting away to each other.

I was half expecting Hulaz to be piloting the craft, but instead, Livik was at the front, raising her arms to connect with the craft. The moment our seats started to suck our bodies into place, we all looked over to Livik to watch her in action.

As soon as her arms reached out to her sides, the craft responded. The silvery-white vines appeared from the sides of the craft, reaching for her glowing skin. They traveled around her hands, gently snaking their way up her arms, and I could feel the power in the air as the connection grew stronger. It was almost as if the craft came alive at her touch. In seconds, we could feel the craft rise from the hanger floor and start moving towards to exit. The craft picked up its speed the second it was clear of the main craft.

I could hear April asking Abigail lots of questions and the others talking between themselves, and I sat there wishing that James was with us all, my heart aching in my chest.

"James will be back with you soon, Mel," Christik said next to me.

She gave me a knowing smile and placed her hand on my arm. Instantly, I felt her calming power flow through me.

"Thank you," I told her gratefully.

I turned my focus to my kids as we travelled, listening to them catch up on news from Christine. She was telling the kids how everyone was getting on with the projects now that everything was safe again. Although Christik still had extra guards around the cruiser just to be on the safe side.

Before long, I could feel the craft slowing down and then gently descending. The anticipation began to thicken in the air as our excitement grew. As soon as the craft touched the earth, the vines surrounding Livik's arms and hands began to unwind, releasing her. Livik turned as soon as the vines melted back into the craft's walls and the exit opened. It was getting dark outside, but we could still feel the dry heat coming into the craft from outside, and a small gust of wind blew in a sprinkling of dust and tiny stones, which scattered at our feet.

Christik glided out of the craft first, but before she walked away, she turned and used her power to make sure we all had something on our feet. The angels honestly never missed a beat when it came to looking after us and our basic needs. '*They never ceased to impress me,*' I thought to myself.

We quickly followed suit and disembarked the small craft, our feet landing on the arid and dusty ground of Peru. As we looked around at our surroundings, I was blown away with how the sky looked. It was growing darker by the second, with more and more bright stars appearing in the early evening sky. I'd never seen so many stars in my life, and it was breathtaking. I couldn't resist looking up to the heavens while turning in a full circle to really appreciate the bright and numerous stars.

"What are those stones for?" April asked in awe as she looked at the stone circles.

"Those are for Earth's defense," Abigail told her, "The angels created the defenses with the early Peruvian civilizations."

"Woah," April exclaimed, suitably impressed.

Christik, Livik and Jakiz glided to the front of us all with smiles on their faces, obviously enjoying our awe and wonder.

"Please follow us," Christik said.

She began to gracefully glide away with the other two angels and us following behind. We seemed to be heading towards the massive Gate of the Gods we'd witnessed being activated the last time we were there. We walked past the other rings of stones as we headed towards it, and I could feel the powerful energy coming from them. The stone rings were still active, their powerful energy feeding the defensive net in the sky above. It was reassuring to know that the angels would be warned straight away when the Marilians tried to invade.

We followed the angels, and as we reached the Gate of the Gods, it was just as impressive as the last time. In the evening colors of the sky, the surrounding rock frame of the gate looked even more pink, and the center, filled with the angel's powerful energy, looked magnificent in the side of the darker rock face.

"What the heck is that?" April asked in disbelief, which had the other kids laughing.

"It is Amaru Muru, the Gate of the Gods," Livik told her with a humorous smile on her beautiful face, "It is one of seven-star passages on your planet that our elders will be arriving through," she explained.

Christik glided forward toward the stone Gate, and her body began to shimmer with the white glow of her power.

"My other angels are ready at the other star passages," she said quietly, as she started to raise her arms.

We were all silent as we began to feel the power building in the surrounding air. A gentle wind started to blow through my long hair, getting stronger with each second. April was obviously feeling nervous as I could see her inching closer to Abigail and Harrison for reassurance.

Soon, our hair was being whipped around our heads as the force of the wind increased. The sandy soil at our feet was trembling with small stones bouncing on its surface. Christik was glowing brightly as her power grew, and just when I thought she couldn't get any brighter; her power burst forth from her outstretched palms, hitting the energy barrier inside the star passage.

The shimmering barrier absorbed Christik's power, and it started to swirl a mix of silver, white and gold in its center. Around and around it swirled as we all watched in awe, none of us knowing what was going to happen next. The shimmering vortex increased in size as it moved, gradually filling the inside of the gateway until finally, the star gate gave off a massive burst of silvery light. For a moment, I couldn't focus, and all I could see was the light in my eyes like the effect of a camera flash.

I held my breath, and I couldn't look away as my eyes started to refocus. Blinking rapidly, I looked at the now pulsing silver barrier before us.

"They are coming," Christik shouted above the noise of the wind and the humming energy of the gate.

As we all stared, a figure was starting to form within the barrier. At first, it was just an outline of an angel, but a broader angel with higher and much wider wings. Within seconds, the shape of the angel was beginning to sharpen, its silvery-white skin becoming more evident, as well as the darker silver hair and feathers on its broad wings. I soon realized that the elder appearing before us was Christik's father. He was definitely a lot more masculine than his other half; Christik's Mother Lindaz, from what I could remember from Stonehenge.

The moment his form solidified, he started to step out from the star gate, his foot and leg passing through the barrier and coming out with ease. When the rest of him exited the barrier, we all automatically took a step or two backwards. Not only was he broader and more masculine than the other angels, but he was taller too, and his size was very intimidating.

Christik glided up to her father, stopping within a few feet, and she dipped her head in respect to him.

"Welcome to Earth, father, my one," she said, with a tone of affection.

Her father looked down on her with love in his stunning peacock blue eyes. Suddenly, his large wings opened before us taking my breath away. They seemed to take up the whole scene before us in their splendor.

He dipped his head to her in return, and then he took two long steps forward. As soon as he reached Christik, his wings surrounded her, bringing her in for a loving embrace.

It was very clear that Christik's father had missed her terribly and that his love for her was just as strong as any human parent. She let him embrace her as she rested her head on his broad chest.

"Are you going to release our daughter, our one; anytime soon so I may get to her, Evest?" A strong female voice said behind him humorously.

It wasn't until Evest released Christik and moved sideways with his head dipped and wings once again folded that we saw Christik's mother, Lindaz. She was just as spectacular as her other half but clearly female in form.

"It is so good to see you, my daughter, my one," Lindaz told Christik.

Her eyes glistened with what looked like unshed tears as she too moved forward, wrapping her large wings around Christik. It was beautiful and amazing to witness such love and affection between them all. Evest looked upon his family with love and awe, and even though it was their moment to share; we all felt a part of it.

After a few more moments, Lindaz released Christik, and she backed away, just enough to get a good look at her daughter.

"We are very impressed with what you have accomplished here on Earth, my one," Lindaz told her sincerely.

"We are also pleased that you summoned us, my one," Evest added, "The Marilians are not to be underestimated. They are a vicious race with a terrible reputation."

Christik's parents then turned their attention to the rest of us, just as the other elders appeared around them. They were all stunning and a sight to behold. There were six of them in total, three males and three females, and because they were stood in pairs; I automatically assumed that they were paired together. The kids and I all dipped our heads to the elders in respect as soon as the last pair arrived.

When we raised our heads again, the elders were looking down on us with warm smiles on their beautiful silvery faces.

"Thank you," Lindaz said kindly.

Suddenly, in unison, the silver-haired elders not only dipped their heads, they also opened their large, dark silver beautiful wings in a bow. They really were a magical sight with light from the gate glistening off them, and I could feel their powerful energy coming off them in waves. As they straightened their bodies and folded their wings, I felt confident for the first time; that we actually stood a chance against the Marilians after all. The relief I felt was very strong, and I wondered if it was just my relief or a shared relief with Christik, Livik and Jakiz.

The kids were very quiet, and when I turned to look at them, they were all stood in wonder with their mouths agape. I had to stop myself from giggling aloud for fear of offending the elders. Christik sensed my humor; she turned to look at the kids and then me with a big smile on her lovely face.

"Elders, I would like you to meet our human friends," she said to the larger angels, "This is Mel and her family, Anthony, Holly, Harrison, Abigail and April," she said, indicating to each of us in turn.

"And this is Nalik, who may be Holly's other half, and Christine, Anthony's other half," she added, pointing to Christine and the glowing angel who was still holding Holly's hand. Christik then turned and approached the elders.

"Everyone, I would like you to meet my parents, Lindaz and Evest, and this is Eliz, Ronak, Nical and Mikaz," she said as she indicated to each elder in turn.

Each of us dipped our heads again with great respect.

"I have organized a feast in celebration of your arrival," Christik explained to the elders, "I will take you to the main craft," she then turned to Livik, "Please take everyone else back; we will meet you there."

Livik dipped her head in farewell to Christik and the elders as they all connected hands, and suddenly, in a split second, they all vanished. We stood still, all taking some time to process what had happened and to watch the Gate of the Gods change back to normal.

I felt the wind dying down as I watched the star passage change back to its previous state. Within minutes, it was as if nothing had happened, apart from our windswept hair and the fact that we were covered in sand and dust particles.

"Well, the elders felt more powerful than I thought they were going to," I told the kids, Livik and Jakiz.

"We have never come across another race as powerful as our own elders," Livik admitted, "They are a true force of good."

"I think we're going to be ok now they are here, Mom," Abigail said, sounding hopeful.

"I think so too, darling, but we still need to plan for a big fight, just in case the Marilians give us a run for our money," I told her gently.

"But you do not use Earth money anymore," Jakiz stated.

Both Angels had very confused expressions, which made the kids burst into laughter.

"It's a human expression," I giggled, "It means they could still give us a tough challenge."

"Ahh, I like that expression," Livik said with a smile, "I might try and use it," she added, which made the kids laugh even more.

"Come on you lot, let's get back so we can freshen up and check on your dad before the feast," I said as I began to lead the way back to the small craft.

CHAPTER 4

I t wasn't long before we were back at our rooms, and we were all still buzzing with excitement, looking forward to checking on James and getting to know the elders.

Livik, Jakiz, Christine and Nalik had gone to freshen up too, and they were going to meet us at the cruiser where the feast was to be held. The angels seemed to enjoy the trip back and were very chatty with the kids, asking all sorts of questions and listening intently to the kids' replies.

When we'd arrived back at the main craft, we found a new bed in the kids' room for April and all her belongings which she'd accumulated on top of it. Her Cheshire Cat grin made it clear that she was very happy about moving in, and so were the others.

They all appeared to be thrilled to have an adopted sister, and I knew that James would treat her as another daughter, just the same as me.

While the boys and I got our showers, Holly and Abigail helped April put away her things. Both girls seemed very keen to get to know more about her, and I knew that April would heal emotionally more quickly with some sisterly love and support.

I just wished that she had come to us sooner and again, I felt a pang of guilt for not having checked on her more thoroughly. I knew I shouldn't have been so hard on myself with everything else going on, but I should have made a bigger effort. We were all far too guilty of putting on a brave face for the sake of others.

After my shower and getting dressed in a lovely sand and dirt-free gown, I sat down with the boys who were chilling in the seating area. Both of the boys looked smart in their tunic and trousers, and Anthony had even made an effort with his hair, which was wild and unruly.

I felt my baby girl gently moving around in my tummy as I listened to the boys' chatting between themselves, and I gave my bump an affectation stroke with my hand. I knew it wouldn't be long before she was doing big movements with her elbows and knees.

It was nice to take a load off my feet after such a hectic and exciting day; bad and good, and I was relieved to no longer have sand and dirt in places where there shouldn't be. '*I wonder if guys have the same issue,*' I thought to myself, but I decided not to ask.

When the girls came into the seating area, they looked stunning. Holly was wearing a stunning pale green silky gown with her hair tied to the side of her neck; April and Abigail also looked beautiful in soft tunics and trousers with silk scarves around their necks, both scarves matching their lovely eyes. They looked more like twins than Abigail and Harrison did.

"Wow, you all look fantastic!" I told them with a big smile on my face and my heart full of pride, "Let's go and see how your dad is doing," I added.

By Beth Worsdell

All three girls headed towards the exit with the boys and Hulaz following behind them.

"Do you think your dad's going to mind that I've moved in with you all?" April asked Holly and Abigail, with a worried tone to her voice.

"Nah, Dad won't mind; he's always wanted a big family, and now he's got one," Holly told her warmly.

"At this rate, we might have the first football team since the angels arrived," Anthony laughed

I shook my head while smiling to myself at their banter. Our family was certainly growing unexpectedly, but I was very happy about it, and April didn't need to be worried. Holly was right about James; he'd always wanted a big family.

The medical room was just as quiet as before with only Zanika, Harrik and James present. This time, James was laying on his stomach with Harrik's glowing hand hovering above his lower spine and Zanika's hovering over his neck. James' handsome face was facing us as we entered, but his eyes were still closed.

My eyes scanned my husband from his head to his toes, and I was so relieved to see that nearly all of his previous bruising was gone. It had been so hard to see the man I loved looking so broken, but now I could visibly see how well Zanika and Harrik were healing him.

The angels looked up and gave us big smiles as we walked towards them, and I took that as a very good sign.

"You are both looking very pleased with yourselves," I said with a responding smile.

"Yes, we are very happy with James' progress. His body is healing quicker than we expected," Harrik said, sounding very positive.

"He may be awake sooner than we thought," Zanika added with another smile.

"You are both amazing for what you are doing," I told them. "You both need to get some rest though; can other angels take over for a bit?"

Zanika and Harrik both looked at me with serious determination on their faces.

"We do not want to leave James," Harrik said strongly.

"We want to stay with him until he is well enough to be back with you and your family," Zanika added.

As Zanika finished talking, the kids walked up to the angels and James. My heart ached in my chest as I watched them. Abigail leaned over James, giving him an affectionate kiss on his cheek.

"Wake up soon, Dad, we need you!" She whispered softly next to his ear.

The boys moved to either side of the bed, each of them taking one of James' hands in theirs, and Holly rested her hand on James' left leg. It was as if they were checking that James was still warm, to prove to themselves that he was still alive.

A small soft hand slipped into mine. When I turned my head, I saw that it was April with a tear slowly trickling down her cheek.

"They love their dad, don't they!" She said in a quiet voice; "I never had that," she added, dipping her head towards the kids and James.

I gave her small hand a gentle, affectionate squeeze, and when she looked up, I smiled.

"Well, you do now, April, and James will love you just as much as we do already," I told her with conviction. April's smile spoke a thousand words!

When the kids walked back over to Hulaz and me after checking on James, they took April over to the chairs so I could have my moment. He really was looking so much better. Zanika and Harrik both smiled at me, and I assumed they could sense my relief and anticipation.

"Please wake up soon, baby, I miss you," I said softly, as I ran my hand down his cheek.

I could feel his stubble grazing my skin as my hand moved downwards.

"Will you definitely let me know as soon as he wakes, please?" I asked Zanika earnestly.

She looked at me with understanding.

"Yes, Mel, we will, we promise you!" Zanika answered sincerely.

Feeling more positive; I turned back to the kids, who were waiting patiently.

"Let's get to the feast; hopefully, they aren't all waiting for us," I told them.

As we walked towards the exit, I touched the com resting against my neck. '*Livik, we are ready to be collected from James' medical room.*' Within seconds, I heard the angel reply. '*Angels are now waiting for you, Mel; we will see you soon,*' Livik answered, and I could hear the excitement in her voice. The elders were obviously causing quite a stir.

Angels were waiting for us the moment we left the room, and they were stunning. Two of the angels had long, red shimmering hair, two had blue hair, and one had green, and as they stood all together dipping their heads to Hulaz and us in respect, they looked like something out of a fairy tale. The kids, Hulaz and I, all dipped our heads in response, thanking them for collecting us.

"If you would all like to hold on," one of the red-headed angels said politely.

Each of us walked towards an angel, placing a hand on the angel's arm, and within seconds, we were arriving outside the cruiser.

My body instantly shivered as a rush of cold washed over me, making my teeth chatter. '*I bloody hate being cold*,' I thought to myself as I tried to warm myself by rubbing my arms. The kids were all hugging each other and rubbing each other's arms while giggling as the angels all looked on bemused.

"If you would like to follow me," one of the blue-haired angels said politely as he used his arm to indicate the entrance of the holding structure.

The angel glided forward with us following behind while the other angels glided behind us. We could hear a thrum of chatter and laughter as we approached the massive wooden doors that were left open, and I could feel the excitement in the air.

As soon as we stepped into the cruiser, my breath was taken away. All I could see were decorations everywhere. Beautiful flower garlands hung over the shop entrances, and flowering vines were wrapped around the pillars, chairs and tables that were dotted everywhere. The angels had basically decorated everything that wasn't alive, and it was stunning. The shops looked very different at first glance, and when I took a better look, I saw that the usual items had been temporarily replaced with tables full of food and drinks, enabling the angels to make full use of the main area.

The cavernous foyer was full of Angels and humans of all ages, who were all mingling together, either stood in groups or sat at the decorated tables. As my eyes scanned the scene before me, I spotted Christik at the back of the foyer near the natural pool. She was talking with her elder parents next to a row of long tables. It was nice to see her so animated and lighthearted with a smile on her face and a sparkle in her eyes.

The elders were a lot taller than everyone else in the room, and their powerful presence made them stand out even more. As we walked towards everyone, Christine and Nalik made their way through the throng of bodies, desperately trying to reach Holly and Anthony. Nalik was literally glowing as he approached my daughter, who started to blush profusely. '*They've got it bad*' I thought as I smiled to myself.

When Christine reached Anthony, she slipped her hand into his, and she gave him the sweetest smile, which he returned immediately. Seeing my kids with their loves made me hope for the future, which I didn't think was possible before.

I was soon stood alone as the kids and angels drifted off to catch up with their friends. Suddenly, I felt like Billy no mates, and I could feel my own cheeks becoming hot with a blush. Luckily, Christik noticed me, and she began to beckon me over to her. I gave her a nod and started to slip through the groups of angels and humans.

Everyone was so polite, either saying hello or respectfully dipping their heads and occasionally asking how the baby and I were doing.

Before long, I'd managed to navigate my way to Christik and the elders, abruptly aware of how much of a short-arse I was in comparison to them.

I dipped my head to the elders and Christik the moment I reached them, feeling a little nervous and quite intimidated. The elders and Christik all dipped their heads in response, and I could feel nothing but affection from them, which started to put me at ease. Christik's mother gracefully glided forward with a stunning smile on her beautiful face, and she took me by surprise as she reached forward, taking my hand in hers.

"Christik has told us of your wonderful news, Mel. We are all excited for your new baby," Lindaz said as her smile grew bigger. "Infants are very precious to our race as we do not conceive as quickly as other races," she added.

The look on my face must have shown my curiosity and surprise at her words. '*You would think healers of worlds would be able to have babies at the drop of a hat,*' I thought as I looked into the elder's blue eyes. Lindaz looked bemused as she watched my facial expressions.

"As our race lives such a long time, Mel, if we could conceive quickly, we would each have more offspring than we would know what to do with!" Christik said with humor in her voice.

"I believe it is as it should be," Lindaz stated.

She looked over my head and scanned the foyer.

"Let us address everyone, now we are all here, my own, my one," Lindaz told Christik.

Lindaz turned to the other elders and dipped her head while indicating to the long table and chairs. As the elders began to glide towards the seats, she turned back to me with her eyebrows raised.

"Please join us at the head table, Mel!" She invited kindly.

I walked forward nervously and wondered where my kids were. I wasn't worried about them. They were in a building full of angels, so I knew they were safe, but it did bother me not being able to see them.

I took a seat at the end of the table next to Christik to allow the elders to sit together. I felt even more like a total short-arse, and I must have looked funny being the only little human at the table. The elders all sat in the available chairs, while Christik remained standing by my side.

"If you could all take your seats, please!" Christik said loudly above all the chatter.

Instantly, everyone in the bustling foyer moved to the nearest table and chairs. There was no them and us. All the angels and humans sat with whoever they were talking too. It was wonderful to see such a friendly camaraderie between our two races. As I looked across our long table while everyone was getting settled, I noticed that all the elders now had the communication devices on, like the angels and some of us humans. It was going to be very convenient for the battle to come. I definitely felt more confident, knowing the elders were going to have our backs.

Before long, everyone had taken a seat at one of the many tables, and the cavernous foyer was beginning to quiet. Patiently, Christik waited for everyone to be silent, and as soon as it was, she began to address everyone.

"Welcome all to the celebration of our elder's arrival," she stated.

Angels and humans alike began to applaud with the angels applauding a little more enthusiastically, which was understandable considering they were of the same race.

"I think I can speak for you all when I say how pleased we are to have you here," Christik said as she glanced at her parents and the rest of the elders at the table.

All the elders dipped their heads to Christik and then to the watching audience. Christik continued.

"It was not an easy decision to summon you here. However, having knowledge of our strong ties to these amazing humans made the decision a little easier," Christik declared. "Thank you, elders, for coming to our aid; we appreciate your presence, and we all look forward to working alongside you," she added with another dip of her head.

Everyone began to applaud loudly and cheer at her warm and heartfelt words, and just as Christik started to take her seat, Lindaz and Evest stood from theirs. Silence immediately swept the foyer in anticipation for the two imposing elders. They were a magnificent couple, and I could understand why Christik was in awe of her parents.

Lindaz and Evest raised their arms before them, and their whole beings began to glow an ice white shimmer. As they raised their arms higher, specks of light started to appear above us all, high in the foyer ceiling. More light specks appeared with each second, and they darted around the ceiling like fireworks.

We were all in awe as we watched the display, none of us knowing why this was happening, but all enjoying the light show.

When the air above us was full, the specks began to form into shapes. Planets began to appear before our eyes of various shapes and colors, and there in the center was the largest planet.

It looked remarkably similar to Earth with vast amounts of blue and white on its surface. The main difference between the planet and ours, from what I could see, were streaks of gold and silver that ran over its surface like shining veins.

"This is our planet, Anunaki," Lindaz said, over our ahhhs and oooos. "As some of you already know, we have visited your planet from our own since life began here.

"We formed bonds with your ancient ancestors over many of your centuries," Evest explained, "working with them to protect your Earth and helping it to thrive. We are sorry that we were not able to arrive before your planet came to a critical point."

The elders looked up, and as we all followed suit, the planets dispersed back into specks of light. The specks swirled for a few moments, reforming into what seemed to be the surface of a planet. It was lush and very green, and wildflowers and trees were growing everywhere. It was our planet, but I'd never seen a place on Earth that looked so healthy. Even the sky looked bluer and sharper.

"This was your Earth before your race began to use fossil fuels, machinery and farm animals," Evest stated without judgement.

"Many races have made the same mistakes as your race," Lindaz added, "the damage to your planet was slow, but as you are all now aware, there does come a point where it is irreversible."

I think all of us humans in the foyer felt pangs of guilt. Most of us hadn't done anything near enough to protect our planet. We all felt responsible for what had happened. As I sat there next to the elders and angels, I felt guilt and shame for the part I'd played in destroying our planet.

"If we had not arrived in time, your planet would not have healed itself," Lindaz explained. "The ice age that would have covered your whole planet would have wiped out humanity and the majority of your animals. However, it would have allowed your planet to heal and start over," she said calmly.

"We are pleased that your race and your planet did not have to go through that process," Evest said warmly, "We know that your race has learned a big lesson from the events that occurred. So, let us eat, drink and celebrate the new beginning for your race and planet. Once we defeat the Marilians, together we will be creating a new Earth you can all cherish and enjoy!" He said.

As the elders lowered their arms, the images above us dissipated. The specks of light fell from the ceiling, vanishing before they got close to the people and angels below, like fading fireworks.

Everyone in the foyer started to applaud as the elders dipped their heads as a thank you. The elders took their seats as Christik stood up, and I could tell by her demeanor that she was very proud of her parents and her race.

"Let us eat," she declared.

Nobody needed telling twice. Very quickly, everyone left their seats, making their way to the food areas, which were once the shops. I briefly spotted Abigail and April, making their way to the food with Tracey and John. The girls were laughing, so I assumed that Tracey was telling them one of her stories or jokes.

"Shall we get some food, Mel?" Christik asked.

When I turned to look at her, she was smiling.

"Yes, that would be great," I told her. "It looks like Tracey is entertaining the girls," I added, indicating towards Abigail and April.

The two girls had actually stopped in their tracks; they were laughing so hard. John was shaking his head at his wife while Tracey was looking at him as if to say, '*What?*'

"I really like Tracey," Christik said as her smile grew bigger. "She confuses me with some of the things she says, but she is very funny and is a friendly, honest woman," she added.

"Yes," I agreed, "she cracks me up too," I confessed.

Instantly, Christik looked very confused.

"Tracey cracks you up?" She asked with her eyebrows raised.

"Yes, it means that she makes me laugh hard," I explained. "Tracey is the kind of woman who can make you laugh so hard that you struggle to breathe. I think we all need a friend like that in our lives," I told the angel with a smile.

Christik returned my smile as we left the table and walked into the nearest food area.

The food selection was amazing, and it really was a feast for the eyes. The angels had outdone themselves, and it all looked amazing. There was a formidable feast of fresh fruits and vegetables that I assumed was a selection from around the world. Many I recognized, such as dragon fruit, lychee and Kohlrabi, but others looked absolutely bizarre. Christik had to tell me the names of many of them. The Romanesco broccoli looked like it came from a completely different planet and so did the mangosteen fruit, which I have to admit was the most amazing fruit I'd ever tried.

After getting a small tray of food each, Christik and I made our way back to the long table, joining the elders who were eating and talking between themselves. It was nice to listen to them talking in our human language, discussing how different our planet looked the last time they visited.

Just as the conversation was getting really interesting as they mentioned an elder who had taken a liking to an Egyptian woman, I heard Harrik in my head. '*Mel, would you like to come back; James has woken.*"

CHAPTER 5

The moment Harrik said the words; my heart started to pound in my chest. I'd known that he was going to be ok because I trusted Harrik and Zanika to heal him, but even so; the relief I suddenly felt was almost overwhelming. I touched the com at my chest, *'I'm on my way,'* I told him, *'and Harrik, thank you!'* I said, with all my heart. *'You are most welcome, Mel, see you soon,'* he answered, and then he was gone.

Christik as always sensed what was happening to my emotions, and she reached over and touched my forearm. Curiosity was written on her face.

"Mel, what is happening?" She asked, her curiosity just as evident in her tone.

"It's great news, Harrik has just told me that James is awake," I told her breathlessly as I tried to control my racing heart.

I could suddenly feel Christik's calming power flow through me, helping to steady my heart rate and shaking hands, and I knew without looking that her hand was probably glowing white.

"Could one of your angels possibly take me back, please, so I can go to him?" I asked.

Christik gave me a smile full of happiness and understanding.

"I will take you, Mel," she said.

"But don't you want to make the most of your parents being here?" I asked, surprised that she'd offered.

I knew that if I had the chance of spending time with my parents, I'd want to make the most of every second with them.

"There will be plenty of time for me to spend time with my parents, Mel. Do not forget that I am well used to being away from them. It is our way of life," Christik said warmly, "Come, we shall go right now."

As Christik rose from her seat, her parents as well as the other elders, all stopped talking instantly and looked at her.

"Is all well, my own, my one?" Lindaz asked.

"Everything is fine. Mel's husband has woken; I will be back soon," Christik told her, dipping her head.

The elders all dipped their heads to Christik and I as we began to leave the table. I was so desperate to get to James that I almost forgot to nod in return, but I reminded myself in time. The last thing I wanted to do was to offend the elders.

As we began to make our way out of the throng of Angels and humans, Christik touched my shoulder to stop me.

"Would you like to collect the children before we go?" She asked.

I had thought about telling the kids straight away, but I decided not to. Not just yet. The kids needed to have some fun just for a while. They'd been through so much in such a short time, and with the Marilians coming, it was going to be a while before they'd get to let their hair down again.

"No, let them have some fun for tonight," I answered; "they need to have a good time while they can," I added.

Christik nodded in understanding and agreement, and then she began to glide forward again towards the exit. Everyone was having such a good time that no one really noticed us as we passed. We were about halfway through the foyer when I started to hear a guitar being played. I surmised that one of the cruiser residents must have had one in their cabin.

Whoever it was played extremely well, and I recognized the song straight away as it was one of my favorites. It was a song called *'Watching over me,'* and it always reminded me of my grandparents. *'They'd be so proud if they could see my kids right now,'* I thought as I followed Christik to the exit.

I hadn't realized that we'd been in the cruiser so long, and it was pitch black as we walked outside. I looked up at the night sky as we walked away from the building, and I was instantly blown away by the number of stars in the sky. The sky was teeming with stars as far as my eyes could see, and they looked so bright that if I hadn't had wanted to get to James as much as I did, I could have happily just laid there on the ground and star gazed for hours.

"So many stars!" I said, more to myself than Christik, "I've never seen so many in the sky."

"You can see so many because there is no light pollution from the cities," Christik explained.

"I didn't know that would make such a difference," I told her honestly.

"Are you ready to see your husband?" Christik asked with a smile.

"Yes, I am," I said with a huge grin.

My heart had stopped its racing, and now I really wanted James safe in my arms. Christik glided forward, and I immediately placed my hand on her offered arm. Within seconds, we were outside the medical room where James was being looked after.

As I tried to control my shivering body; I began to feel our baby moving, it felt as if she were doing somersaults. It was strange because I almost felt as if she was excited too, '*Maybe she is excited*' I thought, '*Maybe she can sense that her dad is better.*'

"Are you ready?" Christik asked as my shivering started to wear off.

"Yes and thank you for waiting," I told her, "I don't want James to see me walking and shivering at the same time," I laughed; "I'd feel like a complete idiot," I added.

I took a deep breath and walked into the bright white medical room. As soon as we entered, I could hear James' voice as he talked with Zanika and Harrik. I just caught the tail end of their conversation, which I believe was about the kids when they were little and always getting into mischief. As soon as he heard my footsteps, he stopped talking and turned to see who was moving in.

James was still on the hospital type bed; only this time, he was sitting on it with his legs hanging over the end. The resounding smile that lit his face when he saw me was breathtaking. Before I knew what I was doing; I was running towards him, flinging myself into his arms. Zanika and Harrik respectively backed away a little as James held me. Relief flowed through my body, and tears began to stream down my face. I was beyond happy to have the love of my life back in my arms.

"I get the impression that you might have missed me just a little bit," James said as I nuzzled my face into his neck.

He smelled so good and familiar that it was soothing to my heart and soul. I had to force myself to pull back so I could talk to him properly.

"Yeah, I might have missed you just a tad," I told him as I indicated with my fingers for emphasis.

James raised one of his own hands and began to wipe away my happy tears from my cheeks.

"Are you and the baby ok?" He asked. His eyes searched mine as if they were going to give him the answer.

"We're fine," I told him, "In fact, now you're all healed, we are better than fine. I think the baby is excited because she started doing somersaults just as we were about to walk in," I said with a laugh.

James seemed to be reassured, giving me another beautiful smile, and he reached down, placing his hand on my swollen tummy. The moment his hand connected with my baby bump; our baby began to move. I could feel her moving towards the gentle pressure of James' hand as if she wanted to get closer to him. James looked up at me in surprise.

"See, she's missed you as much as I have," I said, giggling at his surprise.

James' smile as he felt her was beautiful, and it made my heart even more full of love for him.

"Where are the kids?" He asked.

"They're all at the cruiser. I don't know if Zanika and Harrik have told you, but the elders have arrived, and we are having a celebratory feast to welcome them," I told him, "They don't know that you're awake yet. I wanted them to enjoy themselves while they could," I explained, hoping that he'd understand my reasoning.

"They did mention that the elders were here," he replied as he looked and smiled at the angels who were stood waiting patiently. "I think I'd like to meet the elders and surprise the kids," James said while smirking.

"Are you sure you're up to going to the feast?" I asked, feeling surprised.

"Baby, I'm as good as new!" He stated while sliding himself off the bed.

I looked at Zanika and Harrik, raising my brows questioningly.

"James is correct, Mel," Harrik said with a nod of his head, "Zanika and I have completely healed James. He is as good as new."

James took me into his arms, holding me close to his body. His face brushed against my ear, and I felt his kisses on my neck, sending a shiver down my spine, and goosebumps started to appear on my skin.

"I'm going to show you just how good as new I am when we get back to our room later," James whispered.

I could feel myself blushing immediately, and I suddenly hoped that the angels hadn't heard what he'd said. James chuckled as he felt the shiver ran through my body again. Pulling back and taking my hand in his, he looked to Christik, Zanika and Harrik.

"Let's get this party started, shall we!" He declared with a grin.

His grin was contagious, and I think the angels had heard what he'd whispered as all three of the angels had humorous smiles on their faces. Zanika and Harrik glided forward, both of them offering their arms for us to hold. The moment we touched them; we vanished from the medical room, and in seconds, we all arrived back outside the cruiser.

The massive wooden doors of the building were still open, and this time, I could hear not only the guitar being played but also what sounded like a drum of some sort, and someone female was singing beautifully. My body was instantly shivering like crazy, and although James was shivering too, he took me into his arms to warm me up.

"We'll meet you inside in a bit," he told Zanika, Harrik and Christik as he rubbed his hands up and down my back vigorously.

The three angels nodded and glided gracefully into the building without looking back. No sooner were they out of sight than James released me and took my hand. I thought he was going to lead me into the building, but he actually began to lead me away from the cruiser and towards a cluster of trees.

"Where are you taking me, husband of mine?" I asked with a giggle.

"You'll see," he said with a sexy smirk that started to make my pulse race.

When we reached the trees and were out of sight of the cruiser, he pulled me into his embrace. Within moments, his lips were on mine, kissing me as if his whole life depended on tasting me. My hands ran down his back with firm pressure, encouraging him to get even closer. I could feel my already sensitive nipples getting harder as my excitement grew. My whole body was aching for him, and I could feel myself get wetter as his already hard arousal pressed against me.

James pulled his face away from mine, and as he looked at my loved and plumped lips and the sex haze of my eyes, he bit his bottom lip as if he was trying to keep control. By my next breath, his hands were sliding the thin straps of my dress down my shoulders, allowing my gown to slide off my body.

As the cool night air reached my skin, my nipples hardened even more, making them stand to attention, and he noticed them straight away. James took my left nipple into his hungry mouth as his right hand slid its way down my swollen stomach, finding its way to my now aching sex. His hand felt so good as he softly brushed it against me, teasing me as his tongue circled my tingling nipple.

My own hand ran through his thick dark hair, and when his mouth started to suck, and his hand began to explore, my hand gripped his hair as my excitement built. I could feel his thumb brushing against my clitoris, and I knew I was close already.

Abruptly James stood, his eyes glazed with passion, which I was sure mirrored my own.

"Turn around, Mel," he said.

His voice was husky with desire and need, and he didn't need to ask me twice. I turned around to face the nearest tree, and I felt his hands guiding me until my breasts were almost touching the rough tree bark. I placed my hands onto the trunk so James knew I couldn't move any further, and I could hear him moving behind me.

Within moments his naked body was against my own. I could feel his throbbing erection pushing against the top of my thighs, brushing against my own arousal, making him wet and slippery. His arms came around my body, so he could stroke and caress my breasts, and I instinctively began to writhe slowly against him.

I couldn't stop myself from moaning as he started to move back and forth, his erection rubbing against my aching sex. I automatically started to lean forward, desperately wanting to feel him inside of me. As his hands slid down my body to my hips, I moved my legs wider to give him access. Our excitement seemed to be building by the second, and I knew he wanted me just as badly as I wanted him.

James and I both moaned loudly as he slid his hard erection inside me. I was so turned on that my tightness even surprised me while adding to the delicious pleasure. As soon as he started to slide back and forth, my climax began to build. He had me so excited that I knew it wasn't going to be a long affair. James' thrusts became faster and firmer as I pushed back to meet him, not being able to stop myself from encouraging him to go harder.

It was as if he could sense my need, his erection pushing harder as was his grip on my hips. When he started to moan deeply, it was my ruin. I couldn't stop myself from exploding, and I could feel my sex pulsing and tightening around him as my body released. Within seconds, his body reacted to mine, his whole being tensed as he released too, his groans becoming louder as he reached the same place as me. As our climaxes subsided, I straightened myself up using the tree trunk, and he wrapped his arms around me while kissing my neck.

"You are so hot, woman," he said softly against my ear, making goosebumps appear again on my skin.

"You're not so bad yourself, dude," I told him as I wriggled my backside against his groin.

"We'd better get inside before you catch a chill," he said as he gave my butt a cheeky pat.

After rescuing our discarded clothes and getting redressed, we walked hand in hand to the cruiser. I felt so completely sated and happy to have James back, and all felt right with the world. The music was still playing with fervor, and when we entered the foyer, it was clear that everyone was having a fantastic time.

We hadn't even got twenty steps into the building when there was a shriek from the right side of the room.

"Dad!" The voice said loudly.

Instantly, I knew it was Abigail. Abigail pushed through the throng of Angels and humans as if she were a professional wrestler. She was so driven to get to James that I doubt anything would have stood in her way. James' arms were waiting for her as she broke through the last group of Angels and humans. He scooped her up in his arms and twirled her around, making her squeal and giggle.

"I can't believe you're here, Dad," she told him, "Are you ok now, Dad?" She asked, suddenly serious and concerned.

"I'm one hundred percent better my darling," James assured her, just as Holly, Anthony, Harrison and April also broke through the crowd.

As our kids hugged James, April came and stood next to me. My heart instantly felt heavy as I could see her longing to be a part of the moment James and the kids were sharing.

When James looked up at me with sheer happiness on his face, I smiled and side-nodded my head towards April.

"We have a new member of the family," I told him as my smile grew bigger.

James' responding smile was exactly what I was expecting. I knew through and through that he would be fine about it. He looked at April with the same affection he showed our own kids, and he beckoned her over to join in the group hug he was relishing with the kids.

James didn't have to say anything to Holly, Anthony, Harrison and Abigail. They automatically moved, making a gap for April to join in when she nervously approached them. James, always the amazing Dad that he was, used his nearest arm to scoop her in, making her giggle.

It was fantastic to see such a heartwarming sight. Even the angels and people around us who saw it were getting quite emotional with one or two people getting a little teary.

"Lead me to the food please," James asked them as one by one they released him.

I watched happily as the kids led James towards the multiple shops, which were still filled with food. Nalik and Christine approached me from the crowd, both of them seemingly happy that their partners, my kids, were so happy to see their dad.

"It's amazing," Christine said quietly, "you just wouldn't believe that James nearly died to look at him now, would you!"

"I know, it is truly amazing what the angels can do," I told her as my eyes stayed on James and the kids.

We stood there for a few more minutes as I watched the kids and James laughing and joking while they loaded his plate with food.

"Don't feel like you can't join them, you two," I told Nalik and Christine, "You're part of our family too, you know," I said with a smile.

As I walked away heading towards the long table I'd left earlier, I had a feeling that Christine and Nalik were doing what I suggested. I knew James would find me when he was ready, and I needed to eat badly. Christik was already back at the end table with the elders, and I was pleased to see that my barely touched tray of food was still in my seating place. My mouth watered at the sight.

Christik gave me a little smirk as I took my seat and instantly, I started to blush. She gave her head a soft shake.

"I will say it again," she said, smiling, "You are a passionate race, aren't you."

As her eyebrows raised, I laughed aloud, not being able to keep it in. We ate our food and talked while watching everyone enjoy themselves. Within an hour, James had found me and was sitting next to me as we enjoyed seeing angels and humans actually getting up to dance to the music that was playing.

The elders and Christik all seemed very surprised to witness their angels dancing, but I don't think the poor angels had much of a choice. I'd already witnessed Derek dragging a reluctant Hulaz to the newly-formed dance floor, much to Harrik's amusement, who was watching and smiling to himself.

While we watched everyone having a good time, I heard Lindaz and Evest mention a name to the elders next to them. It was their tone of voice that pricked my attention and interest. The name was Akhenaten, and I didn't know why it sounded so familiar to me, but it definitely rang a bell.

"Who are they talking about?" I asked Christik as I leaned towards her.

"The elders are discussing Akhenaten, who was one of our angels," Christik replied quietly as she also leaned in, "He was with us, the last time we came to Earth."

"Did something bad happen to him?" I asked, "the elders sound sad as they talk about him."

"We do not know what happened to Akhenaten," Christik answered, "The elders and I still miss him. He was my brother," she added.

'*Woah,*' I thought as my mind absorbed her words. '*And we thought only humans had family drama.*'

My surprise must have been evident in my face as Christik's eyebrows raised, and she nodded her head.

"I will tell you about it when we can talk properly," she said with a genuine smile.

CHAPTER 6

By the time we got back to our rooms, we were all absolutely shattered. It had been an exhausting day full of excitement and revelry. Even though James was completely healed, I could tell that the party had taken its toll on him.

We said goodnight to the kids, who all gave James a huge hug, including April, and we closed the barrier between our rooms. By the time I got to our bed after showering and cleaning my teeth, James was already sleeping deeply with his arms and legs out like a starfish.

Trying not to wake him, I climbed on the bed. Luckily, the moment my leg touched his, he rolled over on his side, giving me the room to slide under the sheets. I put my arm around his waist, and it felt so wonderful having him close to me again. My eyes felt heavy as my body became warmer next to his body heat, and before long, I was sound asleep too.

I wasn't sure where I was, but there were trees and plants as far as I could see. I'm standing in long, lush grass up to my knees, and I can hear water running in a stream or a small river. Turning on the spot, my ears pick up on a rustling sound, and I stop and wonder who or what is making the noise. The long grasses before me started to move and out from the foliage appears a red panda.

'*Omg it's so cute*' is the first thought that popped into my head as I watched it forage the ground between us. The panda isn't very big, about the size of the large cat we'd had back home. Its fur on its head and body is a stunning reddish-brown, while its legs and underbelly looked black. The tail on the red panda is bushy and striped with a darker shade of reddish-brown, which also appears on its face between prominent markings of white on its cute face and ears.

It's foraging around as if I weren't there, and I was absolutely fascinated watching it. Like James, I always loved animals, and that was why we always had so many pets before our planet's disaster. I was quite happy to continue to watch the little guy, but something didn't feel right. The hairs began to prickle at the back of my neck, and I suddenly felt the tiny hairs on my bare arms stand to attention.

A noise in the sky grabbed my attention, and when I looked up; at first, I thought it must be one of the Angels' crafts, but as the noise became louder as the object in the sky got closer; I realized that it wasn't. It was a different kind of craft, which was bulky in shape, reminding me of a grub and was fairly big in size. It was a dark sandy color, and it was moving fast, considering it wasn't exactly streamlined.

A heavy feeling began to form in my chest, and I could feel my baby girl starting to move around sharply, almost in a panic. As the words "Oh Fuck," left my lips, beams of fire shot out from the craft right before me. The poor little red panda didn't stand a chance as it instantly burst into flames. As my body was thrown backwards from the force of the fire, the last thing I heard was the red panda screaming in pain, just before my body hit the floor.

THE MARILIANS

I abruptly sat bolt upright in our bed with beads of sweat running down my chest, and I suddenly felt cold and clammy. I could still feel my daughter moving around in my belly, and I could sense her distress. I lowered my hands to my swollen bump, stroking her through my skin.

"I know baby girl," I told her quietly, "We need to save the animals."

I could feel her calming at my words and affection. She knew the animals were in great danger, and she obviously wanted them to be safe before the Marilians arrived. She may have only been a growing baby bump, but I trusted my daughter's instincts, especially as she'd already saved my life and her own when Peter and Kay had attacked. Also, after what had happened at the natural pool when the birds and fish wouldn't leave me alone, I couldn't disregard her connection to the animals either.

I turned to look at the large round window above the seating area, only to see it was still pitch-black outside. *'No wonder James is still fast asleep,'* I thought as I looked down at my husband's sleeping face. He was snoring softly and was dead to the world. I didn't know what to do, and I sat there wondering if I should reach out to Christik straightaway, to tell her about the dream or if it could wait until the morning.

I decided to wait as the kids were all still sleeping too. There wasn't anything that could be done in the dark anyway. I laid back down in the bed, and as I laid on my side, I stroked my baby bump reassuringly. *'You don't need to worry baby girl; we will get all the animals back, so they're safe,'* I mentally told my daughter. I could feel her pushing against my hand as if she was trying to say thank you.

When I woke in the morning, everyone else was still sleeping, so I took a nice shower and cleaned my teeth. By the time I came out of the bathroom feeling human again; James was awake and was smiling like an idiot at me.

"Wow you look too sexy when you're pregnant," he said as he slid off the bed and took me in his arms.

"Don't start getting all frisky, husband of mine," I told him with a giggle, "the kids are all going to be up soon, so you need to get yourself sorted," I added as I reached down and smacked his naked pert butt.

"I'll give you ten minutes to stop doing that," James replied as he pulled me even closer.

I could feel his arousal starting to get even more excited and unfortunately, we didn't have the time to do anything about it. Reluctantly, I pulled away from my naked man, and I gave him one of my stern looks while pointing to the bathroom area.

"Go shower now!" I said with a firmer tone, knowing he was enjoying it.

"Oh, I'll give you an hour to keep doing that too," James replied, as he quickly raised and lowered his eyebrows for emphasis.

I could hear the kids next door laughing and squealing, which seemed to give James the motivation to get in the shower quickly. It wasn't long before breakfast had arrived, and we were all sitting together, eating and talking. It had become part of our routine and one which I really enjoyed, especially as we had James back.

"Did it really hurt, Dad, when Kay threw you off the balcony?" Harrison asked his dad.

James looked very sad suddenly; he knew without being told what the kids had been through, seeing him so broken. He then looked as if he was undecided as to what to say.

"It did, son, I'm not going to lie to you, but it was only for mere seconds, and then I blacked out," he answered calmly.

Harrison nodded in his head, clearly appreciating James' honesty.

"Could you hear us talking to you while you were being healed?" Abigail asked, with hope in her voice.

James gave them the warmest smile, and his eyes lit up with love for them.

"Yes, I could hear you. Not at first but after a while, I could hear you all," he said, "It was great to listen to you reminiscing about when you were younger, and I'm really pleased that you guys remember so much," he told them. "Maybe you can tell April some of your memories and April; you could share some of your own.

April abruptly looked so put out that I wanted to hug her.

"What's wrong, April?" I asked, feeling very concerned.

She looked at me with eyes that looked so sad and tearful they would have made anyone's heart drop.

"I don't have any nice memories apart from when I was with my girlfriend, and we weren't together very long," she answered.

"Why don't you have any nice memories?" Holly asked gently.

"I was always in foster care, being bounced from one place to another," she said quietly, "It's only the little ones that really get looked after well and adopted. I couldn't find my real parents or find out how I ended up being in care, so I decided running away was better than staying. That's when I met my girlfriend.

"How long were you together?" I asked, giving her a warm smile.

"We were together for five months, and she was amazing," April told us. "I met her when I was trying to find a job. She was older than me, and she already had a good job working in a cafe. She'd been working there since school and was basically running it for the owners. She gave me a job and a room to rent. We just clicked, and I loved her," she added, as a tear ran down her soft cheek.

James reached over and pulled her chair, so it slid towards him, and the moment she was within reach, he wrapped an arm around her shoulders.

"You have all of us now, daughter," he told her softly.

My heart seemed to melt in my chest as I watched our kids, one by one, get up from their seats and hug April. As I listened to her sob softly against James' chest, I got up from my own seat and walked over to them.

"This has to be the best family group hug I've ever seen," I told them as I wrapped my arms around the bundle of bodies before me.

When April's sobs subsided, we heard her quiet voice.

"Guys, I think I'm cooking now, and I have snot running down my face," she said with a nervous giggle.

We all released her and moved back to our seats, laughing. When she looked up, she did indeed look a little flushed with snot running from her nose.

"Ahh, what's a little snot between siblings," Anthony told her with a huge grin on his face.

At that point, we all cracked up laughing.

THE MARILIANS

As we finished putting our cups back on the tray, I decided to tell James and the kids about saving the animals. We'd always been a menagerie family, so I knew they'd want to be a part of it. I touched my com at my throat and reached out to Christik. *'Christik, are you busy?'* I asked.

As always, she answered immediately. *'I am with my parents Mel, but I can talk with you. Is James alright?'* She asked.

'James is great thank you, but I had another dream last night, and I think the baby... No, I know the baby wants us to save the animals that have already been released Christik,' I told her.

There was a slight pause while Christik thought about what I'd said.

'Meet us in the main meeting room when you are ready Mel,' Christik said, *'we will be waiting for you, and Mel,'*

'Yes,' I answered.

'Do not worry,' she said, and then she was gone.

"Come on tribe; we've got a mission to do for your baby sister," I said to my family as I patted my baby bump.

All of them looked a little worried, and I couldn't blame them after what happened with Peter and Kay.

"It's going to be an adventure," I told them with a smile.

There were lots of questions of who, what, where and when.

"Be patient family, all will be explained," I assured them.

After waiting for Nalik and Christine to arrive, we all made our way to the big meeting room. James and I didn't mind Nalik and Christine coming with us as they already felt like part of our family too, and we knew Holly and Anthony wanted to be with them.

Christik and her parents were waiting for us when we arrived. The three of them in deep conversation were sitting at the large wooden table. All three gave us lovely smiles and dips of their heads as we entered, and we automatically reciprocated. After hellos and morning greetings, we all took seats around the table, and Christik looked at me expectantly.

"As I mentioned to you earlier, I had another dream last night," I told her, "I haven't told James and the kids about it yet as I didn't want to waste time, especially as we don't have a lot of it," I added in a rush.

"I understand," Christik replied.

I took a deep breath and then continued.

"I dreamt that I was in a forest, but I don't know where, and I was watching a red panda, which was looking for food," I explained. "While I was watching it, I heard a noise in the sky, which got closer, and I realized it wasn't one of your crafts. It was one of theirs, a Marilian craft."

"How do you know if it was a Marilian craft and not one of the angels' crafts you haven't seen yet?" James asked.

I looked at my husband as I felt my heart sink in my chest. I knew he'd be upset when I told him.

"I knew because the craft shot out a beam of fire, which made the red panda burst into flames," I told him gently. "It was so awful, and the blast from the beam threw me backwards in my dream, it was so powerful."

I looked to Christik, Lindaz and Evest, who all had looks of horror on their faces.

"We need to retrieve all the animals that were released, or they are all going to die," I told them desperately.

"We have only released animals in five locations, but it will take a lot of time to find the animals, Mel, and we don't have much time before the Marilians arrive," Christik said sadly.

"It does not have to take a lot of time," Nalik said, surprising everyone as he was normally so quiet.

"What do you mean, Nalik?" Evest asked

We were all curious about his statement.

"As we saw at the pool in the holding structure, Mel is basically an animal magnet at the moment. All the fish and birds were drawn to her and the baby immediately."

The realization hit all of us at once as soon as he said it.

"We just need to go where the animals were released, and I believe they will come to us, as long as Mel is there," he added.

"I think you are correct Nalik. We will have to act fast as we already have much to do," Christik said with strong determination in her tone. "I will organize the containment for the animals and angels to assist us. I will be back shortly."

Christik left the room, leaving us sitting with her parents and a bit of awkward silence; none of us really knowing what to say.

Lindaz looked at the kids with a warm smile on her face.

"Are you all excited to meet your new sister?" She asked.

All the kids either nodded or said yes, politely.

"I have a question about our sister if you don't mind me asking?" Anthony told her.

"Of course, Anthony, you may ask me anything," she told him warmly.

"How come our sister has gifts and wings? He asked. "I mean, I know about evolution stepping up a notch after our planet nearly died, but how is she more like you angels, like Christik told my Mom and Dad?" He added.

We all waited for the answer; everyone one of us were just as curious. I know I'd thought about it a lot since Christik had told us and shown us our daughter.

Evest and Lindaz looked very thoughtful for a minute; then Evest leaned forward, resting his arms on the table.

"The relationship between Holly and Nalik is not that unusual," Evest said as he glanced at Holly. "There are a few planets that we have visited on a regular basis, and your Earth is one of them. There have been angels before who have found their other halves within another race," he added.

"There have been two angels who have found their other halves here on Earth," Lindaz told us, "We have not had contact with either of them since the last time we were here. One of the Angels was in Egypt, and the other was in India."

Evest leaned back into his chair.

"We believe that both angels married their other halves and had children. Which means," Evest said...

"...that generations of humans may be part angel," Holly said, interrupting the elder.

Evest dipped his head in acknowledgment.

"Yes, Holly," he told her, "It is because of that reason that we believe evolution took the leap and made your sister more like us."

"Wow!" James said as he looked at me, and I looked at him.

As the words Evest spoke sink in, I turned back to him, suddenly feeling confused.

"Why didn't Christik tell us all this!" I asked.

Both Evest and Lindaz looked at us with sympathy.

"Christik did not know very much about what happened to the angels," Lindaz said, "she was too young to understand at the time. If she had known more, she would have told you. All Christik knew was that one of the angels was her older brother."

Deep down, I knew that she was right. Christik had always been honest and above board with us. Just as I was telling myself off for even doubting my friend, and James was about to ask another question, Christik glided back into the meeting room. When she took in all our faces, which looked shocked, she suddenly looked worried.

"What has happened?" She asked with concern in her voice.

"There is nothing to worry about, my own, my one," Lindaz told her calmly, "we will tell you on the way," she assured her.

Christik dipped her head.

"The craft is ready, and there are angels ready in each location to help us collect the animals," Christik said, "Let us get this show on the road."

When Lindaz and Evest looked at Christik with complete confusion on their faces, we all burst into laughter, which was a blessing as it certainly lightened the mood and made the shock wear off quicker.

Christik smiled and opened the door wide, allowing us to walk through. The kids were still chuckling as they passed her, and the elders got up to follow. James and I began to follow from the rear.

"You aren't zapping us to the craft?" I asked Christik when I reached her.

"I thought you would appreciate not shivering on the craft," Christik said as she smiled at me knowingly.

"Thank you," I told her gratefully.

While we walked to the hanger where the craft was kept, Lindaz and Evest told Christik what they'd told us about the angels. She was just as surprised as we all were, although she agreed that it explained a lot.

"What my parents have told us is good news," Christik said as we reached the craft.

"Why is that?" James asked as we started to get on board the waiting craft.

Christik followed James and glided to the front of the craft as we all boarded.

"It is good news because it means that Nalik and Holly have a wonderful future ahead of them," she answered, as she smiled at my daughter, who was still holding hands with her angel.

Holly was positively beaming at Christik, and Nalik was glowing his shimmer profusely. Relief flowed through me as I thought about Holly and Nalik's future together. *'There's hope for everyone now,'* I said to myself with a smile.

Watching Christik in action; flying the craft was just as impressive as watching Hulaz. Her actions were the same as she connected with the craft, and her flying skills were just as smooth. Everything the angels did seemed to be flawless, and at times, it was quite intimidating. The only thing that the angels weren't able to do was to tell jokes. Although it was as funny as hell when they tried to come out with some of our sayings and Christik seemed to enjoy retelling them.

Like always, it was hard to guess how long we were flying for. Especially this time because we were all more relaxed, and we were all talking the whole time. It was like a Q & A with the elders. We were all asking them questions, and they were fantastic answering each one. They were especially patient with the kids, which made James and I like them even more.

I felt the craft beginning to descend, and my baby girl suddenly started moving around. I could sense her excitement growing as the craft got closer to the ground. I placed my hand on my bump and stroked her affectionately as her arm or leg pushed outwards, *'Don't worry baby girl; we're going to get them,'* I told her. I winced a little as I felt either an elbow or a knee pushing against my hand.

"Are you ok, baby?" James asked with a worried look.

"I'm good; she knows we're here, and she's just pushed out a knee I think," I told him with a reassuring smile.

James nodded in understanding. I knew he remembered what it was like with the other kids, and all of them had been active babies. When the craft connected with the ground, my heart began to thump in my chest, partly due to the unknown but also with excitement.

CHAPTER 7

W hen the door of the craft opened, it was like being slapped with a wet blanket. The humidity was so bad that I knew one hundred percent that my hair was probably looking as if I'd been electrocuted. It was strange because automatically I expected a lot of wildlife noise when the door opened, but from inside, all we could hear was one or two birds making a strange noise.

Christik began to disconnect herself from the craft, and the vines smoothly uncurled themselves from her arms and hands, melting back into the craft frame. As soon as she was free, she turned around, waved an arm and suddenly, we were all wearing shoes.

It was funny because I was getting used to not wearing shoes now and James, as well as the kids, never seemed bothered by having bare feet all the time either. Luckily, the shoes were so comfortable; they really were like the best slippers ever.

As the elders were closest to the exit, they disembarked first with the rest of us following behind. The air was heavy with the humidity, and it was even more stifling than the trip we'd taken so many years ago to South Carolina. Our trip was at the height of summer when it was a hundred and ten degrees and one hundred percent humidity. I had to assume that we were somewhere very tropical.

When we looked around at our surroundings, some of us turning on the spot, we were amazed at the sheer natural beauty of the place. There were tropical trees and plants everywhere, all moist from the humid air, and some leaves were dripping with their wetness. The foliage was so thick that we couldn't see through it to see what was beyond.

The bird or birds made the weird noise again; only this time the sound appeared to be a little closer.

"I think the animals that we released here can sense you and the baby already, Mel," Nalik said with a smile.

"How is that possible, Nalik? We've literally just landed," Holly said.

"It is as if your baby sister is sending out a signal to them," Nalik explained.

"Where are we exactly?" I asked as I continued to study our surroundings as my hair frizzed even more.

"We are in the Amazon rainforest near Madagascar," Christik answered. "The rainforest is a large part of your ecosystem, and we were saddened to see so much of it had been destroyed," she added with the sadness evident in her voice.

"Humanity forgot over time that the rainforests, jungles, forests and oceans are the lungs for your planet's oxygen supply," Evest added, "just as your lungs keep your bodies alive."

Christik stepped forward, and she reached for her com on her chest.

"Angels, we are here, locate and join us please," she said aloud.

Within the blink of an eye, angels began to appear one by one until there were twelve of them surrounding us. All of them looked magnificent with their shimmering green hair and wings standing out from the backdrop of the rainforest. '*Good job they aren't the guard angels, they would have stuck out like sore thumbs,*' I thought as I smiled at them.

Each of the angels had a container box for the animals, and they were all various sizes. Two of the angels had two large boxes between them, making me even more excited to find out what animals were there.

The strange bird noise sounded again, and this time, it sounded very close. Immediately, we all began to look around for the bird just as another bird called from the other side of us.

"How many birds are there?" James asked as he scanned the trees and undergrowth.

"There are two birds of the same breed," Christik said as her eyes stared at a very large tree behind me. "You call them Potoo birds, and they are normally nocturnal, but they are coming because of the baby," she added, "they are masters of camouflage."

The Potoo bird called again, and it was so close that I nearly jumped out of my skin. Its call was like nothing I'd ever heard from a bird, and it almost sounded as if it was squawking the word, War. My eyes caught movement and, as they focused, I spotted the Potoo bird as it gradually inched its way down the tree it was on.

If the bird hadn't moved, there was no way that I'd have seen it. It was a stunning bird whose body looked more elongated than other birds I'd seen, and its feathers were mainly various shades of grey.

There was the odd tufty feather sticking out from under the folds of its wings, so I assumed that it was still a juvenile.

Movement from higher up the tree made me look up, and I was relieved to spot the second bird. None of us moved as we watched the two juvenile Potoo birds inch their descent. As the lowest bird reached my shoulder level, it turned its head to look at me, and suddenly I was staring into two bright yellow eyes that were very curious. I could feel our baby girl moving excitedly in my tummy.

"This is the coolest moment in my life ever!" April breathed.

"You like animals?" Abigail asked quietly.

"Yes, I've always loved animals," she answered, "That's one of the reasons I hated being in care because I couldn't have a pet," she said sadly.

"We love animals too, and we had lots of pets," Abigail told her, "no wonder you've fitted in so well with us all. You were meant to be our sister."

"Thank you, sis," April said a little tearfully.

I didn't need to look behind me to know that April had tears streaming down her face, and she was probably in Abigail's arms having a hug.

The Potoo bird squawked again, but this time, its squawk was at me as if it was trying to communicate with me. I trusted my instincts and my baby girl, as I raised my arm to offer it my forearm to mount. Without hesitation, the bird hopped from the tree and landed on my arm. He or she was a beautiful bird, and as it sat on my arm, its head began to tilt sideways, one way then the other as if it was sizing me up.

Not being able to resist; I raised my other hand, and I started to stroke the Potoo bird from its head to its tail. It raised its head, which made me realize that it was enjoying the attention.

"The other bird is coming closer, baby; you need to place that one in the box quick," James told me, snapping me out of the affectionate moment.

If I hadn't known how valuable and limited our time was, I might have been pissed off. However, I knew that we had to act quickly, and I gave myself a proverbial kick up the butt.

When I turned around, one of the red-headed angels raised a hand to me and then opened the container box he was carrying. I walked over slowly, so as to not scare the bird, and I continued to stroke down its body while telling it that everything was going to be fine. The bird was calm, but when I tried to place it inside the box, it didn't want to go in.

Instead, the bird literally walked its way up my arm until it was resting its head against my breasts. I was so taken back by the look of affection in its bright yellow eyes that I instinctively brought up my other hand to hold it. James cleared his throat as if to say, '*get on with its woman,*' and again, I told myself off while giggling.

"You have to go into the box, little one, the monsters are coming, and we have to keep you safe," I told the Potoo bird, "I will come and see you when I can," I added as I stroked it again.

I had no clue if the bird understood a word I said, but I think it sensed what I was saying. So, when I tried again; this time, it allowed me to place it inside. As I stood up, the angel closed the door on the container, and he instantly vanished.

"Ok, let's get the other one," I said, feeling a bit more business-like.

I walked back over to the tree as the other Potoo made its way down. It was slightly smaller than the first, but there was still no way to tell if it was male or female. It was certainly a lot more sure of itself as it reached me, hopping straight into my arm and affectionately rubbing its head against my bare skin.

"Affectionate little thing, aren't you," I told it.

I walked straight over to the next waiting angel with her hand raised, and she smiled as I placed the bird inside the box. In a second, the angel and bird were gone. I walked over to James, who was grinning from ear to ear.

"I'm actually quite jealous that you're getting to do this, baby," James said, feigning sad puppy eyes.

I wrapped my arms around his waist and hugged him tightly as I knew that he really was disappointed. James was always the biggest animal lover between us all, which is why he wanted to be a vet now.

"I'm sorry, James; I know it's not fair, but it's not me, remember; it's the baby," I reminded him. "So, when the baby is born; it's going to be something that you can both share together. A daddy and daughter thing," I added.

Abruptly, his eyes lit up as my words registered.

"Wow, I didn't even think of that," he said, suddenly excited.

He turned his head to look at April.

"April did you hear that!" He asked her, "We're going to be able to look after the animals with your new baby sister," he said, grinning like a Cheshire Cat.

I knew he'd said that to April to make sure she knew she was included, and I loved him for it, and so did our baby girl, who was now wriggling like crazy. Pulling back from James, I placed my hand on my bump, and I could feel our daughter's anticipation.

"I think something else is coming," I said aloud.

All of us stood still and stayed silent as we looked for the slightest movement and listened for the tiniest sound. Before long, we could hear twigs breaking on the rainforest floor and rustling of leaves as something moved through the vegetation. As it neared, it definitely sounded like a larger creature.

When the animals broke through the undergrowth, we all nearly took a step back. There were two of them, and they were the strangest animals I'd ever seen. It was as if Mother Nature couldn't decide whether to make a zebra or giraffe, so she did half and half.

Their thick zebra-shaped bodies and large ears were a deep brown, which lightened as the sun hit, but their legs, from their bodies down to their hooves, were striped just like zebras. Just like the Potoo birds; they also looked like juveniles. They didn't seem as timid as the birds and the slightly bulkier one huffed and scraped at the ground, not in an aggressive way but more of a hello.

James and the kids came closer to me, moving slowly so as not to frighten the creatures.

"What are these animals called?" I asked as I reached out a hand to the closet one.

"They are called Okapi," Christik told us all.

"They are so cool," Harrison said as he inched closer to the other Okapi.

I was half expecting the Okapi to back away, but there was no fear in them at all.

"They aren't afraid of us like I thought they would be," I said as I turned to James.

Evest glided forward to stand next to James and me.

"There are no predators here as yet, so these creatures have nothing to fear," Evest explained, "When we repopulate an animal kingdom, we always release the insects first, then the birds and plant eaters. When they are thriving, we then release the meat-eaters.

"That way, nature is in balance and stands the best chance of success," Lindaz added.

"Well, that makes sense," I told them.

I took another step forward and started to stroke the Okapi before me, and its coat felt similar to a horse, only softer and thicker. Harrison followed my example and did the same. Before long, we were all petting the Okapi, and they certainly liked the affection we were showing them, especially the large male that I was petting.

"As much as I'm enjoying this, we need to get them in their boxes," I said.

I could feel our baby beginning to get anxious as we were wasting time.

"Come on, boy, come with me," I said, as I beckoned the male by clicking my fingers.

As I walked towards the angels with the largest containers; the male Okapi started to follow, and then the smaller female began to follow us both. Once the male gingerly entered his box, the female got into hers and, apart from a slight huff, they settled quite quickly. The angels disappeared before our eyes.

Within a couple of hours, we had ten different animals already boxed and taken, and we were just waiting for the last two, which were

Capybaras, to get into the containers. Apparently, they weren't very keen, and Evest ended up using his power to gently persuade them from their rears.

All the animals had been very strange looking compared to what we were used to, and the Capybaras were no exception. They almost looked like giant guinea pigs with longer legs, and the girls thought they were very cute.

When both of the Capybaras were boxed and taken, we all seemed to breathe a sigh of relief. This was short-lived when we remembered that this was just the first location. Our baby girl had settled once the last two animals had been taken, and it was quite a relief for me. I was starting to feel quite drained as the excitement was wearing off.

"On to the next," Christik said as she waved her arm toward the waiting craft.

James walked over to me and wrapped his arm around my waist.

"You both did a great job, beautiful," he said as he kissed my cheek.

"I think it was all this little one," I told him while tapping my bump, "she certainly knows her own mind already."

As we boarded the craft, our kids were all talking about the animals and which ones they liked the best. April was still full of excitement and was asking the elders about not only the animals we'd seen but also creatures on other planets that they'd been too.

The elders began to describe some of the creatures to the kids as Christik connected to the craft and began to take off. I tried to keep up with the conversations between the elders and our kids, but I was so drained already from what we had done and the nightmare I'd had that my eyes became heavy, and as soon as I rested my head on James' shoulder, I was gone.

I didn't wake until James very gently stroked my face and softly called my name. It took me a couple of minutes to wake up properly and get my bearings again, remembering that I was still on the craft. I sat up and looked around, and I saw that all eyes were on me. I felt a little embarrassed, but the sleep had done me a world of good.

"Was I snoring?" I asked, suddenly aware that my mouth was really dry.

"No baby, you weren't snoring," James said, rather unconvincingly.

Out of the corner of my eye; I could see the kids all nodding.

"Liar," I scolded him with a giggle, "I really need a drink and maybe some food before we start again. How long before we land?" I asked.

"We are already here, Mel," Lindaz said with a smile, "We can eat before we disembark."

"The animals will be making their way to you already," Nalik added, "They could probably sense you and your daughter as soon as we got close to the area."

The angels with their usual thoroughness had stored both food and drinks on board before we'd left the main craft. To be honest, food and drinks for the journey hadn't even entered my mind, as I'd been so concerned with saving the animals and making sure the bad dream didn't become a reality.

I was very grateful to the angels for being so thoughtful because I knew that if I was hungry, then the kids would be ravenous, especially the boys.

We all ate and drank our fill, and I felt so much better after eating. I could feel my energy levels rising, and I was ready to start again. The kids were raring to go as well, which was good. Thank goodness, we were a family of animal and nature lovers.

"So, where have we landed?" I asked as we finished the last of the drinks.

"We are now in India," Christik said as she put away the trays and cups, "we have six animals here to collect."

"I always wanted to travel when I was older, but I didn't expect it to be like this," Anthony said to Christik with a smile.

"I am pleased that you are all able to experience this," Christik told him, "I believe the first two animals are arriving," she added.

Knowing that two of the animals had already reached us had our butts moving. Christik opened the craft door, and we all quickly exited into another moist rainforest, and it was just as lush as the first. The temperature was different but not by much, and it was very dark. I couldn't tell if it was late at night or early morning. Six angels were there waiting for us with their containers ready, and all dipped their head in welcome.

Just as we were about to reciprocate the gesture, something big glided through the air straight at me. Not knowing what it was, I instinctively turned my body and raised my arms to shield my face. I couldn't help the loud shriek as I felt it land on my raised arms, and I heard James and the kids yell and shriek too.

When I started to wonder why no one was coming to my rescue, the giggling started. I turned my head to whatever it was that was clung to my arms, just as the giggling turned to belly laughter.

"Mel, you seem to have a big flying squirrel on you," James said through his laughter.

I was suddenly eye to big beady eye with the flying squirrel, and it began to rub the side of its face on my hand. I couldn't help but smile at the squirrel; it looked so content to be near me. Rustling in the nearest trees made me act quickly. I wanted to be prepared for the next flying squirrel. I quickly walked over to the green-haired angel, who had her hand raised and her container open ready. I'd literally just managed to get the flying squirrel inside the box when the other decided it would glide through the air and land right on my back.

"Oh, my god!" I shrieked when I felt it land on me with a thud.

I could feel its front paws gripping around my neck and its back legs splaying across my back. The kids and James were laughing so hard that I was surprised they could still breathe. I straightened myself up and looked at the female angel, whose container I'd just closed with the first squirrel inside. She looked at me with a face that was trying to be serious, and she was definitely trying not to laugh too.

In good humor, I raised my eyebrows, and I tried not to laugh myself. I turned around with a serious face and glared at James and the kids with the squirrel still attached on my back. It was starting to nuzzle into my hair; surprisingly gentle considering how large it was.

"So, you think it's funny, do you?" I said firmly, glaring at them in turn.

Abruptly, they all stopped and looked at me like they were all deer caught in car headlights. I couldn't hold my laughter in any longer.

"Ahhh, I got you!" I said through my laughter.

The look of relief washed over their faces, and then the laughter came again.

"Mom, you had us worried for a minute there," Anthony said, through his giggles.

"I know, honey, I'm sorry, but I couldn't resist," I told him, "Can you remove the squirrel, so we can put it inside the container?"

Straightaway, Anthony and Harrison came to my rescue, gently detaching the squirrel, who seemed most put out. I stroked the squirrel's ear before Anthony put it inside the next box. Both angels vanished with smiles on their faces.

Before long, we had managed to retrieve all six animals, and we were back on the craft to the next location. Between us, we had rescued two lion-tailed macaque monkeys and two purple frogs, as well as the two flying squirrels. The purple frogs were the most unattractive frogs I'd ever seen, but James, Anthony and Harrison thought they were very cool.

We were feeling really proud of ourselves as we traveled to the next location. It was amazing to see and handle so many different animals that we wouldn't have probably seen under normal circumstances, let alone met in person. As we travelled, I could feel a sense of pride forming, *'We are doing an amazing thing right now,'* I thought.

CHAPTER 8

I t felt as if we had only just taken off and when we seemed to be descending again. '*Surely we can't be at the next location already,*' I thought, as we all looked at each other; obviously, we were all thinking the same thing.

"We must have been quite close to the next place," James said, with his eyebrows raised.

"That's good," I told him with a smile, "it means we'll get our task completed sooner."

I should have known that we were already arriving; our baby was already starting to do flips, and I could sense her anxiety level going up. '*Don't worry, baby girl; it's not going to take long,*' I assured her as the craft landed softly.

"Which country are we in now?" April asked.

Her eyes were filled with excitement. In fact, James and all the kids had the same excited look in their faces.

"I believe we are now in China," Evest told her. "We always had a good relationship with your ancient Chinese ancestors," he explained.

Christik's glow was beginning to dim as the craft started to power down, and the vines were quickly receding back where they came from before disappearing completely.

"The Chinese had the utmost respect for their country and the natural balance of nature. It was a great shame that they let their leaders slaughter your creatures for vanity," Lindaz added. "So many creatures were killed for their body parts because of false beliefs that they were medicinal. No one needed those body parts apart from the animals they belong too."

"We could not agree with you more, Lindaz," I told her, "that is something none of us could understand, especially when scientists could prove there was no benefit."

"We will make sure that it never happens again," James told the elders.

His face was so serious that I knew he'd make it his life's mission to protect the animals, and I also knew that I'd be right by his side. In fact, we would all by his side as we all felt the same way.

The elders both dipped their heads to James in respect.

"We know you will, James," Evest said.

"Are we ready?" Christik asked everyone as she glided towards the craft door.

"Born ready!" The kids all said in unison.

They all looked at each other with smiles on their faces. Even Nalik and Christine had said it at the same time. All of a sudden, the craft was full of laughter. Anthony clapped Nalik on the back as he stood from his seat.

"You're going to fit into our family very well, Nalik," Anthony told him with a big grin.

They were still laughing as we left the craft, and the elders were smiling at them lovingly. The elders had taken a shine to the kids and appeared amused by their humor.

"Are your children always this funny?" Lindaz asked with bright eyes.

"Oh, yes!" I told her, "My mom always told me that there are two things that can make any situation better, love and laughter."

"I believe you are right, Mel," Christik said as she glided towards me.

There were only four angels waiting for us this time in the cleaning we'd landed in. We dipped our heads at the angels before taking in the new surroundings. The air felt cooler and crisper on our skin, and a slight breeze made goosebumps appear on my bare arms. We seemed to be in a forest clearing and somewhere close by was a river or waterfall, as I could hear the water rushing against a riverbed or large stones.

It was a beautiful forest with different flowering bushes and trees; all mingled with patches of bamboo. When I saw the bamboo, it brought a smile to my face as I remembered James having an ongoing battle with the plant when we first moved into our house. The previous owners had planted some in the garden, and it spread around the garden like wildfire. It had taken three full years for James to finally get rid of it all and as the memories went over in my mind, I turned to look at James, who had his eyes rolling in his head.

"Is the bamboo bringing back pleasant memories, husband of mine?" I asked while trying to keep a straight face.

"Not nice memories, no!" He answered with pursed lips that had me chuckling.

The kids were all looking at us in confusion.

"Bamboo is not your dad's favorite plant," I told them with a smirk, "I'll explain another time," I added.

"Can we see what the water noise is?" Abigail asked the elders with hope in her voice.

"Of course, Abigail," Lindaz told her warmly.

"The animals will follow your mother and baby sister to wherever they go."

"Awesome, let's go," Abigail said as she pointed in the direction of the water noise.

As Abigail led the way with April, Christine and Holly, we all followed behind. We could hear the leaves rustling as the cool light breeze blew through. The flowering bushes smelled fantastic as we brushed past them, and I have to be honest, I could have happily plonked my arse down on the ground and read a book right there with the water rushing in the background. It was the kind of place where you could forget all your worries and just relax.

"We had only recently started to release animals here," Christik said as we walked close to the water. "That is why there are only four here," she added.

"I must admit I was wondering why there was so few," I told her.

"We are lucky to be in the early stages of the healing process," Nalik said with a serious tone, "It would have been an impossible task if it had been at a later stage."

"And it's a bloody good job that you're now an animal magnet, Mom," Abigail added with a smile.

Nalik and Abigail were spot on with their comments. I dreaded to think what would have happened to all the animals if the situation had been different. It would have been so heartbreaking for all of us women to have helped save the animals, only to see them killed. It made me shudder just to think about it.

It was a lovely walk through the Chinese forest we'd landed in, and we were all admiring the beautiful trees and bushes. The forest was so dense that nothing could be seen other than leaves and the sky above. We could hear the water sounds getting closer with each step. Abigail and April were walking faster than everyone else, their excitement getting the better of them. One second, the girls were there and in another second, they were gone, disappearing behind a thick patch of bamboo.

"Woah!" Abigail said over the rushing water, barely loud enough for us to hear her.

The rest of us sped up to catch up with them, and as we walked around the bamboo patch, we all stopped. The scene before us was breathtaking in every way. We walked out onto a wide riverbank, and we were suddenly standing on pebbles instead of wild grass. Not only was the rushing river very wide but it also traveled downwards, and through the massive clearing it had created; we could see a stunning mountain capped with snow.

"This is so beautiful," I told James breathlessly as he slipped his hand in mine, "I never thought we would ever get to see places like this."

"Neither did I, Mel," he agreed, "With four kids, I didn't think we'd ever be able to afford to travel the world. Now we are getting to share these places and moments with our kids. We are really lucky," James added with a smile.

Lindaz and Evest glided next to James and me, and like us, they were holding hands, which was lovely to see.

"You live on a beautiful planet," Lindaz told us. "We have not been to many planets that have such natural beauty," she added, "we have always felt a deep connection to your world."

"I wish you could have told our ancestors how important it was to protect all this," April told the elders.

Her lovely face showed the sadness she felt. Evest let go of Lindaz's hand, and he glided over to April. Dipping his upper body towards her small frame, he took one of April's hands in his, and he looked deeply into her wide eyes.

"April, we did tell your ancestors," he told her, "We told them, and we showed them how important it was to keep everything in balance with your Earth.

"Unfortunately, we could not stay here permanently, April," Lindaz added, "Every time we left your planet, your ancestors would develop quickly, which is not a bad thing. However, your race would not sustain and protect your planet while evolving.

"It is always the way that the few greatly affect the many," Evest said solemnly. "Vanity, greed and pride are the things which were destroying your world, April.

April bowed her head to Evest.

"Thank you for being so honest with me, Evest," April told him sincerely.

"Always April, we will never tell you untruths," he told her.

THE MARILIANS

We all stood admiring the beautiful scenery for a few more minutes before the girls decided to play toss the stone while waiting for the animals to find us. The boys were quite happy to watch the girls throw the pebbles as hard as they could, and Holly's technique was most impressive.

Before too long, all the kids and Nalik were playing, and Nalik was the only male who didn't appear upset that Holly was winning. She had a very good arm on her, and her stones were definitely traveling the furthest, with Christine coming a close second. The rest of us watched with smiles as the kids tried to outdo each other.

While we stood watching, a distant noise of breaking branches and rustling leaves caught my hearing.

"Something is coming, and it sounds like they're in a rush," I said to James, who was still holding my hand, "Kids, they are coming," I called out.

The kids quickly stopped their game, and the boys, whose turn it was to throw, dropped the pebbles they were holding. We could hear the noise of the animals getting louder and louder. Just as the kids walked over to the angels and us, two creatures burst out from the bushes next to us, making me jump.

There was no way of telling what they were at first as the two creatures tumbled over each other's bodies. There were squeals from both, but it didn't sound like it was aggressive. The seemed to be playing, and as they rolled and tried to detangle themselves; all we make out was thick brown fur and almost black legs.

Christik glided towards the two animals and outstretched her hand towards them with her palm glowing. She looked bemused at the creatures as she let her power flow from her hands.

"There is no time for play right now," Christik told them.

As her calming power hit them, they both comically stopped play fighting and flopped on their backs with their paws splayed out; with faces that almost looked like they were smiling. It was as if they'd been given happy gas and were now happily chilling.

Once they were still, I took that as my cue to retrieve them. They looked like raccoons, especially their faces, with the black patches on their eyes and the markings on their faces and bodies. However, the shape of them was more canine.

I scooped the first one into my arms, and as soon as I held it, it started to nuzzle against my neck.

"Are these a kind of raccoon?" I asked Christik as she held the other within her power.

"They are Tanuki," she answered, "I believe your people would call them raccoon dogs."

"They look a lot like raccoons, but then their proportions aren't the same," James said as he helped me place the one I held inside the first container.

"These Tanuki are closer genetically to your dogs than your raccoons," Evest told James, "As you can see, the Tanuki cubs are very playful."

"I think they are so cute," April added, "Can I get the other one for you, Mel?" She asked with a pleading look on her face.

"Yes, of course, you can," I told her.

I straightened up after closing the box, nodding to the angel before he vanished, and I turned around to face April as she walked over to Christik. The Tanuki was still lying on its back with its legs in the air, looking at Christik as if she were the best thing since sliced bread. As soon as April scooped up the Tanuki, Christik reigned in her calming power. The animal suddenly wasn't chilled as Christik's power stopped, and it desperately looked around for its little partner in crime.

April tried in vain to keep hold of it, while James and I rushed over to help her. Between the three of us, we just about managed to get the Tanuki into the next container. When the angel vanished, we all breathed a sigh of relief.

"If you believe that the Tanuki were a handful, then you should prepare yourselves," Christik told us.

"Why? "What animals are we waiting for next?" I asked with my eyebrows raised questioningly.

Christik's resounding smile had me smiling back in return.

"Two panda cubs," she said. "If I remember correctly, they were more playful than the Tanuki."

Something caught my eye, and when I looked up, the two waiting green-headed angels were both nodding their heads in agreement and were both smiling.

"Were you the angels who brought the pandas here?" I asked.

"Yes, we were," one of the angels answered.

"It took us quite a while to remove the panda cubs from our legs, as they didn't want to leave us," the other angel told us.

"They were clinging to your legs?" Holly asked through her giggles.

"Yes, they were," the first angel said with a smirk.

"Now that would have been very funny to see!" Christine told them warmly.

"Well, while we're waiting for these little rascals, why don't we have some refreshments?" Christik said.

She then turned her gaze to Nalik.

"Nalik, if you could retrieve the drinks and food, please," she asked.

Nalik dipped his head and vanished back to the craft, and while we waited for him to return, we all walked back to the grass and sat down. I was pleased to take a rest as our baby girl was starting her somersaults again.

"Is the baby moving?" April asked as she sat down next to James and me.

"She sure is," I told her, smiling as I looked into her wide eyes.

"Can I feel her move please?" April asked with hope in her voice; "I've never felt a baby move before."

"Of course, you can," I told her.

Yet again, my heart felt heavy with the knowledge that April had missed out on so much normal family life. She inched herself forward and gingerly placed her hand on my swollen baby bump, just as Nalik reappeared with the food and drinks. While Nalik placed everything on the floor between us all, April sat in amazement as she felt her new sister moving around under her hand.

"She's very strong isn't she," April stated, as I felt the baby pushing her feet against the side of my stomach to push her butt out.

"Yes, she is," I agreed, "I believe she is enjoying you stroking her back because she's pushing to get to your hand," I told her.

I took April's free hand in mine and placed it near her other hand.

"Can you feel the little bump?" I asked her.

"Yes," she replied, with even wider eyes.

"That's her butt pushing out, and you are stroking her back," I explained, "I think she's going to like back tickles, just like Abigail," I said with a smile.

At the mention of her name, Abigail quickly looked around to us.

"I still love having my back tickles," Abigail said with a grin. "I would happily pay someone to be my own personal back tickler," she added with a giggle.

"You are so much like your mom," James told her warmly.

"Thank you for letting me feel the baby," April said with a big smile.

"You are so welcome, honey," I told her, "it won't be long before you'll be able to hold her."

Her resounding smile lightened my heart, and I knew she was going to be a wonderful big sister.

Nalik and Holly finished handing out the food, and we all started to eat, drink and chat between ourselves. Although it was a beautiful place; it did seem strange not to hear birds singing. All that could be heard was the water rushing alongside us. I did know that the pandas were close, though because the baby was still moving around, and it almost felt as if she was using my bladder as a trampoline.

Just as I decided to stand up and move around, the first panda quickly padded out from the trees. It stopped and looked at each of us in turn as if it was trying to decide who was friendly. James and the kids all oooo'ed and ahhhh'ed at the panda cub while it looked around, and then the panda locked eyes with me. It was as if he or she was thinking '*Ahh there you are.*'

I decided to kneel instead of standing up, so I was level with the panda. I knew there was no way that I'd be able to lift it. Even though it was young, it was still a chunky little thing. It seemed quite excited as it came my way, and every now and then, it would look one way then the other, possibly checking to see if anyone was going to stop it.

The panda cub had almost reached me when the other panda cub ran out from the trees. It was running straight for the first panda like it had been trying to catch up to it. The little panda abruptly realized that the first panda wasn't alone. Its head whipped around wildly as its eyes looked from angels to humans; the poor little thing couldn't slow down its momentum even though its little legs tried to brake.

I looked from the second panda whose eyes were wide with shock to the first panda whose little expression said, '*?*' And suddenly the two pandas were a bundle of rolling white and black fur, rolling across the grass and then pebbles, heading for the water. In seconds, we were all on our feet and trying to catch the rolling fluff bundle that was going to get soaked.

The kids were all giggling as they tried to stop the pandas, but it was too late. With a splash, the little cubs rolled straight into the cold rushing river, and the moment they hit the water, they fell apart. Both wet cubs were lying on their backs with their little legs waving in the air. The shock of the cold water and the water washing over their faces made them panic.

"Quickly, get them out!" I shouted as the poor little cubs began to squeal with distress.

James and the kids were quickly following the cubs, aiming to retrieve them, but the angels were quicker. Lindaz and Evest quickly raised glowing hands towards the panicking pandas, and as their power shot forward encasing the cubs, James and the kids backed off. We all watched as the elders started to raise the cubs out of the water. They looked like they were inside glowing bubbles, and they seemed so confused, and I'm sure relieved too.

As the cubs were lifted into the air, the water ran off them and out of the bubbles. It was quite funny to see them trying to shake themselves inside the bubbles, failing miserably as they kept losing their balance. Lindaz and Evest began to use their power to dry the cubs while floating the cubs over to Anthony and Harrison whose eyes were lighting up.

"The panda cubs are heavy," Evest told them, "are you ready to hold them?" He asked.

"Yes," Anthony said.

"I'm ready," Harrison told him.

Both the boys held out their arms ready to take the cubs, and the elders aim was precise. The cubs landed softly into Anthony and Harrison's waiting and steady arms, and I think the pandas were relieved to be safe, even though they were in the arms of strangers. The girls walked straight over, desperate to check the cubs over.

"Are you ok, little guy?" Abigail asked the cub Harrison was holding.

Its little eyes looked up at her as it rubbed its little black nose against her hand. April and Holly were both rubbing behind the ears of the cub Anthony was holding, while Christine stroked down its fluffy back.

"Oh my god, they are so cute," April said.

"Did you have a scare, little one?" Holly asked it as it turned its head sideways so she could scratch where it wanted her to scratch.

It was comical to watch the pandas enjoying all the attention, and neither of them seemed to want the attention to stop. As much as I wanted the kids to enjoy themselves, time was getting on, and we still had one more place to go.

"Let's get them in their containers, so the angels can make them safe kids," I said.

The looks of disappointment were clear to see on the kids' faces, and I hated to be the bad guy. Reluctantly, the boys with the girls' help managed to get both of the pandas into the containers. I was relieved when it was done and relieved that our baby girl had settled down once again. As soon as the angels left with the cubs, we all helped to clear up the food and drinks and walked back towards the craft. I was starting to look forward to getting to bed, so I was pretty sure the kids were feeling worn out too.

CHAPTER 9

Within a short time of boarding the craft and taking off, all of the kids were fast asleep. Christine was sound asleep against Anthony's chest, Abigail was asleep against Harrison's shoulder, and Holly and April were fast asleep on either side of Nalik. Poor Nalik looked as if he was afraid to move. I was leaning against James, who had his arm around me, and I could feel his arm getting heavy against me as he too began to fall asleep. For some reason, I found myself wide awake.

Evest and Lindaz were sitting across from James and I, and they both looked so relaxed that I envied them.

"Have you always been together?" I asked, looking from one elder to the other.

Lindaz smiled warmly at me as Evest look her hand and brought it to his lips to kiss it softly.

"Yes, we had always been together," Evest replied with pride ringing in his words. "We were very fortunate to find each other while we were young."

"Did you know straight away that you were each other's halves or soulmates as we call it?" James asked, surprising me.

I hadn't realized that my husband had stirred.

"We both knew straight away," Evest told us.

"Evest could not stop himself from glowing when we met," Lindaz said with a loving smile at her husband. I felt for him as we were healing a planet at the time. The race we were helping thought that it was a warning sign," Lindaz explained. "It took a lot of convincing to make the Catara race understand that it was love that was making Evest glow."

"Wow, I bet you felt awkward, Evest," James said with a knowing smile. "I felt like an idiot because my cheeks glowed bright red every time I saw Mel," James admitted, "I don't know how I'd have felt if I'd glowed all over every time I'd seen her."

"It did not affect me in a negative way," Evest said with a humorous smile, "We angels all have the same reaction to love when we find our other half. I am sure you aren't the only human to have red cheeks when in love."

"You're right, Evest, I've noticed that Anthony's cheeks like to glow red quite profusely. Like father like son," I laughed.

"Cheeky," James said as he tickled my side.

"We are nearly at our next location," Christik said from the front of the craft. "Would you like to wake the children now," she asked.

"Will do," I answered as I reached for Christine and Anthony.

We gently woke the kids as Christik started to descend the craft. By the time we landed, the kids were all awake and were rubbing their tired eyes.

"This is the last location; you will be pleased to hear," Christik assured the kids, "we will be back on the main craft soon."

"Which country are we in now Christik?" I asked her as she detached herself from the craft and glided through between us to the rear door.

"We are back in Egypt," she said as the door opened, and the dry heat from outside rushed in.

The elders waited patiently, letting Christik and all of us out first before following behind. It was surprisingly hot, considering the sun was quite low. The sky was full of warm colors that spread across the sky, giving the long grasses and trees a golden hue. Christik had landed the craft next to another river, but this river wasn't fast-moving like the one we'd left in China. Yet again, Christik's angels were waiting for us when we arrived, but this time, two of the six angels each had large water-filled containers, which was a surprise.

"What on earth are those for?" I asked Christik, pointing at the containers.

"You will see," she answered with a smile.

"I'm starting to think we're rubbing off on you a little too much," I told her.

Straightaway, she looked confused, and so did the elders.

"You have not been rubbing off on me, I would have felt it," Christik said with a confused and serious tone.

The kids and James found Christik's response highly amusing, and I only just managed to keep a straight face myself.

"I mean that you are picking up a lot of our human responses to things, Christik," I told her, no longer able to contain the giggle that escaped me.

"Ahh, I see," she said with a smirk on her lips.

She was getting very good at smirking at the right time too. As I looked around the area we were standing in; I could see lots of large abandoned houses and apartments built into the side of the riverbank on the opposite side from us. It seemed so weird to see buildings but with no noise of people or vehicles. It was truly surreal. The area must have been a bustling place at one time, probably busy with not only the residents but also plenty of tourists too.

"Is this the Nile river?" Christine asked Christik as she pointed to the river that was shimmering with the sun's warm colors.

"Yes, it is," Christik replied, "When we begin to release the animals, we try to make sure that they have a good water supply."

"That seems logical," Anthony said. "You plan it all very precisely, don't you."

"We have to, Anthony," Evest told him, "The fate of planets depends on us.

"That's a huge responsibility for your race, Evest. Doesn't the pressure get to you sometimes?" Holly asked him.

"No, it does not Holly," he told her softly, "We have been healing planets for a very long time. If something does not go as planned, we have each other to get through it," he added.

"I really wish we humans were more like your race," Holly said sadly.

"Many races go through the same stages that your race has been through, Holly," Lindaz told her, "It takes a very long time for a race to realize what is important and what is not. Some races never learn, such as the Marilians."

"I've got a feeling that eventually, the Marilians will end up destroying themselves," James said.

We all agreed with James. It was just a shame that the Marilians weren't going to destroy themselves before they had a chance to get Earth.

"Can we have a swim in the river while we're waiting for the animals to get to us?" Harrison asked, hopefully.

"Yeah, can we, Mom?" Abigail added, "It's so much hotter here; I bet the water feels amazing!"

I turned to Christik, who was smiling again at the kids.

"Is there anything in the water that's unsafe for the kids?" I asked.

"No, Mel, they will be perfectly safe," she assured.

I turned back to the kids, and they were already heading towards the water.

"Don't go too far out please, ok!" I called after them.

The kids had heard me, but all I got were waved hands of acknowledgment as they started to wade into the water. Nalik and Holly were soon swimming together, while Abigail, Harrison, Anthony, April and Christine were splashing and trying to wrestle each other. It was good to see that some things didn't change so quickly. Some sibling fun was just what they all needed.

James came up behind me and wrapped his arms around my waist, resting his hands on my bump.

"It won't be long before this little one is joining in," James said.

"It'll be ages before she is able to join in," I laughed.

"Ahh, you say that now gorgeous, but look at how quickly they've all grown up," he said seriously.

"Mmm, you're right, the time has flown by way too fast," I told him as I watched our kids having a blast., "Why are you brushing against my leg?" I added.

"I'm not," he replied, clearly confused.

I looked down at my left leg, and there sat by my ankle, rubbing its head against my leg was a sand-colored rodent of some kind and another sat next to it, which was looking at me.

"I think we have our first two arrivals," I said.

"We were all enjoying watching the children to notice them arrive," Lindaz stayed with a humorous smile.

"For sure!" James told her with a chuckle.

James released his arms, allowing me the space to bend down and pick up the creature that had taken a shine to my ankle. It felt as soft as a rabbit and was roughly the same size as the rabbits our kids had kept at our home.

"Mmm, what kind of animal are you?" I asked it as I lifted it to my eye level and watched it blink at me.

"They are Hyrax," Christik said, "Shall we get them into their containers quickly before the next animals arrive."

"Yes, good idea," I told her as James picked up the other Hyrax.

James managed to put his Hyrax into its box without any trouble. On the other hand, I had a bit of a nightmare because the Hyrax I was holding didn't want to leave. Luckily, the angel with the container was quick to help, and moments later, both of the animals were safe and gone. The kids were all oblivious to the whole thing and were racing each other in the water, laughing and cheering each other on.

After being surprised by the arrival of the two Hyrax, all of us were on alert waiting for the next animals to make an appearance. There was one thing that I was sure of and that was the fact that I was desperate for a pee. I didn't want to go in the river, especially as the kids were swimming in it, although I was pretty sure that may have been why they wanted to swim. I also didn't fancy going off into the empty buildings either. *'Bushes it is then,'* I thought to myself.

I turned to James, who was scanning the area for the next animals.

"James, I need to go off and pee," I told him quietly.

He nodded at me and turned to the angels and elders.

"We'll be back in a minute," he told them.

Taking my hand, James led me away from the others and into a dense patch of long grass and bushes. I was so desperate to go that I didn't even care that I had no tissue and was going to have to finish *'Oh natural.'* After I'd been, I felt such a relief, until a rat decided to run up my dress that I'd just let down.

"What the fuck!" I screamed, "James, it's a fucking rat, get it off meeeee…...!"

Panic ran through me instantly. I'd never been a fan of mice, ferrets, rats or any other type of vermin, ever since I'd witnessed a girl at school being bitten on the neck by a ferret she'd been petting in our biology class.

"James, quickly!" I screamed.

James came bounding through the grass and bushes to get to me. I couldn't stop myself from shaking as the rat hid under my hair and was rubbing itself against my neck. I was freaking out big time.

James reached me, and I could see his eyes searching my body for the rat.

"It's under my hair, it's under my hair James, get the little fucker off me now. Please!" I pleaded.

James quickly lifted my hair from the nape of my neck, and he plucked the rat off in one motion. I was relieved, and I staggered out of the bushes with my whole-body shuddering, taking a moment to steady my breathing. James followed behind with the rat held in his hands.

"I swear James that if I hadn't just gone for a pee, I would have peed myself when that little shit jumped on me," I told him with a shaky voice.

"It wouldn't have hurt you, baby," he told me gently.

"I don't give two shits James," I said, still feeling very pissed off, "The little fucker frightened the life out of me."

James started to laugh as he walked up to me and took my hand in his.

"Come on, we'll put it in its box quickly, so you can relax," he said with a smile.

"I don't think I'm going to be able to relax James when I know there's another one of those little fuckers coming," I told him seriously.

"Oh yeah, well don't fret, baby, I'll grab it before it can grab you," James said while laughing.

He was clearly enjoying my discomfort, a little bit too much, but I knew he would try and make sure that the other rat wouldn't jump on me.

When we got back to the angels and elders, they were all clearly confused as to what had happened. James walked straight over to the small container one of the angels held, and he placed the rat inside. He then turned to Lindaz, Evest and Christik.

"Mel doesn't do vermin," he explained to them. "She has a fear of them."

"Why?" Christik asked, genuinely concerned.

"It's a long story from my childhood," I told her, rolling my eyes.

Christik quickly picked up on the fact that I didn't want to talk about it any further and so she didn't push it. The elders obviously knew better than to ask too. Trying to take my mind off my skin that was still crawling, I looked down the riverbank to check on the kids. They were all still having a brilliant time and watching them helped to distract my mind. Well, it did for a little while.

"Mel, don't move!" James calmly said behind me.

I froze on the spot, knowing that the other large rat must have made an appearance. I did as James said and didn't move; just the thought of another rat had my skin crawling again. Suddenly, there was a thud as James hit the floor behind me. I felt the whoosh of air against my legs and feet as he landed heavily on the ground.

Turning my body around, I looked down to the floor, and James was now looking up at me with a huge grin. The other large rat was in his outstretched hands, looking around as if to say, "What the heck is going on?"

"You are my hero, husband of mine," I told him with a smile.

The relief I felt knowing that the second rat couldn't touch me was immense. James picked himself up off the ground, and he walked over to the waiting angel immediately. The angel was smiling as James quickly placed the second rat in the container. As soon as the box was closed, the angel disappeared.

"I think you need to warn Mel next time she has to be near any vermin," James said as he turned to Christik and the elders.

"Yes, agreed," Christik answered, giving me an understanding smile and nod of her head.

"Should we get the kids out of the river before the next animals arrive?" I asked Christik while looking at the large water-filled containers.

"No, the children are safe," she replied, "I think they will enjoy meeting the last two creatures."

I was tempted to ask what they were, but I quite liked surprises, so I decided not to. I was feeling intrigued as to what the animals were. The containers were large in height and width. I was racking my brains, going over in my mind what water creatures could be in the river that were harmless, and my mind was blank.

Christine's shrieks shocked me out of my thoughts. She was standing in the water with both her arms raised in the air, and I wouldn't have been surprised if she had been on her tiptoes too, trying to get herself out of the water as much as possible. Anthony was trying to calm her down while the other kids and Nalik were turning around, trying to spot something in the water. Harrison turned to face us on the riverbank while cupping his mouth with his hands.

"I think they are manatees," he shouted over.

As soon as he said manatees, I thought, '*Of course, that would explain the large containers and the fact that they were harmless.*' I'd always been fascinated with manatees or sea cows as some people called them. I turned to Christik, who was standing with Evest and Lindaz.

"Are the animals manatees?" I asked her.

"They are dugongs, a part of the manatee family," she replied with a smile, "They are friendly. Hulaz enjoys spending time with them," she added with a big smile.

"I want to see them," I told James with excitement in my voice.

"Me too," he said, sounding even more excited than I was.

With a big grin, James took my hand and started to lead me down to the water. The kids seemed very relaxed swimming with the dugongs and as the mammals swam up to the kids, the kids would place their hand into the water to stroke them.

Just as before, when I swam in the natural pool at the cruiser; the moment my dress touched the water, it began to shrink and turn into a swimsuit. James' trousers and tunic reacted the same way and now clung to his muscles as tight shorts and skintight top. It was hard not to admire my husband when he was wearing something so flattering, showing off his hard-toned body.

On the other hand, I was feeling rather self-conscious. It had been a long time since I'd been pregnant with the twins, and my dress had shrunk and shaped around my now prominent baby bump. Not only that but my now larger boobs were more evident also. I knew it wouldn't be long before I would start to look like a Buddha statue. Not that James cared, he seemed attracted to me no matter what shape I was, thank goodness.

The water was wonderful on our hot skin, and I hadn't realized just how hot I'd been getting until the water began to cool me down. I couldn't stop the "Ahhh" that escaped my lips as I let myself sink down into the cool river water. Within moments of being in the water; the two dugongs swam over to join me.

At first, I was quite startled as the first one brushed against my side. I wasn't expecting them to be so big, but then I was sure as adults, they would be more than double their size. Considering they were big; they were surprisingly gentle. I was pretty sure they knew I was pregnant and could sense our baby, just as our baby could sense them. James was enjoying the contact with them just as much as the kids and I were.

"They're so gentle, aren't they, Dad?" Harrison called over to James.

"Yes, they are, son," James told him, "and they are very graceful, too."

Holly and Nalik swam over towards James and me.

"We're going to get out now and dry off, Mom," Holly said as she got closer to us and the dugongs.

"Ok, darling," I replied as one of them decided to literally kiss my belly.

I laughed aloud and looked at my daughter, Nalik and James.

"Did you all just see that?" I asked, completely surprised.

All three of them laughed too.

"Maybe they are similar to dolphins," James said with a huge smile, "I've heard of dolphins behaving like that around pregnant women."

Holly was still giggling as she waded out of the water with Nalik holding her hand. I watched them leave, and as they walked up the riverbank, something in the distance among the abandoned buildings caught my eye. I thought I'd seen movement, but that was impossible, as I knew that we were the only people and angels there, '*Am I seeing things?*' I wondered.

"Are you ok, baby," James asked.

"I thought I saw movement up there where the buildings are," I told him.

My confusion must have been clearly evident.

"I know it's impossible, James, but I'm sure of it," I told him seriously.

James looked at me, just as confused as I felt. I knew he believed me, but he also knew it couldn't be possible too. I shook my head and shrugged my shoulders.

"Maybe I'm just tired, or I've had too much sun today," I told him, dismissing what I'd thought I'd seen.

Lindaz, Evest and Christik glided down to the water's edge with the two other angels following behind. Both of the angels were using their power to lift and glide the large water-filled containers.

"We are ready when you are to put the dugongs in their containers, Mel," Christik said.

"Ok, we're ready," I told her and holding a thumbs up.

"James, you may want to move back," Christik told him, "we will need some room, and I do not believe that the dugongs will move far enough away from Mel," she added.

James nodded his head and moved back to where April, Abigail and Harrison were standing. The kids had been avidly watching the creatures interact with me and obviously found it quite funny. As soon as James reached the kids, Abigail jumped on his back just like she used to when she was little. She carried on watching the dugongs, peering over James' shoulder.

When I looked back to Christik and her parents, Lindaz and Evest were standing side by side and were beginning to raise their hands with their palms facing towards me. I could see their hands were starting to glow as they tapped into their power. The glow brightened and just as before with the pandas, as soon as their power built up; it burst forward, hitting the water beside me.

As the elder's power passed through the water and surrounded the dugongs, all I could feel was a tingling on my legs and body. Slowly, the elders raised the creatures, lifting them up while keeping them encased inside huge bubbles of river water. It was so strange to see them so clearly, and as they passed by me and I saw their eyes, there was a deep intelligence there.

The elders floated the dugongs through the air towards the bank, and as they moved them, James, the kids and I followed behind, wading through the water. Just as we reached the water's edge, the two angels removed the tops of the containers to allow Lindaz and Evest to gently lower the dugongs inside. Water flowed over the tops of the boxes as the creatures sunk down, as their weight and the extra water took up the space.

When the angels placed the tops back on, they nodded before vanishing into thin air. As my swimsuit dried and changed back into a gown, I was thinking how seriously impressed I was at how easy the elders and angels had made it look. I thought what a shame it was that the angels hadn't been around every time a whale had been stranded on a beach. They would have made it such an easy job, getting the whales back out to sea.

"Mission accomplished," I said to Christik with a huge grin and feeling full of pride that we'd managed to complete our task.

"I knew you would be back here before long," said a deep masculine voice from a short distance away.

All of us whipped our heads around to see where the voice had come from.

CHAPTER 10

All of us whipped our heads around to see where the deep voice had come from. Standing between two palm trees was an angel with the same golden hair and wings as the angels who had reactivated Stonehenge. Only this angel was larger; almost as big as Lindaz and Evest, and he was dressed in a pale sandy-colored smock; and trousers.

"Brother?" Christik asked quietly, her shock clearly evident.

The male angel smiled at her affectionately. Then he raised his hands, and his body began to glow from his golden hair down to his bare toes, and we watched in awe as his smock and trousers vanished. As we watched in wonder, gold wings began to form and grow from behind him, and he opened the newly formed large golden wings, spreading them out in all their glory and bowing in front of us all. He was a magnificent sight to behold.

"I cannot believe you are still alive, my one, my own," Lindaz said breathlessly, "We thought you might have faded."

All of us looked from the golden angel to Lindaz and back to the angel. We were all stunned and speechless by the appearance of the angel, and I was confused with Lindaz's words; especially when

Christik had told me that angels couldn't die. *'Is fading dying?'* I wondered.

The angel straightened himself up, and he folded his large wings, so they were tucked behind his back once again.

"I hoped that you would all return," the angel said in his deep masculine voice. "I have waited a very long time; I am only sad that it is under such bad circumstances."

"We are happy that you are here my one, my own," Evest told him, "How did you find us?"

"I was dwelling further down the river when I felt you arrive," the angel explained as he glided towards us, "I was fading, so I was not sure if my mind was playing tricks on me. When you activated the Star passages, the Earth's energy revived my body," he added.

"How did you know that we were going to be here, Akhenaten?" Christik asked her brother.

"It was the dugongs," Akhenaten explained, "I saw them swimming in the river, so I knew that you had started to repopulate the animals here. I just had to be patient and wait for you to come back with more animals. However, I see that you are recapturing them. Why?" He asked.

"The Marilians are coming to try and take Earth," I said.

The words flowed out of my mouth before I realized what I was doing. Akhenaten looked down to me, and then he looked at James and the kids in turn.

"Forgive me, I forgot my manners," Akhenaten said apologetically. "I am Akhenaten, son of Lindaz and Evest, of the Angels," he proudly declared as he bowed his head to us respectfully.

Christik glided closer towards James, the children and I, smiling at us as she moved.

"I would like you to meet our friends, Akhenaten. This is Mel and James," she told him as she indicated to us both, "and their children Anthony, Abigail, Harrison, April and Holly. Also, Holly's other half Nalik and Anthony's other half, Christine," she added.

Akhenaten nodded his head to us all again in respect.

"It is a great pleasure to meet you all," he said sincerely.

"My one, we have much to do and so little time. Let us get back to the main craft, so we can all talk," Lindaz told him affectionately.

Akhenaten nodded his agreement to his parents and Christik.

As my family and I stood there still feeling stunned, Christik and the elders started to glide away towards the small craft. Akhenaten followed behind them, so we all followed too. '*Wow,*' James mouthed to me as he took my hand in his, "I know, crazy,' I mouthed back. We were both amazed at the arrival of Christik's long lost brother. The kids were all looking at each other with raised eyebrows.

One by one, we all boarded the small craft, and Christik took her place at the front as the pilot. Akhenaten took a seat next to Evest and Lindaz. I could see the affection in the elder's eyes as they looked at their son. Clearly, they were just as surprised to see him as we were.

Many questions were running through my mind, such as where had he been all this time, and what had he been doing? I was pretty sure I wasn't the only one thinking those things. Everyone was quiet as we lifted off and flew back. The journey was smooth, and I couldn't keep my eyes open; I felt my eyelids getting heavier and heavier.

I awoke to James gently stroking my cheek.

"Baby, we're back. Mel, wake up, baby; we're back," James said softly.

I opened my eyes and tried to get my bearings. When I looked across the craft; Anthony and Nalik were gently trying to wake Holly and Christine, so I wasn't the only one who'd fallen asleep.

"You obviously really needed that sleep, Mel; you were completely out of it," James told me.

"I do feel better for it," I said with a smile.

Christik had already detached herself from the ship, and she was opening the door to the craft.

"I think we should all get some much-needed sleep and something to eat," Christik said warmly, "You should all feel very proud of what we have accomplished. We have saved many animals, and they are now safe," she added.

"Yes, we did a good job, and I know this little one feels a lot happier and settled now they're safe," I said as I stroked my bump.

"We will meet tomorrow in the large meeting room, in the morning," Christik told us.

"Perfect," James replied, "Come on, tribe, let's go!"

We all dipped our heads to the elders and angels before walking away, and as we walked towards our rooms, I could hear my bed calling my name. I was in desperate need of some more sleep, and I was sure that the kids were too. James always seemed to have endless energy, and I envied him. When we walked into our rooms, the small table was laden with food, and the kids didn't need asking twice. They all began tucking into the food straight away.

I didn't think I was that hungry, but as I looked at the food before us, my stomach started to growl and talk to everyone, making the kids and James laugh. The food was delicious and was just what we all needed after our animal saving mission. The kids were full of chatter, talking about the animals and how awesome they were. Within an hour or so, Nalik left to take Christine back to the cruiser, and we were all in our beds. I think I was asleep before my head fully hit my pillow.

I thought I was dreaming at first when I heard Christik's voice in my head. *'Mel, are you ready for our meeting; we are all here. Mel, where are you?'* It took me a few moments to realize what was happening and to sit up in bed. I quickly scanned the room and our bed. James was still sleeping soundly next to me with a smile on his face. *'He must be having a nice dream.'* I thought.

'Mel, where are you?' Christik asked again.

'Christik, I'm sorry, we were obviously more tired than we realized; we were all still sleeping,' I told her apologetically. *'We'll be there as quickly as possible.'*

I turned to my sleeping husband, suddenly feeling bad that I had to wake him from such a nice dream.

"James, wake up baby, we're late," I said as gently as I could.

He must have been close to waking as he turned over straight away with sexy, sleepy eyes.

"You will never guess what I was dreaming about," he said with a huge grin.

I knew exactly what he'd been dreaming about from his grin, the twinkle in his eye, and the peak in the silver sheet at the apex of his legs. I tried and failed to keep a straight face.

"We haven't got time for your shenanigans, husband of mine. We are late for the meeting, and they are all waiting for us," I told him, "You jump in the shower, and I'll wake the kids.

"Shit, ok," he said, as he leapt out of our bed and ran to the bathroom in all his glory, swinging as he went.

I was still laughing as I opened our connecting door between our room and the kids' room.

"What's so funny, Mom?" April asked as she raised her sleepy face.

It was the first time that our newly adopted daughter had called me Mom, and it melted my heart.

"You honestly don't want to know, honey," I told her with a smile. "You all need to get up though as we're late.

As I gently woke the boys, April helped me by waking the girls, and when they were all starting to get up, I left them to it and went back to our room. James was already dressed and was brushing his teeth, so I quickly jumped into the shower myself.

"Looking rather magnificent there, my lady!" James said with a smile as he admired the view.

"Why thank you, kind sir," I answered with a giggle as he started to leave.

Soon, we were all showered, dressed and ready to go.

"Are you all ready for a brisk walk?" I asked, knowing that we needed to get a move on. After nods and yes' from everyone; we left our room, and I walked straight into Harrik, Zanika and five other angels.

"For the love of man, you nearly gave me a heart attack," I told them as I tried to control my racing heart.

"You have a problem with your heart?" Zanika asked as she quickly raised an instantly glowing hand to my chest.

"No, No, I don't have a problem with my heart," I told her quickly as I raised my own hands up. "I meant that you scared me," I explained, "we weren't expecting you to be here."

"Ahh, I understand," Zanika said as she lowered her hand, the glow disappearing, "We are here to take you to the meeting."

"Well, that will save us the brisk walk," James said while grinning.

Each of us reached for an angel, and in seconds, we were appearing in the meeting room where everyone was waiting for us. Christik was sat at the head of the table with Lindaz and Evest on either side of her, and her brother was sat on the other side of Evest. Tracey and John were at the table as well as Beccy, Derek, Andrew and Mimi.

It was great to see everyone, and there were smiles all around, apart from Tracey and John. Neither of them looked happy at all. *'I need to check with them to see if they're ok later,'* I thought. We all took seats around the table, and I could feel the curiosity in the room, and our friends kept looking at Akhenaten. They seemed just as intrigued with him as my family and me.

As soon as we were all seated and the room began to quiet, Christik rose from her seat.

" Good morning, everyone. I am happy to inform you all that the animals we rescued are now settled here on our craft," she said with pride. "It is reassuring that they are now safe. I would like to introduce you all to my brother, Akhenaten," she added as she indicated to her brother.

Akhenaten dipped his head to our friends, and he smiled at them. All our friends smiled back at the golden angel, apart from John, who dipped his head with a solemn look on his face. Tracey appeared to have brightened up somewhat, and her eyes were glued to Akhenaten.

"Akhenaten has been here on Earth since the last time we were here," Christik explained.

"Why did you stay on our planet?" Mimi asked.

The golden angel smiled warmly at her before answering.

"I found my other half while we were in Egypt," Akhenaten explained. "We were helping your ancient Egyptians with a disease outbreak when I met her. I decided to stay."

My mind was going over everything I knew and had learned about ancient Egypt.

"Were you the Pharaoh Akhenaten?" I asked hesitantly, not wanting to look stupid if I was wrong.

Akhenaten looked at me with kindness in his eyes.

"Yes, for a while, I was a Pharaoh," he replied. "I married my other half, and we had children. We tried to keep the balance between humans and your planet. Unfortunately, the lust for power by some hindered our efforts," he added sadly.

"I read about you, your wife and your family," I told him with a warm smile.

I could feel sadness and regret coming from him, and so could Christik and the elders. Leaning closer, Lindaz placed a hand on his wrist, and he returned her gesture with another sad smile.

"Your history is not always correct. History is only the traces left behind by those who have the last say," Akhenaten explained. "Nothing corrupts people more than greed and power."

'*The angel talks a lot of sense,*' I thought as I absorbed his words. Throughout our planet's history, we'd witnessed powerful and greedy people do the most horrific acts. What Akhenaten was saying was difficult to refute.

"What happened?" Tracey asked with great interest, her eyes studying Akhenaten's handsome face.

The golden angel's face appeared strained as the memories flooded through his mind.

"My one and I realized that the Egyptian people did not want to change their ways. After Nefertiti, my one died; I faked my own death. I traveled around your planet, trying to teach anyone who would listen about how to protect the Earth."

"Why did you go back to Egypt, Akhenaten?" James asked.

"Without the contact of other angels, I started to fade," Akhenaten told us, "My body was losing its power, and I was fading. I knew that my race would come back eventually, and I hoped that they would come and find me."

I wanted to ask Akhenaten so many questions, but I knew it wasn't the time. Every one of us was hanging on every word he spoke. We were all clearly intrigued and fascinated with the golden angel.

"I am happy you found us, my one," Evest told his son. "We were going to look for you when the Marilian danger had passed."

"Speaking of the Marilians, how are our preparations coming along?" James asked with a smile.

Everyone seemed put out that James had changed the subject, but we needed to get a move on with our preparations. James was right to try and get us back on course. Sensing the disappointment in the room, Christik rose from her seat again.

"Do not worry; there will be plenty of time to hear of Akhenaten's story after we have defeated the Marilians."

"That's what I like," Mimi declared, "a positive attitude."

"Too right, we're going to kick ass and take names," Tracey added with a humorous smile.

"I would so love to see you literally kick a Marilian's ass, Tracey," I told her. "If anyone had the nerve to do it, it would be you," I laughed.

All our friends sat there, nodding their heads and laughing, even our angel friends were smiling at the thought. Tracey looked around the table as if to say, *'What do you mean?'* making us laugh even harder.

As our laughter settled down, Christik began to raise her hand towards the center of the large wooden table. We watched intently as her hands began to glow with her ice white shimmering power, and there in the center of us all, an image of a town appeared. It was so strange to see the town without lots of traffic. Instead, we could see the hustle and bustle of humans and angels working together.

Most of the people were working on a large white building which may have been a library or a civic building once. They were turning it into a replica of a holding structure, and they were doing a fantastic job.

"As you can all see, our human friends and our angels have been working hard," Christik said. "We are close to finishing all the fake holding structures, and we have nearly all ammunition in place surrounding them."

As she finished her sentence, the image changed to a room inside one of the nearby buildings. Inside the room were stacks of wooden ammunition boxes. There were guns, bullets, grenades and other armaments that I didn't recognize.

"How many people know how to use all these weapons?" Akhenaten asked with concern on his strong features.

"We have many who are trained, Akhenaten," Christik assured him. "Everyone who has been willing to learn has had training from those who have military training. The surviving humans are extremely dedicated to fighting the Marilians for the sake of their planet."

"Hell, yeah we are!" Tracey declared.

Everyone else around the table agreed with nods of their heads, and as Akhenaten looked around the room; he could clearly see everyone's determination.

"Ann, the body painter, and the other artists have been busy practicing as well," Christik added as the image changed again.

We could see Ann and the others standing in the middle of a street, all staring at a row of deserted shops. It was strange because none of us could see anything unusual to stare at.

"What on earth are they doing?" Holly asked to no one in particular.

"You will see," Christik said with a smile.

I tried to look even harder at the image before us, but all I could see were the shop fronts with their dirty windows and grimy sills, with small piles of rubbish in the entrances that had been forced there by the wind. Then I saw a slight movement at one of the storefronts, and as I tried to figure out what I'd seen, a body peeled itself away from the brickwork of the building.

"Woah, that's fucking amazing!" Tracey declared loudly, making us laugh.

As we continued to watch, eight more angels stepped away from the buildings. This time, there was a lot more "Woahs" from everyone in the room.

"It is amazing, Tracey," Christik answered. "As you can all see, Ann and her artist friends are able to camouflage our angels extremely well. This will give us a large advantage when we fight the Marilians.

"But how will Ann and the others be able to paint them in time when the Marilians arrive?" Anthony asked.

"Apparently, Ann has a setting spray, that will keep the paint on our angels' bodies, Anthony," Christik explained. "We do not secrete body oils like humans, so it will stay on, and our angels are able to stay in one position for days at a time," she added.

Christik then turned her attention to Tracey, whose husband was still looking very solemn.

"Tracey has been invaluable with her help," Christik said warmly.

"I was able to locate plenty of buildings for our needs," Tracey stated with pride. "We now have buildings for our weapons as well as for our ambushes."

The image in front of us changed again to the buildings surrounding another fake holding structure. Instead of windows in the building, there were metal boards with long slits.

"We've used metal boards instead of wood because as you all know, the Marilians use fire as a weapon. The metal will get hot, but it will protect our fighters more efficiently," Tracey explained. "The Marilians don't know what our buildings should look like, so that will get us another advantage."

The image began to disappear as Christik's glowing hand started to dim, and as she took her seat, Derek sat forward.

"We've managed to acquire plenty of body armor for our fighters too," Derek said also with pride. "With the angels' help, we visited many armed forces bases and stocked up on everything we could find. We've got full combat gear, including tactical vests, boots and mag pouches. You are all going to look like total badasses," he said humorously.

As I sat there listening to Derek talk, I could help but notice that Akhenaten was still staring at Tracey, and he was slightly glowing more than he was before. Tracey could obviously feel him staring as her eyes were flitting between Derek and Akhenaten. There was definitely something in the air, but with so many people in the room all feeling something different, it was hard to tell who was feeling what.

"It seems that everything is going to plan, my one," Lindaz told Christik with confidence in her voice. "Do you have any idea how long we have before the Marilians arrive?" She asked.

"No, my one, we do not have any idea," Christik told her mother honestly. "That is why we are trying to get everything ready so quickly. We cannot afford to be unprepared."

"Now the animals are safe, at least we can concentrate on finishing our preparations," James told everyone, "My kids and I are planning to get some shooting practice in today if anyone else wants to come with us. Luiza and Shawn are already at the range your angels made," he added.

Christine and Nalik decided to go with James, the kids and a few others. As we all began to leave the large meeting room, Tracey came up to me while John quietly left the room.

"Do you mind if I hang out with you for a while," Tracey asked with a serious note to her voice.

"Sure, of course," I replied, picking up on her conflicted emotions.

I could feel us being watched, and when I turned around to see who it was, Akhenaten was steadily watching Tracey's every movement. When he realized I was looking at him, his eyes connected with mine, and I could feel his confusion and conflicted emotions too.

I dipped my head to the golden angel and said my goodbyes to everyone before leaving.

The huge control center was as busy as ever, with angels working at their curve's consoles. As Tracey and I walked through, we both looked through the massive shimmering glass window and admired the scene. The white rig crafts were still cleaning the ocean water. However, there was now a big difference between the dirty water that was being sucked in and the clean water being pumped out. This time, the two water flows looked more alike in color.

"We're making real progress, aren't we!" I said.

"Yes, we are. I just hope the Marilians don't get the chance to fuck it all up," Tracey replied bluntly.

"You certainly have a way with words Tracey," I told her with a chuckle.

"After what I've been through, with cancer and losing my babies, Mel, life is too short to fuck around with pleasantries," she replied with a grin.

There was nothing that I could say to her comment. I didn't have the first clue of how tough it had been for her, and I would never judge her.

CHAPTER 11

Tracey was very quiet and thoughtful as we walked back to my room. I could almost hear her mind ticking over whatever it was that was bothering her. I still felt very intrigued with Akhenaten's reaction to her as well, and as we'd left the meeting room, I was pretty sure he was glowing a little more brightly than when the meeting had started. '*This is going to be very interesting,*' I thought to myself as we approached my room's entrance.

"After you," I told Tracey, letting her enter first.

I followed behind her, and she walked straight over to the seating area next to the circular window. The warm sunshine was filtering through the glass and hitting the seats of the chairs. I could feel the comforting warmth as my body made contact with the soft chairs.

As soon as I sat down; I touched my com and reached out to Hulaz. I suddenly had a feeling that Tracey might need an angel to talk with too. '*Hulaz, are you free to have a coffee with Tracey and I?*' I asked, hoping she was available. '*I can be with you very soon, Mel,*' I heard her say clearly in my mind. Relief flowed through me as I took in the mixed emotion in Tracey's lovely face.

"What's going on, Tracey?" I asked her softly, "You have so many emotions swirling inside of you that you're making me dizzy," I added with a warm smile.

Tracey's face instantly looked so strained; I had to resist the urge to lean forward and give her a huge hug. '*She'll be a sobbing wreck if I do that now,*' I thought. Tracey looked at me with sadness in her brown eyes.

"I honestly don't know where to fucking start!" She declared; her voice trembling as she spoke.

"Before the end of our planet began, I was diagnosed with breast cancer, and it was already incurable," Tracey explained as she lowered her gaze. "I was one of those women who always put off having the mammograms done. By the time I found my lump in my right breast and went for the mammogram, it was too late."

Tracey took a slow breath to steady her emotions.

"John didn't know how to cope with the news, so he just got angry with me for not going sooner," she said as her voice shook. "When he got angry, I withdrew from him, Mel. I had to come to terms with dying as well as explaining to our twins what was going on, and John didn't help at all!" She stated, her anger at John clearly evident. "That bastard was in denial, and I had to do everything. I consoled our kids, broke the news to family and friends, and on top of that; I had to organize my own fucking funeral," she said in an emotional rush of words.

A massive sob escaped her as she finished her sentence. My instincts took over, and before I knew what I was doing, I was reaching for her and taking her into my arms. Tracey's whole body shook as she let out her tears of frustration, anger and heartbreak.

I held her and stroked her hair as she let it all go. I understood her emotions, and I also knew that most people would feel the same way if they were in her shoes. I couldn't even begin to comprehend what it had been like for her. She was an amazingly strong woman, and I admired her immensely. When her sobs began to subside, she pulled herself away, using both hands to wipe away her tears.

"When the world started to die, all I kept thinking about was saving Ashley and Martin. Tracey said vehemently, "I didn't care about myself or the cancer anymore because it didn't matter. All that mattered was that our twins survived.

I could feel how hard it was for Tracey to be reliving what had happened, but I also understood that she desperately needed to pour her heart out, so she could begin to heal emotionally. I reached forward, and I took her hand in mine, hoping that she would find comfort in my small gesture and the strength to carry on. Her wet and tear-stained face looked up at mine once again.

"Ashley and Martin got sick when the water in our area turned bad," she said quietly. "Fair play to John, he looked and searched everywhere for clean water, but it was all gone. We tried to filter and clean what we found, but it still made the kids really sick."

Tracey took another deep breath, pursing her lips, she let it out as slowly as she could.

"I supposed they got sick so quickly because they were so young," she said. "John and I held them in our arms as they died."

A huge sob wracked her body as she said the words. I could see her facial expression changing from hurt to anger before my eyes as her mind replayed the events of what had happened.

"John just got really angry again," she said with her own anger shining through, "He didn't help me grieve our babies, he just got

139

angry. Angry at me and the world. I felt so alone and to be honest Mel, I was looking forward to the sickness or the cancer taking me, so I could be with my babies again."

I stroked her hand with mine, and I looked deeply into her shining, tear rimmed eyes.

"I would have felt exactly the same way, Tracey," I assured her quietly.

"I don't remember anything else until I woke up in the birthing room, and then I felt the loss of my babies all over again," Tracey told me as her anger turned back to sadness. "I was so upset that the cancer had gone because that was my way of being back with my babies. John really doesn't understand."

"Do you think John grieved the loss of Ashley and Martin while you were sleeping?" I asked gently.

"Yes, I think he did," she said as she lowered her head.

Another tear escaped her eyelashes, trickling slowly down her damp face and landing on the blue silky dress she was wearing. Tracey didn't even notice.

"John has already gone through the grieving process, but I haven't, and he doesn't understand," Tracey explained. "To be honest with you Mel, I'm still angry at the fucker for not being there for me when I was diagnosed, and for not being there for me now while I'm grieving," she added.

"Have you tried to explain that to him, Tracey?" I asked.

Tracey took another deep breath, and her shoulders lifted and fell as she lifted her head to look up to the ceiling of my white room. When she looked at me again, it was defeat that I felt from her and saw in her brown eyes.

"I've tried, Mel, but there is no talking with him," she said with resignation. "I blame his mother," she added with a weak smile, "she was one of those women who believed that boys should man up and not talk about their emotions. She was an emotional fortress, and I always felt sorry for John's dad, being married to someone so cold."

Do you think you and John can get past this?" I asked, but in my heart, I already knew the answer.

"No, I don't think we can, Mel," she replied in defeat. "It's gone way past that. He's made me feel so alone for so long that I actually don't want to be with him anymore. I have tried though, Mel. I just can't pretend any longer," she said sadly.

There was a tap at the entrance to my room, grabbing our attention.

"Come in," I said as I slipped my hand from Tracey and walked towards the entryway. Hulaz glided into the room with a stone tray of coffee, juice and fruits between her glistening slender hands. The moment she saw Tracey and I, she dipped her head and gave us both a lovely smile. Behind her was Mimi, and I was pleased. I felt that Tracey needed all the friends she could get to help her through such a terrible time.

"I hope you don't mind me crashing the pity party," Mimi said with her infectious smile, "I saw Hulaz arriving outside and thought you might like one more."

"Abso fucking lutely," Tracey told her with a returning small smile.

Hulaz placed the tray on the small table in front of Tracey, and as we all sat down on the soft chairs, Tracey poured the drinks. The angels hadn't yet acquired the taste of coffee, so Tracey automatically offered Hulaz some juice. The coffee was just what I needed, and as I watched Tracey hugging her coffee in between sips, it was clear she was in need of a hot drink too.

"So, what's new, what's going on, ladies?" Mimi asked with her usual exuberance.

"I think John and I are done," Tracey said bluntly with a weak smile.

"Holy shit, really?" Mimi asked with a surprised face.

"Yep!" Tracey stated, "I've been explaining everything to Mel, and while I was telling her all about it; I realized how true it is. We're over. We haven't loved each other like a married couple are supposed to for a long time. I think he knows it too," she added.

Mimi's eyes were wide with surprise, and she was clearly stumped for words.

"Woah, so what are you going to do now?" Mimi asked with concern in her voice.

"I'm going to take a room here on the main craft. If that's ok, Hulaz?" She asked as she turned her gaze to the blue-haired angel.

Hulaz dipped her head to Tracey and gave her a smile.

"Of course, Tracey, you are welcome to stay here as long as you need to," Hulaz told her graciously.

"What are you going to say to John?" I asked, feeling worried for her.

"He already knows that I'm moving out, and to be honest, I think we're both secretly relieved," Tracey admitted.

Mimi slid her butt forward on her seat, and she suddenly had the look of a naughty schoolgirl with a big secret.

"I don't want to throw an iron in the works, but did anyone else notice that Akhenaten kept staring at Tracey and was glowing?" She asked quietly.

I bit down on my lips, trying not to giggle at the comical look on Mimi's face. Her eyes were abruptly wide with excitement and mischief.

"Mimi, you are so bad!" I admonished with a giggle, no longer able to keep my humor contained.

"No fucking way, you're pulling my leg!" Tracey told her in shock.

I looked at Hulaz, then Mimi and back to Tracey, who was now staring at me as if to say, '*Well?*'

"It's true," I admitted while trying to keep a straight face. "He was staring at you a lot, even though I think he was trying not to. I did notice he was glowing a little when the meeting started as well," I added.

"Akhenaten was glowing brighter towards the end of the meeting, that's for sure," Mimi said excitedly with raised eyebrows.

"He may be trying to not to fall for you as you are already married," Hulaz interjected, "He is older than many of us, so he has more control over his power and emotions."

"I don't know what to say," Tracey admitted while still hugging her coffee to her chest.

"You do not have to say anything, Tracey," Hulaz told her kindly. "You need to concentrate on yourself at the moment. You do not need to concern yourself with Akhenaten and how he is feeling."

"By the way, what's this I hear about angels being able to change the size of their bits to suit their sexual partner?" Mimi asked Hulaz with a ridiculous grin and one raised eyebrow.

"What, seriously?" Tracey asked while also looking at Hulaz.

I couldn't stop the laughter that escaped me. I knew the girls were going to react this way, and it was cracking me up. As I laughed,

I could feel my baby girl moving around as my hand rested on my bump. Hulaz was obviously amused as well.

"It is true," Hulaz admitted with a smile, "Our race is lucky enough to be able to change the size of our genitalia to suit our other halves needs."

"But… but you don't have any bits," Tracey stammered as she waved her hand in front of Hulaz's body for emphasis.

That made me laugh even harder, and Mimi burst into fits of laughter too. I was laughing so hard that tears were streaming down my glowing face.

"I do have genitalia," Hulaz said kindly, "Look."

With that, Hulaz rose from her seat, and as she looked down on the three of us, her whole body began to give off a bright ice white shimmer, and she suddenly began to grow small pert breasts, and a vagina was forming at the apex of her slim thighs.

"Fucking hell," Tracey shrieked, her hand pointing at Hulaz's breasts, then her vagina and back to her breasts.

"No fricking way," Mimi laughed, "and you can have any size too? She asked.

"Yes," Hulaz answered.

In a split second, the angel's breasts began to grow until they were the size of large melons.

"Oh my fucking god, that is amazing!" Tracey declared as she burst into a fit of laughter too. "You angels are awesome!"

"OMG, stop!" I tried to say, "You're killing me, I can't breathe."

I was laughing so hard that I was struggling to catch my breath. Mimi was holding on to the small table for support as her laughter grew louder. As we all tried to get control of our laughter, Hulaz's shimmer started to dim as her breasts and vagina began to absorb back into her body.

"That's the craziest thing I think I've ever seen," I said as I tried to slow my breathing and take in some extra oxygen.

"So, your male angels can do that too?" Mimi asked as she sat back in her seat.

Hulaz sat back down in her chair, reaching for her fruit juice from the table.

"Yes, our male angels can do it too," she replied.

"Any size their partner needs?" Mimi asked to clarify.

"Yes, too any size," Hulaz said, clearly amused.

"Bloody Hell, Tracey. Maybe you should get it on with angel golden balls, at least you'll never have to ask, is it in yet?" Mimi said as she burst into fits of giggles again.

"OMG, Mimi, trust you to think of something like that," I said as we all burst into uncontrollable laughter once more.

Even Hulaz was laughing this time, and it was a lovely musical sound. It was quite a while before any of us were capable of talking. We took our time, sipping our drinks until our stomachs stopped hurting from giggling so much. It was nice just to enjoy each other's company, and I for one couldn't wait until we could do girlie time on a more regular basis.

"Ladies, this was just what I needed, thank you," Tracey said with true sincerity.

"Oh, me too," I told them, "everything's been so tense for so long, it's great to have a laugh with wonderful friends."

"Too right," Mimi added.

"I am happy you invited me, Mel," Hulaz said warmly, "I enjoy spending time with you all."

"We enjoy your company too, Hulaz, and your party trick is fucking epic," Tracey told her with a giggle.

"Party trick?" Hulaz asked, confusion on her beautiful face.

"You know," Tracey told her as she put her hands to her boobs and did the motions.

"Oh," Hulaz said as we all began to laugh again.

By the time Tracey and Mimi had left my room, I felt as if I'd done a hundred sit-ups. My whole stomach ached from laughing, but it was a good and welcome feeling. It felt so wonderful to be alive, especially with such amazing people. Hulaz stayed for a couple of hours after our friends had left, and it was lovely catching up with the angel. After she left, I knew I'd have some time to myself before James and the kids came back, so I decided to take a walk down to the birthing room where the encapsulated animals were stored.

The walk to the birthing room was a quiet one, with only a few angels passing me as I made my way. I noticed that things were changing between us and the angels in a positive way. Whereas before I would just get a dipped head response from the angels I passed, now I was getting verbal greetings using my name. I suddenly felt quite sad at the thought of the angels leaving once the battle was over. I knew the angels would still visit our planet, but it wasn't like they were able to pop over for a chit chat every week, especially as their job was saving planets all over the universe.

As soon as I walked into the birthing room and took in the sight of the massive glass wall with all the encapsulated animals inside, my sadness melted away. It was hard to feel anything but sheer awe at the sight of all the animals. I walked up to the glass and peered inside, wondering just how thick the wall was. There were rows and rows of capsules behind the closest ones I could see, all filled with the shimmering fluid and baby animals of all varieties. On each capsule, I could make out the organic device that was keeping them alive. I could see so many different animals, all at various stages of growth depending on their size and every so often, there was a flicker of movement as one of them kicked or twitched.

"We have a lot to be proud of, don't we," a male voice said from behind me, making me jump.

I spun around to see Harrik standing a few feet away with a smile on his handsome face.

"Goddammit, Harrik, I wish you angels would make a noise when you walk. You scared the living daylights out of me," I told him as I patted my chest and racing heart. "You seriously need to cough or make a noise so I can hear you coming, or I may end up having this baby sooner rather than later."

"My apologies, Mel. I did not mean to startle you," the angel said as he dipped his head.

"It's ok, I'll probably get used to it just as you all leave," I told him lightheartedly, "We certainly do have a lot to be proud of. It's exciting to think of all these animals roaming free soon."

"Christik told us that you might like to help us release the animals when the time is right," he said as his sapphire eyes sparkled.

I felt butterflies in my stomach, at just the thought of James and the kids being part of the angels' release program. Instantly, I knew how thrilled they would be to be asked.

"Harrik, my family would absolutely love to be involved," I told him with a huge grin. "I think I'll let Christik tell them the good news."

Harrik and I spent an hour talking about the animals, and after we left the birthing room and I headed back to my room, I reached out to Hulaz.

"Hulaz, could we go and check on the animals that we rescued tomorrow, please," I asked.

My baby girl was feeling restless, and I thought the contact with the animals might settle her down a bit.

"Of course we can, Mel," Hulaz replied right away, "I will collect you in the morning."

"Thank you," I told her as I entered our suite.

I hadn't realized that it was already getting late, and the excited voices I heard as I walked in told me that my family was back from their shooting practice. There were paper targets all over the floor with holes everywhere, and the kids were teasing each other over who had taken the best shots.

"It sounds like you all had a good time at shooting practice," I said as I made my way to my husband.

James reached for me, wrapping his arms around my waist and giving me a light kiss.

"I think we have some sharpshooters on our hands, Mel," he said with pride.

Abigail was positively beaming as she picked up her target and held it up for me to see.

"April and me are the sharpshooters!" She declared excitedly, "Show Mom your target, sis."

April's face lit up at Abigail's words, and she picked up her target too.

"I don't like to brag," she giggled, "but Abigail and me nailed it!" She sang as she grinned at our youngest daughter.

"We can't even deny it," Harrison said as he jokingly shook his head. "The girls were a lot better than we were. Remind us not to get on their bad sides."

The girls thoroughly enjoyed teasing their brothers throughout the evening while James and I watched and enjoyed their banter. We could still hear them as they got ready for bed, right up until the barrier closed between our two rooms. As James and I snuggled up to each other in our bed, I knew sleep wasn't far away.

"You know that the girls aren't going to let our boys live this down, don't you," James said as my eyelids became heavy.

"Oh, I know," I giggled quietly as I let sleep take me.

CHAPTER 12

I woke in the morning feeling refreshed and wide awake. James and the kids were still asleep as I showered, and I didn't hear anything until I finished and came out of the bathroom.

"Morning, beautiful," James said as soon as he saw me.

He was sitting at the small table, which was now covered with breakfast, and all he was wearing was a pair of trousers. I had to take a moment to appreciate his firm muscular body, which still gave me the tingles.

"Morning, handsome," I replied, giving him a sexy smile.

It was hard not to flirt when you had a hottie for a husband, especially when he didn't realize how damn hot he was.

"I think the kids are just waking," he said as he handed me my morning coffee, which instantly made me smile.

We were just finishing our breakfast with the kids when Hulaz arrived. James and the kids were going to help Christine and her dad with some building work, something that I definitely wasn't able to do for a while. Luckily, my family didn't mind hard work or getting their hands dirty.

"Ha hum," Hulaz said as she attempted to do a fake cough. Straightaway, I knew that Harrik had told her what I'd said the day before. "Good morning to you all," Hulaz said as she gracefully glided in.

"Morning," I told her as I smiled knowingly at her, "I'm ready when you are."

After giving James and the kids hugs goodbye, Hulaz and I made our way to our room's exit.

"Would you like me to flit you to the animals holding room?" She asked.

"Um no, I think I'd like to walk," I told her as we made my way to the corridor. I still didn't relish the aftereffects of flitting. I always preferred to be hot than cold although the shivering didn't last quite as long as it did when I was first flitted by the angels.

Hulaz and I small talked on the way to the animals' holding room. She explained in depth how everyone was doing at the holding structure and how much preparation was left. It seemed that while the kids and I had been wrapped up with James being hurt and the elders' arrivals, everyone had their noses to the grindstone. Hulaz didn't think it would be too long at all before we were all ready.

By the time we arrived at the animals' holding room, my baby girl was doing somersaults inside me. Every so often, sticking a foot up near my ribs, making me take a sharp breath.

"Are you alright, Mel," Hulaz asked as I gasped.

I gave her a reassuring smile.

"I'm fine. I think she knows we are close to the animals. She's excited," I told her as I ran my hand over my bump.

By Beth Worsdell

I followed Hulaz into the holding room, and I was yet again stunned by the size of the rooms on the main craft. As we entered, the two dugongs were on our left inside a large natural-looking pool. It was similar to the pool inside the human holding structure, with trees and plants around it, growing in between large rocks. There was lush grass beneath my bare feet, which felt soft and cool as we walked further inside. The dugongs looked more than happy as we walked past their pool, swimming leisurely without a care.

The angels seemed to have gone above and beyond to make the animals feel safe and happy. There were various trees and plants that had been planted in clusters, to suit each species' needs. While I stood and admired the angels' handy work, the animals began to slowly appear. Some came out from the foliage on their own, but most of them came out to see us in their pairs.

The only two I wasn't keen on seeing again were the two large sand rats, but I knew I'd have to get over my aversion to vermin eventually. It wasn't their fault that my skin crawled at the thought of touching them. '*Get a grip woman*,' I admonished myself, but it was very hard to get the thought of the biting ferret out of my mind.

With most of the animals being so little, I decided to sit on the floor, so they could all reach me. My baby girl could sense all the animals, and she was beginning to roll inside me. The pandas were the first to reach us, and as they neared, they appeared to start racing each other, each trying to be the first. They were so funnily clumsy that they both ended up in a heap of black and white fur next to my knees.

Hulaz and I both laughed as I tried to untangle their chunky little paws while they made cute little noises of indignation. Once they were both free, they seemed quite content to cuddle up next to my thighs and have their heads rubbed; next to their ears and have their bellies tickled. If they could have purred like cats, I think they would have done.

Next to reach us were the two Okapi, who came to us hesitantly and slowly.

"It's ok, you're safe," I told them.

I knew that they couldn't understand what I was saying, but I hoped that my tone would calm their nervousness. Hulaz and I were patient as they approached, and when they were close enough, I reached out a hand to stroke the female's neck. My touch seemed to soothe her nerves, and the male began to brush his nose against my hair, occasionally having a sniff.

Before long, we were surrounded by the animals we'd rescued, and I was being smothered with affection. Even the Potoo birds were affectionately rubbing their beaks against my hip. My baby girl was pushing against my abdomen as if she wanted to get closer to them. I had a feeling that animals were going to be a big part of my family's life from then on.

Hulaz and I were enjoying our time with the animals and while I was making a fuss of the dugongs as they came to the side of their pool; Christik's voice spoke loud and clear in my mind. '*Mel, we need you at the holding structure, please come quickly,*' she said.

The moment I heard Christik's words in my mind and her tone as she said them, I knew something was very, very wrong. Immediately, Hulaz picked up on my worry and racing heartbeat.

"What is wrong, Mel?" Hulaz asked with concern marring her beautiful glistening face.

"Christik needs me at the holding structure. Hulaz, can you take me there now, please, something bad has happened?" I asked in a rush of words.

Thoughts of Peter and Kay entered my head, and I was abruptly worried that we'd missed a Marilian, and more people had been corrupted. It wasn't just Hulaz that could sense the growing worry and dread building inside me. The animals could sense it too. Not only were they all looking at me as Hulaz placed her hand on my bare arm, but they were all making low distressed noises too.

"Don't worry!" I told them, just before Hulaz and I vanished from the room.

In seconds, we were standing outside the holding structure with the bright morning sun on our faces. While I tried to control my shivering, Hulaz looked around to see if anyone was around.

"Christik must be inside," she said as she began to glide towards the large and heavy wooden doors.

The holding structure was looking dramatically different. Ann and the other artists had been extremely busy, not only body painting the angels but also camouflaging the holding structure too. It was no longer the bright white building it was before, appearing like a stationary cruise ship. Now it was painted in various shades of greens, browns and all the warm colors in between.

As we got closer, I noticed that Ann and her friends had actually painted trees and bushes on the outside, '*no wonder it blended so well with the surroundings,*' I thought.

When we walked through the doors and into the main entrance, Christik was waiting with Lindaz, Evest and Akhenaten by her side. Hulaz and I both dipped our heads in respect as soon as they looked our way. All four of them reciprocated, and when they looked up again, sadness was written all over their expressions.

"What has happened?" I asked as my heart began to pound harder in my chest. '*Please don't say James or my kids*,' I thought as my heart began to sink.

"Something has happened to John," Christik said quietly and calmly, "Tracey is with him in their room. Please come with us, Mel, Tracey needs you," she added.

As we made our way up to Tracey and John's cabin, all I kept thinking was '*how much more can poor Tracey take*?' It was heartbreaking to have a friend that I cared for and loved go through so much heartbreak and loss. '*Please Let John be ok*,' I said in a mantra.

Christik arrived at their cabin door, and it was already slightly open. She stood to the side of the door frame and allowed me to go in first.

The cabin was smaller than the one James and our kids used, but it was bright and spacious with the same neutral colors with added shades of blue.

"Tracey?" I called as I walked further inside.

"Mel?" Tracey called out in a sob.

Her voice seemed to come from the right of me, where there was another door. I assumed that it was their bedroom, and I felt a little strange invading their privacy, but I knew that my friend needed me.

Light streamed through the circular window in their bedroom, and it shone on their bed where John was laying, making him look as if he were glowing. Tracey was kneeling on the floor beside his still form, and I could see tears running down her face, dropping silently onto John's hand, which she was holding between hers.

"Tracey," I said again as gently as I could.

"He's gone, Mel!" Tracey sobbed, struggling to get the words out, "I don't know how, but he's gone."

"Oh god, Tracey, I'm so sorry," I told her as my heart ached with sadness.

Christik glided into the room quietly. Moving past me; she softly sat on the bed right next to John and Tracey. None of us said a word as Christik's hands began to glow their bright, white shimmering glow. She placed her right hand on Tracey's trembling shoulder, and I could see her power flowing into my heartbroken friend.

As Tracey's sobs and shaking settled, Christik placed her left glowing hand on John's still form. John looked so peaceful as if he was just sleeping; his face looked so relaxed that he even appeared younger.

Tracey looked up from where she knelt, her eyes and mine were watching Christik's glowing hand as it hovered a few inches away from John's still chest. It was as if time stood still as we waited for Christik to say something, anything. We watched as her power flowed into John's body and then appeared to flow back to Christik's hand.

"I am afraid John's heart stopped beating, Tracey," Christik said gently as she looked into Tracey's waiting gaze, "There was nothing anyone could have done to stop this. It happened very quickly, and no one could have predicted it."

"I could have done something if I'd have been here with him," Tracey wailed as her emotions heightened again, "I know CPR, I could have got his heart going again!" She cried out.

Christik's hand flowed bright in Tracey's shoulder, her power helping to soothe Tracey's broken heart and her guilt.

"Tracey, please trust me," Christik said softly, "Your husband's body formed a blood clot for some unknown reason, which moved into his heart. There was nothing that you could have done."

I could feel strong emotions coming from behind me, feelings of despair and frustration. When I turned my head to look behind me, Akhenaten was stood in the doorway to the bedroom, looking as if he didn't know what to do with himself. The golden angel was conflicted. I could feel his need to hold and comfort Tracey, but I could also feel his resignation. He knew that now wasn't the time.

Akhenaten's feelings of love towards Tracey had grown, but he was obviously old enough and experienced enough to know that she would need time to grieve for the husband who she still loved, even if it was a more platonic friendship love. I gave Akhenaten a knowing and sympathetic smile. I understood what a difficult situation he'd found himself in, and I hoped that he felt my compassion.

Christik's hands were beginning to dim as I looked back towards her, and as Tracey continued to sob quietly, Christik stood back up.

"Tracey needs you more than me at this time," Christik said as her peacock sapphire eyes looked deeply into mine.

I nodded as she passed me, making her way to the cabin's main room. Kneeling down next to my distraught friend, I took Tracey into my arms, and I held her tightly. Her body shuddered within my grasp as her tears flowed freely.

157

"I should have stayed, Mel," she sobbed, "I should have been here."

You saw John's face Tracey, he passed away at peace," I soothed. "He knew you loved him, and I know he loved you, and he certainly wouldn't want you torturing yourself with unwarranted guilt," I added.

"The angels could have saved him, if I'd have been here," Tracey stated as if trying to convince herself that her statement was true.

I stroked her back as I held her tightly.

"You would have been sleeping too, Tracey," I told her, "You wouldn't have known it was happening, even if you had been here."

I could feel her rationalizing my words as I held her, and her body began to slump as she admitted to herself that I was right. The angels and elders were patient as I consoled my friend. None of them saying a word. It wasn't until I heard James' voice that I started to release Tracey from my arms. I knew that the angels couldn't move John until Tracey left the bedroom. James' voice was full of worry and concern.

"Where are they?" I heard him ask the angels as he burst into the cabin.

"They are in the bedroom, James," Christik replied calmly.

Tracey and I rose from the floor as James entered the bedroom. I could feel his protectiveness towards not only myself but our friends as well. Within moments, James had his arms wrapped around both of us.

"I'm so sorry, Tracey," James said softly into Tracey's short curly hair.

I could feel Tracey nodding her head at his words.

"Let's get you to our cabin," he told her.

James was always calm and levelheaded in a crisis, and we let him lead us to the cabin that he'd shared with our kids while I'd been sleeping.

Christik, Akhenaten and the elders stayed behind, and I assumed they would move John once they knew what Tracey's wishes were for his body.

James escorted us into the cabin, and it was a relief to be away from John's lifeless body. Neither Tracey or I wanted to leave him, but I knew we had to eventually, and it would have only got worse if we had stayed longer.

Tracey sat herself down on the small couch, nestling her body on the corner. She brought her knees to her chest, wrapping her arms around them.

"I think we could do with some hot drinks, James," I told my husband.

James nodded his head, and he left the room, I assumed to speak with Hulaz.

I sat next to Tracey, not knowing what to say to the woman who had lost everything, her home, her kids, and now her best friend and husband. I sat back in the couch and began to go over everything in my mind.

"I can't believe this is happening, Mel," Tracey said so softly I barely heard her. "I'm wondering what I did in a previous life to deserve all this."

I took a slow deep breath to try and control my own feelings of frustration and sorrow.

"I've always believed that everything happens for a reason Tracey," I told her gently. "John is with your children now, and maybe that was what was supposed to happen."

Tracey looked up at my words as if realization had hit, her eyes suddenly wide with hope.

"You think that's true?" She asked with hope, "that John is now with Martin and Ashley?"

I did believe it.

"Yes, Tracey, I do," I told her confidently.

As soon as I spoke the words, Tracey slid from the corner of the couch, back into my arms, and I let her cry her pain away as I waited for James to come back.

When James and Hulaz arrived with a stone tray of honey, coffee and water, Tracey and I were still in the same position. Tracey was no longer crying, but both of our faces were still damp. As James laid the tray on the small table in front of us, Hulaz used her power to move two more chairs next to it.

It felt good holding the coffee between my hands, feeling the heat soak into my palms and fingers. Tracey had sat herself up and was back in her previous position, now hugging her coffee cup between her own trembling hands.

"Had you and John ever discussed what you would both want, should either of you pass away, Tracey?" James asked, delicately.

I couldn't believe he was asking the question so soon, but then; we didn't have anywhere to put John's body respectfully for any decent length of time. It was a tough question for James to ask but necessary.

"Tracey's eyes were red and puffy when she looked up and held James' gaze. James' eyes were full of compassion and empathy.

"Yes, we talked about it years ago when we lost John's mom," Tracey said as her lips trembled.

"What did John say he wanted?" James asked.

"He wanted to be cremated and have his ashes buried with a tree planted on top," Tracey answered, her voice breaking with emotion.

"Did he say where he'd like his ashes buried, Tracey?" I asked softly.

"Next to a beach because we liked to do beach walks with our twins and our dog," Tracey said.

James discreetly touched the com on his wrist as he reached for his coffee. '*I don't think she should be alone for now, Mel*' I heard in my mind as he looked at me. '*I agree, she can stay with us on the main craft,*' I replied. '*Me and the kids can stay here in the cabin for a few days,*' James said as he gave me a loving smile. '*You ladies can rally around her then. I'll let the girls know,*' I told him, '*I love you, baby.*'

James gave me a knowing and loving smile before his attention turned back to Tracey.

"Tracey, Hulaz and Mel are going to take you to the main craft. You're going to stay with Mel if that's ok with you," James stated.

All Tracey was capable of doing was nodding her head in agreement. I saw James touch his com again as I sipped at my coffee. When I went to place my cup back on the stone tray; Hulaz walked into the room with Akhenaten.

"We will take you back now," Hulaz said kindly.

The moment Akhenaten laid his eyes on Tracey, his body's white shimmer glowed a little brighter. As he was older and more experienced than most of the angels, he obviously had a lot more control over his emotions than Nalik. I could see the concentration on his handsome, chiseled face that he was reining his affection in. His body started to dim back down as I watched.

When Christik entered, I knew it was time. James took the arm of Hulaz, I reached for Christik's arm, and Akhenaten gently took Tracey's hand in his. The moment Akhenaten made contact with Tracey's skin; blue electric sparks burst from their touch. Tracey's eyes looked wide in surprise as she turned her attention to Akhenaten.

The golden angel looked down on Tracey with understanding as he softly held her trembling hand.

"I can be ...just a friend to you," he told her quietly.

Tracey was so stunned by the reality of everything that had recently happened, that all she was capable of was a nod of her head. Akhenaten was the first to disappear with Tracey, then Hulaz flitted with James, and Christik and I were the last to leave the cabin.

When we arrived at our room inside the main craft, Trudy and Mimi were waiting for us. James walked over to me, and he took me in his arms.

"You've got this, baby, but you only have to call me, and I'll come back, ok," James said quietly next to my ear.

"Thank you," I replied. "I love you, James," I added with all the love in my being.

Losing someone you know always seemed to give you a better appreciation of those who were still in your life. And after everything we'd been through and now losing John, our good friend, my appreciation of my family and friends was growing again.

James walked over to Akhenaten, who was still staring at Tracey, and he touched the angel's forearm.

"Could you take me to my kids please," James asked, breaking the angel's concentration.

Akhenaten broke his gaze as if he'd been in a deep daydream. After nodding at James, they both disappeared, leaving us ladies alone with Hulaz and Christik. I assumed because Evest and Lindaz stayed at the holding structure, that they had offered to transport John's body, allowing Christik to be with us, her friends.

The rest of the day and through the night was a mix of emotions with all of us listening to tales of John's life, the good, the bad and the funny. We all knew that Tracey needed to talk about John and begin her grieving process. Sometimes, we listened quietly, and sometimes, we cried, especially when she was talking about her cancer. Sometimes, we laughed so hard that we cried and nearly peed ourselves because of the funnier stories Tracey told us.

It was as if we were all riding Tracey's emotional rollercoaster. By the early hours of the next morning, we were all asleep. Tracey and Mimi had fallen asleep on my bed. Trudy and I had taken two of the kids' beds, and the two angels slept quietly in the seating area in the comfy chairs.

None of us woke until late morning when Lindaz arrived with a tray of drinks and food. I think we were all grateful for the refreshments, and it wasn't long before we were all tucking in. Hulaz and Christik looked as perfect as ever, with their beautiful shimming hair in place and their sparkling sapphire eyes. On the other hand, we humans looked like we'd all been through an assault course. Our hair was all over the place, and our eyes were pink and puffy from all the crying and laughing.

"I understand the ways of humans," Lindaz said to us all as we ate and drank. "We would like to help you cremate and honor your husband, Tracey."

"Thank you, Lindaz, I'd appreciate your help," Tracey replied with a crack in her voice.

"I am afraid that, due to the Marilians' imminent arrival, we do not have the luxury of time," the elder stated softly.

We all found ourselves nodding in understanding, and we all knew that as harsh as that was, she was right. We didn't have the luxury of taking our time. The Marilians could arrive anytime, and we needed to honor John quickly, but with the utmost respect that he truly deserved.

"I know you're right, Lindaz," Tracey told her. "I've never been one to fuck around anyway. I'd like to get it over with, so John's ashes are safe."

"We will make preparations for you, Tracey, contact me through your com to tell me what you would like us to do," Lindaz told her.

Lindaz and the angels graciously left my room, leaving us girls alone, and I was the first into the shower, desperately needing to freshen up. When I came out of the bathroom, Mimi and Trudy were nowhere to be seen. Tracey was sat on one of the chairs while staring at the round window, and her hand was touching her com around her neck.

"Are you doing ok?" I asked quietly, not wanting to make her jump.

"I'm doing ok, I think," she said with tear-filled eyes. "I was just telling Lindaz what John would have wanted. I'm glad she offered to sort it out for me because I don't think I'm capable right now," Tracey added.

"I don't think I'd be capable either, if I were in your situation, honey," I told her honestly.

Tracey jumped from her seat and walked toward me.

"Thank you for being such a good friend, Mel," she said, with so much feeling it nearly brought me to tears again.

"You are so very welcome, Tracey," I told her sincerely.

Tracey released me, and she headed for the bathroom.

"The girls are getting showers; they'll be out in a few minutes," Tracey said before disappearing into the bathroom.

Just as my butt touched the seat of the chair next to the window, Hulaz reappeared with some drinks and breakfast. She sat down next to me, and we small talked until all the others had finished getting ready. It was nice to shoot the breeze and discuss less heartbreaking topics. Before long, the others had joined us, and we were all looking more human again.

As we finished our food, Hulaz suddenly stood up with concentration all over her face for a moment, before looking down to us.

"It is time," she said, "the elders and the others are ready, Tracey."

Tracey's face was one of utter surprise.

"Fuck me sideways, that was quick," she squeaked.

We were all stunned at how quickly John's cremation had been organized, but these were ancient angels we were dealing with, and with their power, they could do or organize anything in a flash.

"Are you ok to do this, Tracey?" I asked nervously. "I can always tell them that you aren't ready."

"Yes, I'm ok. I want to get it done before the Marilians can fuck it up," Tracey said bluntly.

"We will take a small craft to the location. We do not want you all to be shivering when we arrive," Hulaz said with a smile.

The quick journey in the craft was a quiet one. None of us felt like talking much, and even though I'd eaten some breakfast, my stomach was churning as if I'd not eaten for days. I supposed it was nervous stress that I was feeling. Let's face it; no one wants to say a permanent goodbye to someone they cared for or loved.

We landed softly in a beautiful area near some rolling sand dunes and a stunning beach. The sky was clear and blue, and the sun was making the waves glisten before they turned white and lapped at the golden sand. We all looked and admired the scene as we disembarked the small craft. It was heavenly to feel the sun on our faces while listening to the waves crash.

As we glanced around, we all became aware of a group of people standing in the nearest meadow. They were quietly talking between themselves and in front of them was a circle of angels, which included the elders and our angel friends.

In the center of the angel's circle was John, dressed in white trousers and smock. He was laid on top of a beautifully carved, pale-colored wooden altar, and over his still form was a thin golden sheet, thin enough where John's features could still be seen.

CHAPTER 13

The lush wild grass was soft on our feet as we were walking towards them all. Tracey walked with purpose, and I could tell she was trying to be strong. All eyes were on her as she walked up to our group of friends, coming to a halt before them. One by one, everyone took turns to say how sorry they were and to give her a hug. It was clear how grateful Tracey felt to have them all there and how much she was liked and loved.

After all the hugs and condolences were finished, Tracey turned towards the circle of angels, and her eyes widened at the sight of John's motionless body. James and I automatically flanked Tracey, and we both took her hands in ours.

The angels and elders looked beautiful stood in their circle with the sun making their shimmering hair glisten even more than usual. Lindaz, Evest and Akhenaten were either side of Christik, who was obviously going to officiate the ceremony. Our other angel friends in the circle all looked just as saddened as the rest of us, and when Tracey's eyes met theirs, they all gave her a knowing sad smile.

Christik began to raise her arms to waist height with her palms facing the blue sky. One by one, the elders and angels followed suit before Christik began to speak.

"Losing one of our own is losing part of ourselves," Christik said with reverence. "John was a part of us and earth. He gave respect, strength and purpose to everyone he met."

Christik looked to Tracey, and with a wave of Christik's hand, we were all suddenly holding flowers of various kinds. Tracey looked down at the sprig of beautiful blue orchids she now held in her hand, and she began to walk towards her husband's still body.

As she reached the angels, they parted to let her through. All of them began to take a knee and lower their heads to Tracey in deep respect. Tracey only had eyes for John's still form. We watched with heavy hearts as she walked up to the altar, placing the blue orchids on John's chest with her hand resting on top.

"I've known you since we were kids at school; you were my best friend before you became my husband," Tracey said with a shaking voice.

Tears began to slowly run down her flushed cheeks, silently dropping to the grass at her bare feet.

"You gave me the gift of two beautiful babies, and I will always be grateful for every moment we spent together, with each other and our children," she told him, "I hope Mel is right and that you're with our babies right now, John," she said as her voice broke, and her shoulders slumped.

Akhenaten immediately left the circle of angels, gliding quickly to his beloved's side. The moment his arm encircled her shoulders, and his hand touched her skin; we could all see his power pulsing and entering her body. Her gratitude was clear when she looked up into his sparkling blue eyes.

"Thank you," Tracey whispered.

THE MARILIANS

As Tracey and Akhenaten turned and walked back towards us, leaving the circle of kneeling angels; we all began to walk towards them, forming a loose line. Each of us took a moment to place our flowers around John and say our goodbyes. Meanwhile, Akhenaten never left Tracey's side. He was being the strong friend she so desperately needed, and he could help her in a way that we couldn't.

After everyone had said their farewells to John, the angels started to stand as Derek, who was the last person in the line, left his flowers. John looked so utterly peaceful, covered in the sheer gold sheet and surrounded with flowers of every color and shade.

I was expecting the angels to close the gap in their circle, but they didn't, leaving a clear view of John and the altar he was laid on. Christik raised her arms again, but this time, her palms faced John, and instantly the other angels and elders did the same. They moved like synchronized swimmers, all following Christik's movements. When Christik opened her wings, and the others did the same, it was a magnificent sight.

"We honor you, John, with love and friendship," Christik said as all the angel's hands began to glow brightly.

We all watched in awe as their bright white power started to travel from their palms to the altar. Johns body began to elevate in a glow of white and gold as if he were in a cloud of glitter. We could see John's body starting to glow beneath the gold sheet, and as the brightness grew, a sand-colored stone urn appeared on the altar beneath him.

With a sudden burst of light, John's body became part of the sparking cloud, shimmering before us. It was the most magical cremation I'd ever seen.

With surprise and widened eyes, we watched as the glittering particles started to slowly swirl and descend into the stone urn. It wasn't long before every trace of John was contained within the container, and the ceremony was over.

We were all silent as the angels and elders reined in their power, lowering their arms and folding their wings behind them. Christik walked forward with grace and gentleness as she took the urn from the altar and walked toward our grieving friend.

"Thank you," Tracey told her as she took the urn, bringing it up to her chest, "That was beautiful, and John would have been seriously impressed," she added with a small weak smile as tears trickled down her face.

Christik dipped her head to Tracey respectfully.

"We have a place for your husband to rest," Christik said gently.

With that, Christik began to walk towards a cluster of wild blue flowers that were growing in the grass, just before the sand dunes started. As we all got closer, there in the center of the flowers was a shallow hole that the angels had prepared. Akhenaten reluctantly released his touch on Tracey as she began to lower herself to kneel beside the waiting hole.

I was so busy watching Tracey that I hadn't noticed Lindaz and Evest coming alongside of us, until Tracey stood up again after placing the urn inside, and she looked at them. The elders were now standing either side of the hole and Tracey, with Christik stood in front of her, and their hands began to glow once more.

Christik and the elders faced their palms toward the ground, and the loose soil started to rise up from a mound. We watched silently as the moist soil rose and fell gently on top of John's urn until it was gone from view.

Akhenaten glided forward towards Tracey, and as soon as he reached her, he held out his palm and in his outstretched hand was a small seed of some kind. Without saying a word, Tracey took the seed from him, and she gently pushed it into the soft earth where her husband's ashes were buried.

When she took her place beside us again, she smiled as she took in the sight of us all comforting each other. James was stood behind me with his arms wrapped around me, and everyone else was doing the same. I could feel Tracey's pain, and so could Akhenaten. As soon as she turned to face the elders, he was at her side once more, letting his soothing power help her.

The elders' power began to brighten and pulse where Tracey had planted the seed, and before our eyes, a shoot of green began to emerge from the earth. We are all astonished to see the green shoot grow into first a tree sapling and then a small healthy tree.

Within minutes, the tree grew to the size of the angels, and we quickly realized that it was a lovely weeping willow. Its delicate thin branches started to bend as more leaves and delicate pink blossoms appeared.

"Wow, it's beautiful," Tracey quietly murmured, reflecting our own thoughts.

As the small blossoms opened, the elders' power lessened, and they lowered their arms.

"John would be happy with his tree and being next to the beach," Tracey said, more to herself than anyone else.

Her gaze then moved to the elders and Christik.

"Thank you again. You have made John proud," Tracey told them as her eyes welled with unshed tears.

Lindaz, Evest and Christik smiled at her warmly with understanding and love.

"We have the holding structure prepared for John's wake, so everyone can celebrate John's life," Evest said as he waved his arm towards the small craft.

Akhenaten led Tracey towards the craft, and we all followed, telling each other what a beautiful and wonderful ceremony it had been. As James and I walked behind Tracey and Akhenaten, I could hear him quietly telling her that she could visit the weeping willow anytime she wanted and that he would gladly bring her. *'That angel would do anything for her,'* I thought myself.

When I turned to James, I knew he'd heard Akhenaten, and he gave me a nod, clearly as impressed with the angel as I was. Just as we began to board the small craft, another arrived for our friends, and the journey back was short and full of mixed feelings. We were all so saddened by the loss of John, but we also felt happy that he had such an amazing send-off.

When we arrived back at the holding structure, the entrance was framed with blue flowers, and their flagrant scent drifted on the warm breeze. I could hear the sounds of people talking and the young children laughing as they played. It was soothing to the heart and soul to hear their giggles.

Walking into the foyer, it was hard not to be impressed by the effort of the angels. They'd really put themselves out with their preparations. There were plenty of tables and chairs for everyone, and in the center of each table was an elegant platter of various foods decorated with edible flowers.

Christik and the elders led us through the center of the foyer, and lots of people came up to Tracey to give her a hug, say how sorry they were and to tell her what a good man John was. The rest of us greeted friends as we made our way to the top tables that had been left empty for us.

As soon as Tracey got to our table and sat down with Akhenaten at her side, she leaned over towards us.

"I think I want to say my piece and get it over with," she said quietly, "I don't think I can hold it together much longer."

Her face looked strained and tired, and I could tell that the day had taken its toll on her.

"We understand, Tracey, you do what you need to do, honey," I replied with a warm understanding smile.

Tracey nodded before standing from her seat and facing everyone.

No one seemed to notice that Tracey had stood and was waiting to speak other than us and the people at the closest tables. Feeling Tracey's unease, Akhenaten used his power to release what looked like a small silver firework that whizzed up above our table. Straightaway, everyone turned to face our table to see where the noise had come from. When they saw that Tracey was standing, they all became silent. Tracey took a deep breath and cleared her throat.

"Thank you all for being here for John," Tracey said nervously, "I know you all got to know John in the last five years, and you probably realized quickly, that he would have done anything for any of you."

As soon as she finished her sentence, there were many shouts of agreement from people in the room.

"John was an amazing father to our twins. He was never too busy to spend time with them," Tracey continued, "He was also my best friend from childhood, and I loved him," she added, as her voice began to crack with emotion.

Not being able to say anything else, she sat back down in her seat completely drained. Luckily, Christik took Tracey's cue and stood to address everyone.

"Let the celebration of our friend John's life begin," Christik declared with a strong and clear voice.

Everyone in the room gave respectful applause before grabbing their stone cups and raising them.

"To John!" Everyone called out in unison, before taking a sip of their juices and water.

The rest of the evening was a wonderful tribute to John and the friendships he'd made. Many came up to talk to Tracey to tell her how he'd helped them in some way, including my own children. John was definitely going to be missed by everyone. I think that Tracey felt safe to leave once she was sure that the last person had spoken to her. Discreetly, she leaned towards James and me.

"Could I go back to your room, Mel?" She asked earnestly.

I could see clearly that she'd had enough and wanted to have some quiet time.

"Of course, honey," I told her quietly, "I'm sure everyone will understand."

"I'm going to take Tracey back, baby," I told James before tuning to Akhenaten and Christik.

"Could you both take Tracey and me back to my room, please?" I asked.

I didn't need to ask the angels twice. We were soon discreetly making our way down the side of the foyer as everyone was talking amongst themselves. The few people who actually noticed us leaving just gave us a sympathetic nod and a friendly smile. As we neared the exit, I spotted my kids, who were sat at two tables with their friends and angels. Holly spotted us straight away, so I touched the com at the top of my breasts. *'We're going back to our room, darling,'* I told her. *'You're going to go back to the cabin with your dad. Please tell the others.'* I didn't need to explain, Holly's expression made it clear that she already knew why. *'Ok, Mom,'* she replied with a knowing smile.

When we arrived back at my rooms, Christik gave Tracey a hug, wrapping her in her arms and wings. I could see Christik's power glowing from within the cocoon she'd made around our friend. As soon as Christik drew away from Tracey and stepped away, Akhenaten stepped forward, taking Tracey's hand in his. Tracey looked up into Akhenaten's sapphire blue eyes, and the angel's brows furrowed as he tried to control his shimmering glow.

"I am here for you if you need me," he said with a voice full of emotion.

I could feel the conflict Akhenaten was feeling, protectiveness, love and helplessness. Akhenaten released her hand, and he reluctantly glided away following his sister. Within seconds, they both flitted into thin air. Tracey turned to look at me with confusion written all over her face, before shaking her head and walking into my room's main area.

Following Tracey into my room, I watched as she walked over to the round window and looked out. I knew she would talk when she was ready, so I sat down in the seating area and waited patiently. Minutes slowly went by before she finally turned around and came to sit next to me. My friend looked so drained that my heart ached with sadness.

"It was a beautiful ceremony, wasn't it?" Tracey said softly.

Her voice mirrored the sadness in her face, and her thinned lips made me think that she was trying to stop herself from crying again.

"Yes, it was beautiful," I told her, "More beautiful than I could have imagined."

"Mmm... I couldn't have asked for a better way to see him off," she stated, "I think he would have been pleased."

I nodded my head in agreement.

"I didn't even like him when we first met, you know," Tracey admitted. "He was an arrogant bastard, who thought he was god's gift to womanhood."

I was very surprised to hear her say that. It didn't sound like the John we'd known at all.

"Really?" I answered with an eyebrow raised.

"Oh yeah," she said with a weak smile. "He couldn't believe that I wasn't attracted to him. It was a shock to his system."

I couldn't help the smile that formed on my lips. I could just imagine Tracey putting him in his place for being a walking ego.

"So how on earth did you end up together?" I asked curiously.

Tracey smirked at the memories that popped into her head.

"Well," she said as she walked over and sat down on the chair next to me.

"I'd always known him from high school, and we were sort of friends. Then, when I was a new nurse at our local hospital, he came into the ER department with a very embarrassing injury," Tracey explained.

I could tell that talking about John and their shared memories were helping her heal, even though she wasn't aware of it.

"You can't just leave it at that, woman," I told her. "Tell me more!"

My facial expression must have said it all because Tracey suddenly begins to giggle. Then, just as abruptly, she stopped herself and covered her mouth with her hand.

"You don't need to feel guilty for remembering you and John's shared memories Tracey," I told her reassuringly, "I'm sure John would be laughing at the memories too, if he were here."

I could feel her guilt subside as she absorbed my words.

"Yes, he'd be cracking up, just thinking about it," she admitted.

When she raised her face to look at me, I raised my eyebrows at her.

"Well, spill it, woman!" I declared, making her smile again.

"John was with someone else when he ended up in the ER department and my section. Apparently, she'd wanted him to last longer in the bedroom, and she'd talked him into wearing a cock ring," she explained while trying to keep a straight face.

"And?" I said with a smile.

"Well, it became apparent that she didn't check the size of the ring before putting it on him. So, when he got hard, the bloody thing was strangling his little friend, if you know what I mean," Tracey explained with a grin.

I couldn't believe what I was heard as I giggled at Tracey's face. Poor John must have been in total agony, but it was so funny. I was so glad Tracey hadn't told me before. If she had, there was no way I'd have been able to look John in the eyes again.

"Oh, my god, Tracey," I said through my laughter, "what happened?"

Tracey clamped her bottom lip between her teeth as she tried to keep a straight face, but I could see her humor dancing in her eyes. She took a steadying breath before speaking.

"I have to say that I actually felt sorry for the arrogant fucker," she said, "He was so vulnerable at that point and was feeling so sorry for himself. I couldn't bring myself to tease him about the whole situation like I wanted to when he was first admitted. His poor cock was swollen and throbbing as if it had been hit with a hammer. So, I had to ice it to reduce the swelling and then lubricate it with a gel to get the cock ring off."

By this point, I thought I might pee myself a little because I was laughing so hard. It wasn't just what Tracey was telling me; it was the actions she was doing while telling me. She was obviously enjoying my reactions to her story. I waved a hand at her for her to continue.

"It took two of us to get the ring off his cock. One of my nurse colleagues had to hold him down, and I had to yank the bloody thing off," Tracey laughed. "I'd never seen any patient so relieved, and he was so grateful once it was all over; he melted my heart," she admitted.

"So how earth did you get from that situation to actually dating him?" I asked, feeling even more curious.

"Well, he was so grateful to have his todger intact and functional that three days after it happened, he turned up at the ER with a massive bouquet of flowers for me and the other nurse," Tracey said while smiling again at the memory. "He wasn't the arrogant fucker that he was before, and he asked me out on a date. Seeing a different side of him made me realize that it had all been an act. After a week of dating, I knew he was the one," she added quietly.

The rest of the night was full of tears, laughter, and more tears, as Tracey reminisced about her history with John. I knew it was healing her broken heart. I don't know which one of us fell asleep first, but I knew we were both mentally and physically exhausted.

CHAPTER 14

When I woke the next morning, Tracey and I were laid on my bed, and I had my arm resting against her waist. The sun was streaming through the round window, and I had no idea if it was still morning or closer to midday. Tracey was still sleeping soundly, and she certainly needed it. I slid off the bed and decided to shower and freshen up. My face still felt a little puffy from all the crying and laughing.

By the time I came out of the bedroom, Tracey was awake, and she was tucking into breakfast.

"I didn't know you could do magic," I told her with a smile.

Her responding smile was a bit brighter than the night before, which was reassuring.

"Hulaz just came with the tray; it's almost as if those angels are psychics," Tracey said with a raised eyebrow.

I smiled again as I sat at the small table to join her. I poured some coffee from the tray and relished the delicious smell before taking a sip. '*What would I do without my coffee*,' I thought.

"So, what would you like to do today?" I asked Tracey.

I wasn't sure how Tracey would be feeling after such a hard-emotional day and night, so I didn't want to assume anything. When she looked at me, I could see and feel a steely resolve flowing through her. She'd put her big girl pants on.

"As much as I'd like to curl up in a ball and sob my heart out; we haven't got time for that shit!" She stated determinedly, "Those Marilian fuckers could arrive any day, and I want us to be prepared."

I was blown away by how strong my friend was. No wonder John and now Akhenaten had fallen in love with her. If I hadn't had been straight, I could have had a serious crush on her myself.

"Well, ok then," I said with a smile, "So, what's the plan?"

"I've already located all the buildings we need, so let's check the last two out and make sure everything is going to plan," she answered.

After reaching out to James and the kids after breakfast, Holly and Nalik decided to come with us. James was going to be busy getting the ambushes ready with Derek and the other ex-service people. April and Abigail were helping Ann with the other artists, and lastly, my boys were helping Christine and her dad, who we still hadn't met. The thought made me feel a little guilty, but we didn't have the time to worry about it.

Nalik took us ladies to the first building in one of the small crafts. The sky was cloudy by the time we got there, and it felt like it was going to rain. The clouds looked dark and heavy in places, and the air was cool on my skin. We were quite close to the fake holding structure, and I could see it in the distance. Nalik landed the small craft in a now unused pharmacy car park, and we began to follow Tracey to the building. The building she'd picked was brilliant. It was a large red-bricked old library, which seemed to tower over all the other buildings.

We followed Tracey inside, and we walked through a very old-fashioned foyer and reception area. It was lovely to see and admire all the old wood they'd kept and the vintage lamps, *'that is history right there. James would really appreciate this place,'* I thought to myself.

Tracey led us through the library until we reached a very old staircase, and we followed her up. The dark wooden steps creaked as we climbed and because the stairs were so narrow; we had to ascend in single file.

"I could fart right now, and none of you could save yourselves," Tracey stated from the front.

"Oh my god, woman, I can't believe you just said that," I told her as we all burst into laughter.

"I'm just saying," Tracey said with a giggle, "I'm not saying I would, I'm just stating facts."

Climbing up steep steps while laughing wasn't the easiest thing to do.

"What is a fart?" Nalik asked in utter confusion at the word and our laughter.

"I'll explain to you later," Holly told him through her own giggles, which grew even louder as she took in his confused expression.

"Oh Nalik, you have a lot to learn," I said through my laughter, barely getting my words out.

The moment we all stepped into the first-floor room, we became silent. Suddenly, the situation had become very real. There were stacks of various guns, ammunition magazines, body armor, night-vision goggles, and much more.

"Wow, you have all been very busy," I said in awe.

I walked through the dark wood-paneled room, taking stock of everything in there. I was amazed at how much everyone had procured from the local military bases. When I got to the other side of the room, which was framed by a large bay window, I was also impressed with the stunning view of the town. I could see all the buildings and most of the roads from where we were. Tracey came and stood next to me.

"Now you can understand why I picked this building," she said, "If you look to the right of the holding structure, there's a large park. There's nowhere else that's close with room to land a craft," Tracey explained. "The Marilians won't have a choice but to land there, and we'll be able to see where they go from here.

Tracey certainly had a tactical mind, and I greatly admired her cool, calm and collected manner. She was certainly a force to be reckoned with.

"How are we going to get everyone into place ready to fight?" I asked, hoping one of them would know.

"Do not worry, Mel, we have everything in place," Nalik assured. "Everyone who will be fighting has an angel assigned to them. As soon as the Marilians begin to approach your planet, the angels will collect their human counterpart and flit to their pre-arranged place," he explained.

'*Wow, everyone really has been busy,*' I thought to myself.

"What about the people who can't fight, such as the older people, children and pregnant women?" I asked, "Where are they going to be?"

Nalik smiled warmly at all of us as we all looked at him as if to say '*Well?*'

"Christik has a safe place in mind for you and the others who will not be fighting," he said confidently, "I believe she is activating the location later today."

As soon as he said it, Stonehenge popped into my head, and I couldn't stop myself from getting excited.

"Nalik, do you think that we could watch the place being activated?"

All of us turned to look at Nalik with puppy eyes full of hope. We must have looked hilarious because the angel looked back with a smirk and humor in his sparkling, peacock eyes.

"I will ask Christik if it is possible," Nalik answered with a full-blown smile.

"Thank you Nalik," I told him warmly before turning to Tracey again. "Ok lady, where to next?"

"There an underground garage close to the library that's going to be used for an ambush," Tracey said matter of factly, "we need to make sure it's set."

The underground garage was just as unkempt as the surrounding buildings. There were weeds sprouting from every cement crack and gap, giving another indication that nature really was trying to reclaim the land. As I looked at the weeds and overgrown vegetation, I wondered if we would ever reuse all the empty buildings again, and if we did; how long would it take? Our future was so uncertain, but with the angels' help, I truly believed that it could be a brighter one.

Tracey led us down a concrete slope and into the parking garage, and just as I wondered how on earth we were going to see anything, lights suddenly came on.

"How the heck did that happen?" I asked, taken by complete surprise.

Tracey smiled knowingly from the kneeling position she suddenly had.

"It's amazing what can be done with solar power, isn't it," she said with a smile, "John and the other guys managed to locate the solar lights from the big abandoned hardware stores."

"That's fantastic," I told her, "we're going to need as many as we can get after the angels leave."

Tracey nodded, stood up, and continued to walk further down the slope, which was now brightly lit. As we followed her, we could see more guns and ammunition on either side of us, which had been neatly organized for quick use. I was suddenly grateful for all the target practice, but then as I thought of my own kids shooting the weapons and going up against the Marilians; my heart sank in my chest. *'I'll be so glad when this is over,'* I thought as I followed behind Tracey.

Further into the garage, I began to notice military vehicles lined up in the parking spaces. Any non-military vehicles that had been abandoned had been moved and were neatly parked further away.

"You found these military trucks too?" I asked Tracey.

"The guys did," Tracey said proudly. "It was amazing what they found at the abandoned bases. The angels helped us store everything in the right places."

As Tracey's eyes scanned the supplies, she looked as if she was mentally ticking off everything that was there.

Holly bent down to a neat spread of handguns that had been laid out on a wooden crate. Tentatively, she picked one up and surprised me by checking if it was loaded.

"You seem very capable with that gun, Holly," I told my daughter.

Holly looked at me with a new confidence that I hadn't seen before.

"I've done some shooting with Luiza before," Holly explained. "I've also been getting in some practice every chance I've had, too," she added.

"I do not want you to be in the coming battle, Holly," Nalik told her with a sadness to his tone.

Her responding glare made it clear that she was offended. The angel quickly raised his hands as if in surrender.

"It is not because you are female Holly," Nalik quickly told her, "I do not want you to get hurt or killed," he admitted, lowering his head.

Holly placed the handgun back amongst the others on the crate before turning back to face her angel.

"I understand, Nalik because I feel the same about my family and our friends," she told him softly, "I don't want any of us fighting the Marilians, but we don't have a choice my own, my one," she said as her hand cupped his shimmering face.

As my daughter and Nalik's eyes locked; the angel began to glow. I could feel the connection between them, and it was very strong. I knew Nalik would do anything to protect her, and the thought was very reassuring.

"I wish James and the kids had their own personal angels to protect them," I said to Tracey quietly.

As Holly lowered her hand from Nalik's face, he turned to look at Tracey and me.

"They do," he said, looking surprised that we didn't know, "They have all been assigned an angel to protect them and fight with them. They will be the same angels who will flit them to their places."

"One fucking guess who my angel bodyguard is," Tracey laughed.

Nalik looked at her with a serious face.

"It is Akhenaten," he stated.

That made Tracey laugh even more.

"No shit, Sherlock," Tracey told him, making Holly and I burst into laughter too, "Anyone would think we're a bunch of pussies. Not the badasses that we are."

Nalik suddenly seemed very sad.

"We don't want to lose any of you, Tracey. You have all lost too many already," the angel told her.

Tracey looked at Nalik guiltily.

"I know Nalik, you're right," she told him.

Tracey took a deep breath and gave us all a thin smile.

"I think we're good to go," she stated confidently, "I already know the other buildings are ready, so we can head back now."

We followed Tracey out of the parking garage into the natural light and headed back towards the small craft. Just as we rounded an empty street corner, I suddenly stopped. I could feel another presence, and I knew it wasn't Tracey, Holly or Nalik. It wasn't an evil presence; in fact, it was emanating a nervous excitement.

"What's wrong, Mel?" Tracey asked as she stopped beside me.

Nalik and Holly stopped behind me just as confused.

"Someone or something is here, but I can't see where," I told them as my eyes scanned the streets.

It was so weird feeling something and not being able to see it, but at least I could tell that it wasn't malevolent. All of us began to scan the streets and buildings, looking for anything off.

"I can't see anything," Holly said as her eyes darted from building to building.

"I can feel them too, Mel," Nalik said as his eyes also roamed the scene, "there are angels close by."

It suddenly dawned on me why Nalik and I could feel the angels but not see them.

"Ok, you got us, you can come out now," I called aloud as I giggled to myself.

By the expressions on Holly and Tracey's faces, they'd realized what was happening too. We all stood there, straining our eyes to see if we could see the angels who were hiding. Something moved against the front of a deli shop, and I gasped in surprise as the angel peeled herself from the window signage.

"That was fucking awesome," Tracey blurted out.

It wasn't until the angel walked towards us that we realized it was Hulaz. It was strange to see her body painted now she was away from the shop. She looked odd with half a poster painted on her face and right shoulder, with the colors of the glass covering most of her remaining body. It was also weird not to see her shimmering as she usually did. Even her hair had been tied back and painted.

Hulaz laughed as she walked towards us.

"You're enjoying this way too much, lady," I told her in good humor.

"Ann is a talented woman," Hulaz replied with a smile, making the letters on her face look even more bizarre. "I am enjoying this new experience. It is making me more confident that we will be able to surprise the Marilians and have an advantage," she added.

Just as she said the last words, three more angels peeled themselves from the buildings. They'd been so well-camouflaged that there was no way we would have spotted them.

"Bloody hell, you're right about Ann's talent," Tracey blurted out, "there's no way the Marilians are going to know you're there."

As the other three angels approached, they all dipped their heads in respect. Two of the angels were covered in painted brickwork, and the other was partly painted to look like a shop door. I'd looked directly at the shop across the street where he'd come, and I hadn't spotted him. We dipped our head back in response.

"We will come back to the main craft with you," Hulaz said as she indicated the way.

"You all look amazing. How long did it take Ann to paint you all?" I asked Hulaz as I walked beside her.

"It took many hours, but Ann had help from the other artists before the final details were added," Hulaz told us. "I understand from Christik that you are coming with us to prepare the refuge later today," she added.

I hadn't realized that Nalik has already asked Christik, but I shouldn't have been surprised. When I glanced at Nalik, he dipped his head to me and smiled.

"Yes, we're looking forward to seeing it," I told Hulaz.

She didn't seem to be giving away any details either, which intrigued me even more. We made our way back to the small craft, and once on board, we headed back to the main craft.

Tracey, Holly, Nalik and I were all having lunch with Hulaz back at our room when James and the kids came back. The kids seemed to be buzzing, so I could tell that they'd enjoyed themselves. James walked straight over and came up behind me, wrapping his muscular arms around the top of my body and kissing my ear. The kids all said their hellos; then sat on the floor and began to tuck into the food.

"How did it go, baby?" James asked as he released me and sat in the remaining chair.

"It was good," I told him with a smile, "Tracey's fricking awesome; she's found the perfect buildings for everything we need."

"I told you all; I was a badass. I don't know why you're all acting surprised," Tracey stated smugly.

As our laughter at Tracey wore off; James and the kids told us all about how they got on. I was pleased that the kids had done so well, and it reassured me that they were doing so well.

When Christik arrived, we'd already finished eating and were raring to go.

"Are you all ready?" Christik asked as she gracefully glided into the room.

"Are you going to tell us where we're going, Christik?" Abigail asked politely.

Christik smiled at our daughter, affectionately.

"Nalik thought it would be a nice surprise for you all. So, you will have to wait to discover where we are going," Christik told her. "Come, let us go!"

We all followed Christik to the hanger part of their ship where a small craft was waiting for us. Everyone started to board the craft apart from Nalik, and just as Holly noticed that he'd stopped moving, I noticed a look between the angel and James. '*That's interesting,*' I thought.

"Why aren't you boarding the craft, Nalik," Holly asked, clearly disappointed.

I could sense that Nalik was uncomfortable having to disappoint our daughter.

"I am sorry, Holly, my one, but I will have to meet you there," he told her. "Do not worry, I will see you soon."

Holly nodded to Nalik before boarding, and I happened to notice a shared knowing look between James and the angel. '*What the heck was that?*' There was definitely something going on, but I didn't want to ask my husband in front of everyone.

I waited until we were all seated and had taken off before touching my com and reaching out to James. '*Ok, husband, spill it!*' I told him, '*what's going on between you and Nalik?*'

James looked at me with his sexy smirk on his face and his eyes twinkling. '*I know nothing of what you're referring to, sexy,*' he said smoothly in my mind.

'*Oh, like that is it!*' I told him while trying my best to give him a stern look. It wasn't helping. The bastard liked it when I was being stern, and I could tell by his increasing smile that he was enjoying the situation and my reaction, way too much for his own good. *'You know I have my ways of getting everything out of you!'* I warned.

'Oh, bring it on baby; I will let you torture me for hours,' he said seductively while wiggling his eyebrows.

It was hard not to start laughing at his cheeky and defiant look. *'You will be begging for mercy,'* I told him with a raised eyebrow of my own.

'We'll see,' he answered, *'we'll see.'*

I was so busy talking and listening to everyone on board that the time flew by, and before we knew it, Christik was telling us that we were arriving. I leaned forward and looked through the gap between Christik and the glass window at the front of the craft. All I could see was choppy dark water and clear sky. I could feel the craft lowering and making contact with the water, creating a jolt. As I looked through the front glass, the water was traveling up the glass window, and we were descending into the sea.

James, Tracey and the kids followed my gaze and looked through the glass themselves. All of them held the same look of surprise.

"The safe refuge is underwater?" I asked Hulaz.

"Yes, it is," she replied with a smile.

"Where are we," I asked her, dying to get more information.

"We are close to the country of Cuba," Hulaz said.

My mind was racing, going through everything I knew about Cuba, and to be honest; it wasn't much. I couldn't recall hearing of anything like Stonehenge being there or near the country. I was completely baffled.

We seemed to be lowering into the depths slowly but steadily, before coming to a full stop under the sea. Christik released herself from the craft, allowing the silver vines that had been wrapped around her arms to recede and melt back into the craft's hull. She turned around as soon as she was free and smiled a knowing smile.

CHAPTER 15

A s soon as Christik smiled, I knew we were going to witness something weird or magical. The excitement that was building in the small craft was palpable, and my heart was racing in my chest. Even my baby was doing flips in my swollen belly as she sensed the excitement too.

Christik raised her hands to the sides of the craft again, and her hands began to glow white with her power. This time, instead of the vines appearing, the craft began to swirl with colors. Instead of the craft being white; the hull was becoming pearlescent just like the corridors in the main craft. Just as I was wondering why Christik would want to change the color, the craft gave off a strong shimmer before changing again to become transparent.

"Woah, what the fuck!" Tracey blurted out, mirroring our own shock and awe.

It was as if we were sitting inside a bubble and not the angels' craft. I knew we were deep in the ocean, but the weird thing was that the craft was doing something to the water. We could see various fish swimming around the craft as if it was daylight down there. When one of the visible fish decided to swim up to the craft, right next to where I was sitting; I was again reminded that all creatures were drawn to our baby. The girls began to laugh as a fish started to tap the craft with his mouth, making it look like it was blowing a kiss.

"You released fish here," I asked in surprise.

"Yes, we did," Christik said, "We released them in a few areas where the water was fully cleaned."

"What is that over there?" James asked, pointing to something on the other side of the craft.

We all turned to look in the direction that James was pointing to, and there, a short distance away, settled on the ocean floor were ancient ruins. There wasn't much left of whatever it had been, but as I looked, I could tell it wasn't a natural formation.

"There are ancient ruins down here?" I asked Christik, wanting to confirm what my eyes were seeing.

"Yes, Mel," she said with a smile. "Many of our earliest settlements are now underwater; we wouldn't be reactivating them if it were not for the Marilians. It will be the safest place for those who are not able or willing to fight," she explained.

"But how can we survive down here? There's hardly anything left of it. At least with Stonehenge most of the building blocks were still there," I told her, as worry began to build within me.

"There is more here than you can see, Mel," Christik assured, "My angels are arriving," she added while pointing to the ruins.

As I looked at the ruins before us, I could make out what looked like three pyramid-shaped structures, as well as two large squares made of rock and other smaller structures. It certainly looked as if a large society had lived there once, and I wondered if it had just been the angels, or if like Peru; they'd lived together.

While all these thoughts ran through my mind, something gold rapidly shot through the water towards the ruins. It was traveling so fast that it could have been a torpedo. What was strange was that the craft we were in didn't move an inch with the force of the movement. Whatever it was, and I assumed it was an angel, was cutting through the water as if it wasn't there.

Just as I started to get nervous, thinking that the angel wasn't going to stop and was going to crash into the ruins, the angel suddenly released its golden wings. Its wings shot up behind it, either side of its long steaming golden hair, and with graceful ease, the angel then spread its wings to slow itself down until it landed just outside of the ruin's perimeter.

It was only when the angel landed on the sand that I realized the angel was a male. He stood motionless, looking at the ruins. Within seconds, another golden angel was shooting through the water towards the other, landing within feet next to the first and then another and another.

The angels appeared to be making a circle around the ruins. They looked amazing; all still like shimmering golden statues with their wings out and their long, gold hair floating around their heads. None of them appeared to be breathing. I couldn't see any air bubbles coming from their noses or mouths.

It was getting harder to see the ruins after a while. All the local fish were still being drawn to my unborn baby and were now beginning to block our view.

"As cute as it is being surrounded by the fish; I can't see a bloody thing now," I said, feeling frustrated.

"I'm struggling to see anything now too," Holly added.

"Maybe you can do something about it, Mel," Christik said with a smile. "She is your baby; maybe you should ask her to help with the sea creatures."

Just as she said it, there was a thud against the craft. When I looked to where the noise had come from, all I could see were massive tentacles. A huge octopus had literally decided to attach itself to the craft, and now none of us could see anything. Christik gave me a knowing look.

I looked down at my growing baby bump and placed both hands on it. I knew our baby was awake because she hadn't stopped moving around since we'd been underwater. She'd even had hiccups for a little while, and I smiled at the thought.

"Ok, my little one, we need your help," I told her gently, hoping she knew that I was talking to her, "I know you want to be close to the sea creatures, but we can't see a thing, sweet girl. Can you ask them to swim to the bottom of the craft, darling, so we can all see what's going on?" I asked her.

I could feel her turning inside me.

"Look. She's doing it," James said excitedly.

"Woah, she's awesome!" April added in amazement.

I looked up to witness the various fish swimming to the bottom of the craft, and because the whole hull of the craft was transparent, we could see them underneath our feet. Some of them were stunningly colorful, and it was amazing to watch them as they shoaled together. I turned my attention back to the large octopus, just in time to see it using its tentacles to move down the craft until it was below us too.

"Thank you, baby girl," I told our baby while stroking my bump with my hand.

I moved back to my place alongside James, and I continued to watch the angels shoot through the water and land. There weren't many spaces left in the angel circle around the ruins, and I couldn't wait to see what they did next.

"The anticipation is fucking killing me," Tracey said breathlessly. "I heard all about what happened at Stonehenge, and I wished I'd been there to see it."

"It was very magical," I admitted; I wish you'd been there too.

As the last few golden angels arrived and took their places in the circle, our excitement grew. We were all wondering what was going to happen next when eight more angels shot through the water; only this time, they were the silver angels. Instead of adding to the angel circle, these angels all took a place in front of the ancient structure remains. Three of the silver angels landed in front of the three pyramid-shaped ruins, while the others landed in front of the square structures and smaller ruins.

All of the silver angels had their wings spread out exactly the same as the golden angels. None of us knew what to expect next. We were all glued to the scene as the golden angels began to raise their arms out to their sides with their palms facing the seabed. The angels' hands began to glow, and their power started to pulse toward the ground. From our distance, it was hard to trust our own eyes as the sand began to move under the angels' magic.

As we stared in awe, tiny gold and silver flecks began to rise from the seabed surrounding the angels. It was as if the angel's power was sucking up all the gold and silver from below the sand. Within minutes, each of the golden angels had swirling gloves of gold and silver beneath their hands. None of us said a word; we were all speechless as we watched.

Just as the globes of gold and silver became large enough to nearly touch the angels' hands, the silver angels raised their arms in the air. Their now glowing palms were facing the remains of the buildings they faced. Eight of the golden angels suddenly sent one of their shimmering globes to the waiting silver angels whose outstretched hands were waiting.

The silver winged angels didn't flinch as the globes of silver and gold reached them, and as soon as the contact was made; vines began to appear from the shimmering balls. The vines were just like the vines that came out of the earth healing crafts. As they grew, more vines appeared, splitting from the first, and they all headed for the ruins in front of the angel.

"Wow," Harrison said while we watched the vines reach the ruins.

The vines slithered around the ruins as if feeling their way before beginning to take shape. They seemed to be reforming the original frames of the ancient structures. They moved and settled in place, forming walls and ceilings, steps and enclosed walkways between each building. As the globes shrank to nothing; another eight golden angels sent more gold and silver to the waiting silver angels, and so it went on. The ruins were coming alive before our eyes.

When the last of the gold and silver was used, the silver angels lowered their arms. '*I wonder if these angels realize how amazing they are,*' I thought as I took in the splendor before me. There was now a gold and silver city glistening on the seabed, but one that still couldn't be used. The vines had created a decorative lattice framework, but that was all. As I was wondering what the angels were going to next, the golden angels began the same process all over again. Only this time, it wasn't gold or silver rising and creating balls beneath their palms; it was mother of pearl.

When the tiny flecks of shell collected into the same size swirling globes, the angels sent them again to the silver angels. This time, the silver angels sent the flecks of shell in glistening streams, straight to the gold and silver framework, and we watched speechless as the mother of pearl filled in the spaces between the vines. Suddenly, there were real buildings forming under the sea, and before long, we were all looking at the most beautiful city I'd ever seen.

We were all staring at three magnificent pyramids, two large square buildings and many smaller structures. It was an amazing sight to take in, and we were all absolutely flabbergasted.

"Welcome to the city of Cubanaz," Christik said, snapping us out of our amazed trances.

"So, this was one of your cities?" I asked, still feeling stunned.

Christik nodded her head.

"Yes, Mel, although originally it was made of local stone, so as to not disrupt the local environment," Christik explained.

"Well, I don't think anyone is going to mind spending time here," I told her.

"How are they going to breathe down here?" James asked.

Tracey and the kids were still completely in awe of the whole situation with their mouths agape, looking from James and I to Christik.

"Watch, and you will see," Christik answered gently.

All of us turned our attention back to the beautiful city and the angels. We looked just in time to see the silver and gold angels leaving. Each of them looked up and then forced their open wings down, shooting themselves through the ocean and back to the surface. When the last of the angels had gone, we all waited for the next thing to happen. None of us had any idea what it could be.

"Look!" April said excitedly as she pointed to the left of the city.

It took a few moments for my eyes and brain to figure out what I was seeing. It looked almost like the rig crafts that the angels used to clean the Earth's oceans, but this craft looked slightly different. As it got closer, I could still see two large structures on either side of it, similar to the inlet and outlet pipes of the water cleaning crafts, but these were not quite the same.

We watched the craft get steadily closer to the city, and as it got to within fifty feet or so, it began to slowly descend. It made contact with the seabed with ease, and as soon as the contact was made, vines started to grow from the bottom of the craft, and large structures either side of it seemed to open. The vines softly dropped to the sand and traveled in all directions until they reached the city's buildings. As the vines touched the stone bases, they passed through like a knife slicing through warm butter.

After a few minutes, the vines stopped, and the watercraft began to glow slightly. We could see some of the vines changing color, some turning from white to light blue and others changing to pale green.

"We are now removing the water from inside the city and replacing it with oxygen for you all," Christik told us.

Within moments, tiny air bubbles were starting to appear from the pyramids and the other buildings.

"Are there leaks, Christik?" James asked, concern evident in his tone.

"No, James, do not worry. It is our way of keeping pressure; we do not want to cause you any harm," she reassured him, "The city will have a constant supply of oxygen and all the supplies that will be needed."

From where we watched, we could just make out flashes of light coming from inside the buildings, bouncing off the mother of pearl on the rooftops.

"My angels are arriving with the supplies now. Would you all like to see what the city looks like from inside."

There were yes' from all of us, and Christik smiled at our quick responses. I think she enjoyed showing us so many new things and seeing our reactions to them.

"Please take your seats," she told us.

As we all sat back down; April looked concerned.

"What about the fish and the octopus? They're still surrounding the craft?" She asked, looking at Christik with worry written all over her young face.

"They will not be harmed, April," Christik told her kindly, "They will be collected while we are inside."

Christik took her place at the front of the craft, and the moment her fingers touched to sides, the vines appeared and wrapped around her arms. As soon as we began to move, the fish and the octopus disbursed, before swimming after us. As we slowly moved towards the city, I began to realize just how big it was. The shimmering light from both crafts bounced off the gold, silver and mother of pearl, making the city look like it would be more at home in a fairytale rather than under the sea.

My mind thought back to the tales of Atlantis and other underwater ruins that had been discovered around the world.

"Christik, have you ever heard of Atlantis?" I asked as she steered us closer to the nearest tunnel leading to one of the large square buildings.

"When we built the city you refer to, we called it Atlantiz," Christik said as she steered, "Its remains are in the Mariana drop, or trench as you call it. We settled there after your planet was hit by a large comet, which wiped out most of your creatures. It took a long time to clean the air and water enough for your creatures to thrive again," she explained.

"So, you all lived deep in the ocean," Harrison asked, suitably impressed.

"Yes, Harrison," Christik answered.

"Well, no wonder nobody was able to find it," he laughed.

"How did people hear of it if they couldn't find it then?" Anthony asked.

I could tell by his face that questions where running through his mind, the same questions were running through mine.

"When we interacted with your earlier civilizations, some of their leaders were brought to Atlantiz. We wanted them to take us seriously and by seeing our city, they did," Christik explained. "Unfortunately, we could not return as often as we would have liked. It was too easy for those civilizations to revert back to their old ways of greed and power.

Christik turned her attention back to steering the craft. We were getting closer to the tunnel, and because the craft was still transparent; we had an excellent view of what Christik was doing. Smoothly, she pulled up at the tunnel, and just as I wondered how we were supposed to get in, the craft and tunnel melted together before our eyes, creating a circular entrance.

You'd think after everything I'd seen since I'd woken up; I wouldn't get surprised anymore, but that was not the case. Everything the angels did had me in awe of them.

Christik led us into the tunnel, and a cool, refreshing breeze flowed over my skin. It was like being in an air-conditioned building, but I could still smell the scent of the ocean in the air. It was hard to wrap my head around the fact that we were so deep underwater. We walked down the beautiful tunnel, the mother of pearl shining with iridescent colors, and we headed for the large square-shaped building.

The entrance to the building was the ancient stone with the silver and gold vines entwined in a stunning arch. As we walked in, our eyes darted everywhere as we tried to take in every detail. The angels had been extremely busy in such a short space of time, and no wonder; there were so many flashes of light as they flitted in and out with the supplies.

There was a middle aisle, which we began to walk down, and on either side of the aisle were tables and chairs, beautifully decorated with shells of all shapes and colors. The shimmering light from the mother of pearl ceiling and walls had given the cavernous room a magical feel that made my heart race. As my eyes scanned down the room, I looked towards the far end just in time to see Nalik appear.

Holly's angel seemed nervous as he stood at the far end of the room, and my heart began to race even more. I touched James' back to get his attention, indicating with a small side nod to where he should look. The moment he laid eyes on Nalik; a huge grin appeared on my husband's face '*What does that bastard know that I don't?*' I thought.

James looked back to me, looking very smug. '*The shit.*' I didn't have a clue what was going on, but it didn't take long for Holly to notice her angel had arrived. Holly's face lit up when she saw him, and Nalik smiled back nervously as his body began to glow. He looked at her with complete adoration as he lifted a hand to beckon her. The rest of us stopped in our tracks. Even the other angels in the room stopped what they were doing to watch Holly as she made her way to her angel.

James took my hand in his, and he gave it a loving squeeze before stroking my hand with his thumb. I couldn't take my eyes off our daughter as she made her way to Nalik. I could feel an excitement growing in the air and coming strongly from James. It suddenly dawned on me as to what was happening. Hope and pride began to build within me.

When Holly reached Nalik, he was almost pulsating with light as his emotions grew stronger. He gently took Holly's hands in his own, and then he knelt before her. Nalik quickly glanced at James, who gave him a quick encouraging nod before looking back to Holly. I could see the angel's peacock eyes sparkling, even from where we stood.

"Holly, I knew you were my own; my one; my other half, as soon as I saw you and felt your presence," he told her confidently. "I cannot imagine my life without you. Will you marry me and be my one, my wife in the eyes of your people?" He asked with hope in his words.

I believe that if Holly could have glowed like her angel, she would have done. She looked at Nalik as if he were her whole world, and my heart melted in my chest.

"Yes," Holly told Nalik with the confidence of a grown woman.

CHAPTER 16

Holly's face was a picture of love and adoration for her angel. She reached out a hand, and she softly cupped Nalik's face as he started to rise from the floor. The look of pure adoration was clear to see in Holly's and Nalik's eyes. We could all see that she loved the angel as much as he loved her. Nalik continued to glow as Holly touched his face; he was clearly mesmerized by her.

"I will marry you, Nalik because I love you, more than I thought I could ever love someone," she told him with conviction."

Nalik's glow brightened even more.

"I do not want to wait, Holly. Will you marry me here, now?" He asked hopefully.

Holly looked from Nalik to James and me. Under normal circumstances, I'm sure I would have been in shock at the thought of our eldest daughter even considering rushing into marriage with someone so quickly. However, nothing was normal anymore, and I was just grateful that our daughter had found happiness and her soul mate.

I turned to look at James, and he was grinning at Holly and Nalik as if he'd just won the lottery. When I looked back to Holly, I had a matching grin, and my heart was full of love for her. Holly grinned back at us and turned to Nalik.

"Let's do it!" She declared.

Instantly, the excitement in the room escalated, and the angels that had stopped moving began to move into overdrive. As we started to walk towards Holly and our future son in law, angels were disappearing and reappearing all around us. Some of the angels reappeared with food or drinks, placing it on the nearest tables while other angels were appearing with our friends.

I had to assume that the angels were telling our friends what was going on because they were arriving with smiles on their faces. The happiness that was filling the room was contagious. When we got to Holly, she was smiling from ear to ear. I gave her a responding smile.

"Would you like to change for your wedding?" I asked her warmly.

Holly looked at me as if I'd just offered her the biggest box of her favorite chocolates.

"Hulaz and I can take you and Holly back to your room, so Holly may get ready," Christik said with a smile.

The angels seemed just as excited about the wedding as we all were.

"That would be brilliant, thank you, Christik," I told her.

Without another word, Christik and Hulaz stepped towards me and my daughter.

"We'll see you in a few minutes," I told James and the kids, just before vanishing from the room.

By our next breath, Holly and I were standing outside our rooms with the angels, and both of us were shivering.

"Let's do this," I told Holly with a chattering smile.

"We will come back for you shortly as there is something Hulaz and I need to do," Christik said.

Before we had a chance to reply, the two angels flitted, leaving Holly and I standing looking curiously at each other.

"Shall we?" I asked, waving an arm toward the entrance.

Holly walked into our room with purpose, and I could tell that she was absolutely confident that she was making the right decision.

"I'm going to take a quick shower first," Holly stated before walking towards the kids' room and bathroom.

Ten minutes or so later, Holly walked back into the room, and she was wearing a beautiful pale lilac dress with her dark hair flowing to the side and down her shoulder in a loose braid. She looked so happy that she was almost glowing like her boyfriend. There was a tap at our archway entrance, making both of us turn.

"Come in," I called.

Christik and Hulaz glided into the room, and this time, their arms were full.

"We thought you may appreciate a little human tradition," Christik said kindly with a knowing look.

She held up a stunning white silk dress, which was delicately adorned with small pearls and tiny colored shells, it was gorgeous. When Hulaz held out her full hands; we realized that she held a gold and silver entwined tiara, which also had pearls and shells on it. Holly and I were both in awe.

"Christik, Hulaz, they are so beautiful!" Holly told them while beaming.

"They are very beautiful. Thank you so much, both of you," I told the angels as I started to feel quite choked up. '*Fucking hormones*,' I thought to myself.

"I'm feeling quite emotional myself," Christik said quietly to me, with another one of her knowing looks.

"Let us get our beautiful bride ready, shall we," Christik said as she verbally put on her big girl panties.

Moments later, the angels and I were stood looking at Holly in her bridal wear, all trying not to get too emotional. Holly looked a vision in white, and with the pearls and tiny shells, she looked perfect for a wedding in an underwater city.

"I wish I could see myself," Holly told us with a touch of sadness to her voice.

My heart sank because I remembered what I was like on my wedding day to her dad. I'd stood in front of my own mirror and memorized how I looked in my dress, and I wanted the same for my daughter.

"You can, Holly," Christik said.

Christik moved forward, and she raised her right hand with her palm facing towards Holly. Her hand started to glow as she began to make circular motions, and a small silvery disc started to appear. Christik kept making the circular motion with her hand; her circles getting larger as the disc grew in front of Holly. My daughter's eyes widened as she started to see her reflection in the silvery disc.

Within moments, the moving disc was as tall as Christik and as wide as the three of us. Holly looked at herself with astonished eyes.

"I don't look like a young girl anymore," she said softly.

"No, you don't, darling. You look like the beautiful woman you've grown up to be," I told her.

"Nalik is a very lucky angel," Hulaz said with a smile.

"Yes, he is," Christik and I chorused, making Holly laugh.

"Are you ready?" I asked Holly.

Holly nodded her head and walked to me as Christik stilled her hand. The shimmering mirror disc instantly faded into nothing. We all made our way back to the corridor and once there, Christik and Hulaz placed their hands on our arms, flitting us back to the underwater city of Cubanaz.

Luckily for us, the angels had the forethought to flit us to the corridor just outside the large building. Holly and I were shivering for a couple of minutes before it started to subside. It wouldn't have been a good look for Holly if she'd been shivering with chattering teeth down the aisle. *'James, we're here in the corridor'* I told my husband through the com.

'Ok, I'm coming baby,' he replied excitedly.

Moments later, James reached us in the corridor, and when he saw Holly, he stopped in his tracks.

"Holly, you look amazing, that Nalik is one lucky bastard," he told her.

Holly's face began to blush.

"Thanks, Dd. Let's get this show on the road, shall we," she said, "would you both walk with me?"

James and I looked at each and back to our daughter. We nodded with pride on our faces.

"Ok, I'm ready," Holly said confidently with the most wonderful smile.

Holly led the way into the cavernous room with James and me behind her, and the angels taking up the rear. The room looked amazing. The angels had really gone to town with their decorations, while Holly had been getting ready. Pale streams of material draped the backs of the chairs, and beautiful shell arrangements were center pieces for the tables. They'd even hung drapes of material around the sides of the room, where the stone met the new part of the building, fixing it into place with more decorative shells.

The room was packed with people. Every table was full, and they were all smiling at Holly. It wasn't until that very moment that I realized how many close relationships James and our kids had made while I'd been sleeping. It was reassuring to know that should the kids need help and support, it was there. Seeing so many smiling faces was very humbling. We were lucky to have so many attending Holly's day, and I made a promise to myself that I would make an effort to get to know more people.

I looked down the aisle, and Nalik was now standing at a gold and silver woven arch, decorated to match the rest of the room. He was glowing profusely, and he only had eyes for Holly. Holly walked forward, and as she reached the first two tables on either side of the aisle, the people sat there held out flowers to Holly, which she took with a surprised look and a warm smile. She carried on making her way to her angel, and every time she came to more tables, more friends gave her flowers.

By the time Holly reached Nalik; she was holding a gorgeous bouquet of flowers of all possible colors. It was a wonderful gesture from all Holly's friends, making them a true part of what was about to happen. Holly smiled brightly at Nalik as James and I sat in the empty seats Anthony, Harrison, April and Abigail had saved for us. Hulaz joined us too, taking the seat next to her other half, Harrik. Christik glided around the couple and placed herself on the other side of the beautiful arch. The whole room became quiet, and all of us watched Holly, Nalik and Christik with anticipation and excitement. James reached out and took my hand in his.

Christik looked at Holly and Nalik with an affectionate smile.

"To find your other half is a wonderful thing," she said, "you were blessed to have found each other, Holly and Nalik. It is clear to see that you belong with each other and are two halves creating a whole. Holly, would you like to say something to your own, your one?" She asked our daughter.

Holly's smile grew even bigger as she looked into Nalik's eyes, which were sparkling with love.

"Nalik, I didn't expect to find love or my other half, but I knew that I was drawn to you as soon as we met. I can honestly say that I can't imagine my life without you and your love. You make me feel complete, and I love you more than I can express," she told Nalik with her emotions shining through every word.

"Nalik, would you like to say something to your own, your one?" Christik asked.

Nalik moved forward, and he reached for Holly, laying his hands over Holly's as she held her bouquet; his hands started to glow. A silky red ribbon appeared in his hands, and we watched as it wrapped around the stems of Holly's bouquet. He held Holly's gaze as his hands dimmed back to normal.

"Holly, the moment I saw and felt your presence; I knew that we belonged together," Nalik declared to Holly. "I knew that you were my other half and that I was in love with you the moment you looked at me. I am beyond grateful that you feel the same way. I will love you for all of my existence."

Holly looked at Nalik with tears of happiness trickling down her pink flushed cheeks. I could feel the strength of their love as I'm sure everyone else in the room could.

"Holly, are you willing to be the other half of Nalik's soul and being, as long as he lives?" Christik asked.

Holly's eyes stayed transfixed on Nalik's, not diverting once.

"Yes, he is my own, my one," Holly said with confidence.

"Nalik, are you willing to be the other half of Holly's soul and being, for as long as she lives?" Christik asked.

Nalik's glow began to pulse again as he stared deeply into Holly's eyes, and his hands softly stroked hers.

"Yes, she is my own, my one," Nalik said loudly and clearly as if he wanted to make sure that everyone heard him.

Christik smiled at them both affectionately.

"I pronounce that you are now one," Christik declared as she held out both of her hands.

Resting on each of her palms were two beautiful but simple rings, one slightly larger than the other, and both were made of mother of pearl, which glistened from Nalik's glow. Nalik turned to Christik, taking the wedding ring she offered, and then he turned back to Holly. He took Holly's left hand in his, sliding the delicate shell ring onto her left ring finger. Her resounding smile made it clear how happy she was. She reached out to take the other ring from Christik's palm, giving Christik a smile that said, thank you. Holly took Nalik's left hand, and she gently slid the ring onto his ring finger. His smile was as big as Holly's, and my heart melted in my chest.

"Holly and Nalik, you are paired," Christik declared loudly, excitement in every word.

Christik clapped her hands, and delicate flower petals began to rain from the ceiling as everyone in the room started to clap and cheer profusely, many of us standing. Nalik reached for Holly, and he took her into his arms, her arms immediately circling his waist, and when he lowered his face to hers to kiss her, she didn't hesitate. When their lips met, Nalik's glow was almost blinding.

Holly and Nalik looked very bashful when they pulled away from each other, but they still broke out in huge happy smiles. Both of them looked from one face to another, returning smiles and congratulatory nods.

"Let us celebrate!" Christik said over the claps, cheers and whistles.

We couldn't wait any longer. My family and I rushed forward, wrapping Holly and Nalik in our arms to hug them and tell them how happy we were for them. I knew I was being a typical gushing mother of the bride, but I couldn't stop myself, and I didn't really care. I was just so thrilled that our daughter was so happy.

Holly and Nalik joined us at our table, and they were gracious as everyone took turns to come over and wish them all the best. So many people gave them gifts, but this wasn't a traditional wedding. There weren't any stores to buy from or a gift list to go by. Every single gift they received was made by the person who gave it, and they were all made with the person's heart and soul, making them even more special.

The rest of the day and evening was spent eating, drinking, dancing and singing. Quite a number of people knew how to play instruments, and the angels had brought them for their owners. I hadn't known until that night that some of the survivors had formed a band, and they were brilliant. We all danced to music from many different genres, the boys whizzed Abigail and April around the makeshift dance floor, James and I danced, and even Holly had Nalik dancing with her. Which he actually seemed to enjoy.

By the end of the evening, everyone was having a great time, especially April. A lovely young lady had been gazing at April all night, and she'd finally plucked up the courage to come over and talk to our adopted daughter. It was amazing to see April thoroughly enjoying herself. As people started to leave, I realized how tired I was, and it wasn't long before the kids were ready for their beds too. I leaned over to Holly, who was resting her feet from all the dancing and was watching Abigail dance with Nalik.

"Holly, are you are Nalik staying at your cabin in the holding structure?" I asked her.

"No, Nalik has a room on the main craft not far from your rooms," she explained, "He wants me to be close to you guys."

"Ahh, Ok, we're going to get the kids back, so we'll see you tomorrow, darling," I told her. "We're so proud and happy for you."

"Thanks, Mom," Holly said as she rose from her seat, coming around the table to give me a hug, "Just think, Mom, our next celebration will probably be for this little one being born," she smiled as she softly patted my baby bump.

Tracey decided to stay and was going to go with Trudy for the night, so we left Holly and Nalik to enjoy the rest of their night. The kids were really tired, and I could barely keep my own eyes open. Harrik and Hulaz very kindly flitted us all back to our rooms before going back to their own. Anthony, Harrison, April and Abigail barely had enough energy left to hug us, before they all fell into their beds. They were already fast asleep less than ten minutes after arriving back. As I stood in the archway between our room and our kids, my heart melted with love as I looked upon their peaceful sleeping faces before closing our bedroom barrier.

Moments later, I was laid in James' arms as he made soft kisses along the top of my back and shoulders. I could feel goosebumps appearing on my skin as his touch sent tingles through my body. As tired as I felt, my husband still got me hot and horny. I pushed up against his firm hard body, and I could feel his solid erection against my back. I knew I was already getting wet, just thinking about him being inside me.

"Bloody hell, you turn me on, woman," James said as he nuzzled his face into the back of my neck and my hair, "I want to taste you."

"Mmm..." was all I could manage as he re-positioned himself, so his hard erection was pushing and rubbing against the apex at the top of my thighs. My husband didn't need me to say anything more. By my next breath, James was up on his knees, and he was looking down on me with a hunger in his eyes. With one hand on my knee, he ran his other hand down my hip, along the length of my leg from my thigh to my ankle, relishing the softness of my skin. When his hand began to slide between my thighs, I knew I was in for a treat.

I watched James intensely as he used his firm hands to part my legs, encouraging me to lie on my back. With his hands on my thighs and his throbbing arousal pointing in my direction, he took a moment to admire my larger pert breasts and prominent darkened nipples. Just the look in his eyes made my sensitive nipples harden even more. James moved closer, placing his hands on either side of my forearms, enabling him to take each of my nipples into his hot mouth. He didn't linger long, trailing kisses and his wet tongue down my body, teasing me and he knew it. I couldn't stop myself from squirming against his solid muscular arms.

When James' tongue found the hot mess at the top of my thighs, I thought I might burst. He slowly ran his tongue up and down my sex, lingering a little longer on my clitoris every time he moved up. I could feel my climax trying to build whenever he swirled his tongue on it. My hands reached down, my fingers slipping through his thick dark hair and I gripped. My actions were only encouraging him further, and he passionately assaulted my clitoris. My back arched as I felt my climax take over, and I could feel myself clenching inside.

James didn't wait for me to recover, his hunger for me was raging in his eyes, and it was making my pulse race even faster.

"Lay on your side, baby," he said, almost in a sexual growl.

I knew he was trying to control himself and be more gentle than normal. I wanted him so badly that I just rolled on my side without saying a word. James took my ankle gently in his large hand, and he raised my leg, making me completely exposed. He didn't waste another second, gently and slowly sliding into me with purpose. Both of us moaned as he filled me, and the throb of his arousal made it clear that he was already close. I relished every second as he slid himself in and out.

At first, James took things slowly, letting my climax build to match his, but when I urged him to go faster; he didn't hesitate. With each thrust, my orgasm got closer, and I could feel myself tightening around him as I found my release. His back arched with his final thrust as he filled me with his own climax.

It took a few moments for us both to recover, and when I turned my head to look at him, he was staring lovingly at me with a sexy grin on his face.

"You really are the most magnificent woman I've ever seen," he almost purred.

"You're only saying that because you've just emptied your brains, husband of mine," I giggled.

"I don't keep my brains in my balls, woman," he said as he tried to sound offended.

"Oh, the decisions you've made over the years after sex would dispute that fact my husband. That's how we ended up with so many kids," I laughed.

"I can't really argue with that, baby," he said as he slid himself against my back, wrapping his arms around me again, "We certainly had fun making them," he chuckled.

Within minutes, we both drifted into a deep sleep.

CHAPTER 17

Weeks and weeks had passed, and absolutely nothing had happened. We'd all been keeping ourselves busy preparing for the forthcoming battle, but with every new day that came and went, we all became a little more relaxed and complacent. More and more women had opted to wait until after the battle to birth any more animals, leaving me somewhat redundant. They wanted to be part of the fight, and my admiration for our race had grown.

We truly were one race now, and all the social barriers that people had seeded and rooted were now as dead as those who'd started them. There were so few survivors left that it wouldn't be long before everyone was a bit of everything.

We'd spend a lot of time with our friends, and I'd made a real effort to meet as many of the other survivors as possible, as well as James' and the kids' friends. The angels had made a big effort to build relationships with the survivors too, and Christik was very happy to tell us of the progress the Viziers and their angels had made in the other locations.

My bump felt like it was growing by the day, and our daughter was running out of room to do her somersaults, although she did enjoy trying. Her feet wedging underneath my ribs wasn't fun and trying to get a full night's sleep was becoming impossible. Unfortunately, I couldn't expect the angels to be at my beck and call every time I was woken up with raging heartburn, and to be honest, I needed a crane to be able to turn over in bed.

I was resting in my room when Tracey, Mimi, Trudy arrived for a girl's night. It had become a regular event, and James loved hanging out with the guys to reminisce about past sporting events. Sports was one of the things that the guys really missed, especially the big games, such as the Super Bowl and the soccer World Cup. James had even talked to the other survivors about teaching the kids the various sports games, so the knowledge wouldn't be lost.

There were many things that we were trying to make sure weren't lost, and the angels were happy to help us write down and log important knowledge and information for our future generations. After all, our kids couldn't just search Google anymore, or watch a YouTube video, and not everything had been written in a book.

I looked down at my feet, wondering if they looked puffy when the girls knocked and then hollered as they walked in. Mimi, Tracey and Trudy were all smiling, so I knew straight away that they'd had a good day.

"You all seem very happy with yourselves!" I said as they walked over and took turns giving me a friendly hug, "Are Hulaz and Livik coming over?"

"Livik is helping Christik and Lindaz with something, but Hulaz is definitely coming over, and she's bringing some snacks with her," Trudy said.

"Helping Christik and Livik with what?" Tracey asked immediately.

Mimi raised her eyebrows at Tracey like a teacher looks at a naughty school kid.

"I'm a nosey fucker, so sue me!" Tracey told Mini with a smirk and mischief in her eyes.

Mimi rolled her eyes and sighed, knowing that Tracey was going to do whatever the hell she wanted. Tracey turned her attention back to Trudy.

"Well lady, what are they up too, and why weren't we invited?" Tracey demanded.

Trudy was as cool as a cucumber, and she stared back at Tracey with an unwavering stern look.

"I'm not telling you what they're up to, woman, and we weren't invited because we aren't artistic," Trudy told her while trying not to laugh.

Tracey glared at Trudy for a moment, and then she released a huge sigh of defeat as her shoulders dropped.

"Fuck me, you're good!" Tracey told her, "even John would have crumbled at that look."

They both plonked themselves down in the comfy chairs next to me.

"You're both in a really good mood," I told them just as Hulaz arrived with the snacks.

We all dipped our heads to the angel as she walked towards us, and she returned the nod with a beautiful smile. We all thanked her as she placed the stone tray laden with food on the table before sitting down next to Trudy.

"Oh my god! Is that avocado!" I asked in a squeak of excitement.

I'd never been one to get excited over food, and James certainly hadn't married me for my cooking, but things were different now. When there was a new food that we could eat because the angels had been growing our food, it was always a major event. Not all the seeds that our scientists had saved were viable, and even with the angel's power, it had taken time to repair the seeds to how they should be.

"Yes, it is avocado, Mel. A human someone told me you were in need, and I found out that some were ready," Hulaz said with a big smile.

James was the someone, and I loved him for trying to keep up with my pregnancy cravings. Even when they were in the middle of the night, and I had to have something. The poor guy needed a fricking medal.

I reached for a slice of green delight, and as I ate it, I felt like I'd died and gone to heaven.

"So, ladies, why are you both in such good moods?" I asked as I gave Hulaz a wink.

The angel loved a bit of gossip as much as we did.

"We've just seen Holly and Nalik. They look so happy," Tracey said.

"Tracey and Akhenaten are getting it on!" Trudy blurted out, positively bouncing in her seat.

Nalik and Holly's married life was blooming for sure. James and I were absolutely thrilled for them both, and luckily, we still got to spend lots of time with them because they wanted and loved being part of the family. However, Trudy's news about Tracey and Akhenaten was a serious news update.

"Spill it, woman!" I told her jokingly, giving her the '*I'm waiting*' eyebrow lifted look.

Tracey actually blushed, which surprised all of us.

"This is going to be good!" Trudy chuckled evilly while rubbing her hands together.

Tracey rolled her eyes at her friend while trying to keep a straight face.

"Ok, I confess!" Tracey declared, instantly grinning like the cat who'd got the cream, "

Hulaz, Trudy and I were instantly on the edge of our seats, poised for the new information Tracey was about to divulge. She held up her hands in surrender.

"Alright. I admit it; Akhenaten and I have been seeing each other, and things are moving quicker than expected," she said, sounding unsure. "It still feels as if John died yesterday, but being with Akhenaten feels so right. I feel like I'm betraying John, but I think Akhenaten is the one."

I could sense that we all felt torn. We were friends with John, and we all cared about him, but life was so precious now.

"John understood what a blessing finding love is, Tracey, and I think he'd want you to grab this chance of happiness while you can," I told her.

"Mel is right, Tracey," Hulaz added with a soft smile.

"So how far have you and Mr. Golden balls got then?" Trudy asked as she raised and lowered her eyebrows repeatedly at our friend.

Tracey actually blushed a deep pink, and she looked extremely guilty.

"Well, you little minx!" I declared, bursting into laughter.

"You did the deed, didn't you?" Trudy asked as she began to laugh too.

"You and Akhenaten are a whole?" Hulaz asked excitedly.

"Yes, Yes and Yes!" Tracey declared with a huge smile lighting up her face, "Yes, I am a little minx, that's why Akhenaten loves me. Yes, we have done the deed, repeatedly, and yes, we are whole. Akhenaten is my one, my own."

The three of us were all beaming at Tracey; it was clear that she was very happy.

"So, is it true that the male angels can change the size of their you know what's to any size?" Trudy asked with wide eyes.

Tracey's blush appeared to glow to another level.

"Mmm, yes it's true," she said with a grin, "Any size, I checked and unlimited stamina."

That was it, Trudy and I began laughing so hard that we were both struggling to breathe, and Hulaz was laughing at our reaction. Before long, we were all cracked up, especially when Tracey started to indicate with her hand just how big. She was just like a fisherman showing how big his catch was.

"Well this explains why Holly is always smiling," Trudy stated.

"Damm lady, I don't want to think about that, she's still my baby girl as far as I'm concerned. I've only just started getting used to her being married, and I don't want to think of my daughter doing the deed with anyone, even an angel!" I declared.

Trudy held her hands up in surrender as Hulaz and Tracey laughed.

"Anyway, getting back to you; you hot mess of a woman. How on earth did you keep up with Akhenaten if he's got endless energy?" I asked, raising an eyebrow at our outrageous friend.

Her responding smiled told us that she had a great answer.

"Well," she said, pausing to build our already growing interest, "It turns out that during our hot encounters, Akhenaten shared his energy and power with me."

"What!" Trudy exclaimed in disbelief.

"I know right, it's fucking crazy, but I can go all night too, and I swear it's the most minding blowing sex I've ever had," Tracey declared, "It's as if the fucker can read my fucking mind."

I couldn't help laughing at her words, and Hulaz began to laugh too. Tracey and Trudy looked at each other as if we'd lost the plot.

"Ok, what's so fucking funny you two," she demanded as she placed both of her fists on her curvy hips.

"He can read your mind, you loon!" I told her.

Hulaz and I could see by their faces when they remembered the times when the angels had known what we were thinking and feeling. Suddenly, we were all bursting our sides with laughter.

"Oh, my god, I fucking forgot, no wonder he knew that I liked kinky shit," Tracey squealed as her face started to go red.

"We take pleasuring our other halves very seriously because we can feel their pleasure," Hulaz told us with a very serious look on her face.

"Damm, Trudy, you and I are missing out lady," I told her with a grin, "we need to trade our two in for a couple of amorous angels."

Hulaz seemed a little shocked, but she didn't say a word. It wasn't in her nature to judge. I placed a hand in her arm.

"Don't worry, Hulaz your angels are safe. It's taken me this long to train James, and he definitely knows what I like. I don't want to start all over again with someone else," I giggled.

Hulaz smiled, and I knew she was only concerned for our husbands.

"Are you and Akhenaten going to get married?" Trudy asked excitedly.

"We haven't really had that conversation, but he's told me that I'm his one, his own," Tracey admitted.

Hulaz slid herself forward, so she was on the edge of her seat, and she took Tracey's hand in hers.

"If Akhenaten has told you this after you have joined, then in his eyes, you are already married," Hulaz said in a serious tone.

For a moment, Tracey looked stunned, and I could feel her torn emotions again, her grief for John and the enormous guilt that she couldn't shake.

"Tracey, we don't know what's going to happen when the Marilians get here. We may not be here the day after they invade. I think you should grab this chance of happiness with Akhenaten. You've both been through hell and back. You really do deserve to be happy," I told her with all my heart.

The room began to feel heavy with emotions, and even Trudy could feel it. As I looked at Tracey, a single tear slowly trickled down her cheek, leaving a thin wet trail.

"I agree with Mel, Tracey," Trudy said softly. "Tomorrow is never promised to any of us anymore, so grab every day with both hands."

We sat there, all nodding our agreement. There was a stretched silence as we all contemplated Trudy's words, but we were all such good friends that the silence wasn't awkward in any way. After minutes had passed, Tracey stood from her seat, and she walked over to the only window. She seemed to be looking up at the stars in the night sky, and with no light pollution anymore, there were thousands upon thousands to be seen.

"If Akhenaten believes us to be married already, then I don't think we need to worry about a wedding ceremony right now," Tracey said as she turned to face us. "I think I would rather wait until after the Marilians have been and gone. I would like to have a very, very long honeymoon period," she added.

"Bloody hell, woman!" I exclaimed, "from the sounds of it, you've already been on your honeymoon period, you nymphomaniac you."

The rest of the evening was full of lighthearted giggles, holding our sides belly laughing, including the odd snort from Trudy. Which only made us laugh even more. We were all savoring our time together.

It felt quite late in the evening when James and the kids got back, and it still felt strange not to see Holly walk through the door with them. The kids all appeared to be tired, and I was looking forward to finding out what they'd been up to all afternoon and evening. James, however, didn't look happy whatsoever. Abruptly, Hulaz stood from her seat, and her face looked ashen.

"I am afraid that I have to leave you, Mel," she said with a serious tone.

As Hulaz glided out of our room, I looked back to James, and a sense of dread washed over me, from my head to my toes. It was as if someone had poured ice-cold water over me. My baby started to move and kick as my heart began to pound rapidly in my chest, and my breathing started to quicken. My eyes connected with James, and I could see the fear in them.

"They're here, aren't they?" I asked, but I already knew the answer.

The kids stopped in their tracks, and their faces spoke a thousand words.

"Yes baby, they're here," James said as his lips thinned, and his brows furrowed.

"How long have we got?" I asked, dreading his answer.

"Christik thinks we have about a day and a half before they reach our atmosphere. We're very lucky that the angels' crafts just outside our atmosphere picked them up so quickly on their sensors," he told us all.

"We're going to have be quick to get everyone who isn't fighting to Cubanaz, the underwater city," I said as I looked at our kids' faces.

My heart was slowing down, and my protective instincts were beginning to take over, not just for my family but for every single remaining survivor. I could feel the adrenaline rushing through my system.

"Who else knows?" I asked.

James seemed more determined with each second that passed, and I knew that his protective instincts were kicking in the same as mine.

"Christik and the other angels are telling everyone else now. I need to get you to the hanger ready to leave, so the kids and I can start getting ready," he said matter of factly.

I was very tempted to demand that I should stay with them, but I knew James wouldn't have it, so I nodded and turned to my kids. The thought of them fighting made my blood run cold.

"Please remember everything you've been taught and stay together, ok, you'll be stronger as a team," I told them as I looked into their innocent faces.

'This is going to change them all forever,' I thought. I approached the kids and gave all of them a big hug in turn, savoring the moment, and by the time I finished hugging them, I had to force myself to walk away.

"Are you ready, baby?" James asked.

I knew he was desperate to get me on board the smaller craft and safe, so he didn't have to worry.

"Yes, let's go," I told him, fighting off the tears that threatened to shed.

We left our room, and as we headed towards the hanger; angels constantly glided past, us obviously rushing to prepare for the fight. James and I didn't speak all the way to the craft, but I felt some comfort just having his hand in mine. Worrying thoughts were rushing through my mind, and I guessed that James was the same.

By the time we arrived in the angels' hanger, my sense of dread was back. I couldn't bear to be away from James and the kids, and the thought of James walking away and leaving me made me feel distraught. James didn't need to sense what I was feeling because it was written all over my face.

"You have to do this, baby," he said.

I felt like my heart was being crushed in my chest.

"I know," I told him, "but that doesn't make this any easier, does it."

My husband pulled me close, and he wrapped his arms around me. I could hear his heart pounding when I laid my head against his chest. It was taking all my emotional strength to keep my tears at bay.

When he released me, I turned away, unable to look at my husband again for fear of breaking down. I boarded the waiting craft with the other women and kids who had been on the main craft working or seeing their angel friends. It didn't seem real that it was happening; the Marilians were finally arriving.

As I sat on the craft looking at all the women and kids' scared faces who were boarding or who had already sat down, I realized that I couldn't go to Cubanaz. I wanted to protect my husband and kids, and I knew that being in the underwater city without them was going to be torture. Right there and then, I made up my mind '*I'm staying to fight,*' I told myself. I knew it was the right decision the moment I made it. I rose from my seat, and I had to push my way through the people who were still trying to board as gently as possible. One or two gave me curious and worried looks as I struggled to get off the craft.

As soon as I was free from the small ship and away from the people, I stood for a moment, bent over with my hands on my knees, desperately trying to catch my breath and steady my pounding and racing heart. I could sense that my baby girl felt like I was doing the right thing, which made it a little easier to calm down. '*What should I do now?*' I thought as my mind reeled with fresh uncertainty. '*Get some battle gear on, yes that's what I need to do,*' I told myself.

By Beth Worsdell

I felt a determination that I hadn't felt for a long time, and the kids and James kept popping into my head, making the feeling grow more intensely. With the newfound purpose coursing through me, I began to stride out of the hanger to make my way back to our rooms. I passed so many angels on my way down the pearlescent corridors, and many of them looked utterly surprised to see me, but none of them said a word. They only looked at my face and felt my emotions before continuing on to wherever they were going, '*yeah, nothing's going to stop me protecting my family.*'

When I reached our rooms and went inside; there was no one to be seen. Without wasting any time, I went to the bathroom area where James had left his spare battle gear. His fighting gear was made up of army and navy combat kits from the bases, where the guys had got their supplies from. The men didn't care whether it was army gear or navy gear, they just took what looked to be the best protection. It was a true blessing that I was slight and athletic in build with a normally smallish waist, and that James was a large muscular man in comparison. Otherwise, there was no way that I would have been able to fit into the battle gear before me.

Bit by bit, I put everything on, the combat trousers, which were snug around my bump, to say the least. The combat top was tight around my now very pert and larger breasts, and luckily, the holders for ammo were adjustable. I used a lace from a spare pair of boots to tie my hair in a French braid, and by the time I was finished, I felt ready to take anyone on.

CHAPTER 18

As I stood in the back of our main living area, I felt like a badass pregnant version of Lara Croft from Tomb raider. Something deep inside was telling me that my baby girl and I were protected, and I trusted that feeling. I knew that James was going to be furious when he discovered that I hadn't left with the others to go to Cubanaz, so I decided that I would need some back up before facing him.

I touched the communication device at my throat, and I reached out to the elders, '*Lindaz, Evest can you hear me?*' I asked with my mind.

'*We can hear you Mel, and I can still feel you on board,*' Lindaz said with confusion ringing in her words. '*Where are you?*' She asked.

'*I'm in our rooms, I couldn't leave with the others,*' I told them both, knowing Evest could still hear everything, '*Something was telling me to fight and that I'd be needed.*'

There was a pause before they spoke again, and I suddenly felt nervous. '*We understand, Mel. We will come and get you,*' Evest said kindly. Within seconds, there was a tap at the archway entrance to our rooms, and when I reached the archway, both of the elders were stood there waiting for me. Evest's face wasn't giving anything away, but

Lindaz had a slight smirk on her face as if to say, '*Yeah, as if you were going to stay behind*'.

"Shall we go?' Evest asked with a warm smile.

"Yes, let's do this, we need to kick some Marilian butt," I told them both.

Lindaz turned and smiled at her other half.

"I like this feisty human," she said as she actually winked at me, taking me by surprise.

Her small gesture made me feel even more confident that I was doing the right thing.

"Where are we going?" I asked as I followed the gliding angels, trying to keep up with them. They were so much bigger than Christik and the other angels, and they always seemed to glide quicker too.

"We are going to the main meeting room first, to speak with Christik our one, and the viziers," she explained.

I wondered why they didn't just flit us to the meeting room, but then I remembered how thoughtful their daughter was, and she'd probably already told them both that I wasn't too keen on doing it. When we reached the meeting room, it was filled with Christik and our angel friends. Christik, Hulaz, Harrik, Livik and Zanika were there, as well as Nalik. They all nodded in respect to me as I entered the room with the elders, and none of them seemed that surprised to see me apart from Nalik.

"Mel, what are you still doing here?" He asked with concern, "James thinks that you are safe in Cubanaz!"

"You didn't really think she would not stay and fight with us, did you Nalik?" Christik asked with a smile on her beautiful face.

I returned her smile as her eyes connected with mine. Nalik didn't say another word. He only smiled as if to say, '*I should have known better.*'

Christik turned to Hulaz, who was standing next to her in front of the large wooden meeting table.

"Hulaz, if you would please."

Hulaz faced the table, and she began to raise her arms with her palms facing outwards, and they began to glow the silvery-white as she tapped into her power. Straightaway, the communication orb began to appear before us, filled with shimmering squares. One by one, the squares filled with the faces of the viziers from all the other main crafts that were scattered around our planet.

As soon as the last square was filled in the shimmering and glowing orb, Christik began to address them first, dipping her head in respect.

"Viziers, as you are all aware, the Marilians are here, and it is a matter of hours before they arrive. Are all our friends who are not fighting safely in our underwater cities?" She asked them.

One by one, they all confirmed that the other human survivors were safe, and the holding structures were empty, apart from angels who were lying in wait.

"We will be leaving shortly to be with our human counterparts; please make sure that your camouflaged angels and your ambushes are ready for action," she ordered, "Also, make sure that the water supplies are full for our use."

The viziers all acknowledged her orders, and the elders seemed suitably impressed with how Christik was handling the whole situation. As I stood with them, I could feel their pride as they watched their daughter with interest.

"Make sure all our angels stay with their human counterparts, Viziers, we cannot lose any more life," Christik told them before dipping her head in farewell." The angels exchanged dipped heads in respect to their leader, and one by one, the squares inside the orb disappeared. As soon as they were all gone, Hulaz lowered her dimming hands back down to her sides, and the orb was gone.

When Christik and the angels turned to leave the meeting room, Evest held up his slender but large hand to stop them.

"I know we have not used them for a while off our planet, but I think we should bring the Longs to earth to help us," he told Christik, "Tianlong, Shenlong, Yinglong and Qiulong.

All of the angels were suddenly wide-eyed with surprise or maybe shock. I wasn't quite sure which.

"They have not been off our planet since the ancient Chinese era," Christik said in a definite surprised tone.

"We may need them, Christik, and I think it would be wise to err on the side of caution, do you not think so," Lindaz told her.

I stood there like an idiot, looking between the elders and the angels, wondering what the hell they were talking about. When it didn't seem like anyone was going to say anything, I couldn't stop myself.

"So, what are these long things?" I asked, not able to remember the words properly.

Christik turned to face me.

"They are what you would call dragons," she said, "We have not brought them here since our last visit with your ancient Chinese civilizations."

Things were really starting to fall into place and make more sense with the angels. My mom had always loved anything oriental, and I believed it was due to my grandfather having traveled all over the world when he was in the navy. She still had gifts he'd brought her from his travels up until the day she died. Most of the gifts she had were decorated with stunning dragons. I was totally stunned to find out that they were actually real.

"I can't believe dragons are real, this is crazy, James and the kids are going to go nuts," I told them.

I knew they didn't understand what I meant just by their faces.

"You know what they're like around animals. Can you imagine how they'll react when they find out that mystical dragons are actually real!" I blurted out.

They all smiled at the thought of my family's reaction.

"So, how are we going to get them here and quickly?" I asked as I looked at Lindaz.

"The Longs, or dragons as you call them, will come through the same star passage that we arrived through," Lindaz said calmly.

"Then let's get going," I said to them, still feeling like a true badass.

Before long, we were all on a small craft heading back to Peru with Christik piloting. I was stressing out about James and my kids, wondering where they were and what they were doing. I wanted to be with them desperately, but I knew we needed to get the dragons first. The thought of the dragons still didn't seem real, and I couldn't wait to meet them. I could feel that my daughter was excited, her emotions felt very strong as she wriggled around.

Harrik was sitting next to me on one side, and Hulaz was on the other; she reached over, and she took my hand in hers. Her calming power gently flowed into me from my hand, up my arm and through the rest of my tense body. I could feel all my tight and tense muscles relaxing immediately. It was better than any massage my husband had ever given me, '*Not that I'd tell James that*, 'I thought.

"You do not need to worry about your family, Mel," Hulaz told me quietly, "They are with their angel counterparts, don't forget, and they will be protected."

It didn't really matter how reassuring Hulaz was because I knew I wouldn't be able to fully relax until I was with them.

"We are here," Christik said as the craft began to slow down.

The craft descended smoothly, and it touched down on the arid, dusty ground without even the slightest jolt. Christik disconnected with the craft, and I watched as the silvery vines melted back into the sides of the ship. Christik turned and faced us all.

"We all know how feisty and mischievous the Longs can be, so we need to tell them immediately that they are here for a battle," she said with a slightly worried tone.

The angels and elders nodded in agreement, and as Christik passed me to open the craft, I heard her in my mind. "Stand with the elders Mel, the Longs are very powerful, and I do not want you to get accidentally hurt." I nodded to her, and my nervousness began to grow. I let the angels and elders disembark the craft first, and I followed behind Evest.

Peru was hot, and the sun was high in the sky; its heat warmed my skin within seconds. We walked and glided the short distance to the Gate of the Gods, and as we approached, I was again in awe of its size and natural beauty. The sun shone on the pink stone and glistened against the gold that was still embedded in the grooves and the disc inside the alcove. Without saying a word, Christik approached the gate while the rest of us stopped about fifty feet away. Lindaz and Evest flanked me instinctively, which made me feel a little safer.

Just like before, Christik raised her arms with her palms facing the Gate of the Gods, and her hands started to glow bright white as she tapped into her power. The hieroglyphs in the long, gold groves began to melt, and the disc started to heat and become molten too. Within minutes, the gold was a fluid liquid, and I watched in amazement as the golden shining disc started to swirl. The wind whipped up around us, and I could feel the dry soil being blown against my legs. Faster and faster, the gold moved, making a whirlpool; then all of a sudden, the gate was gone and in its place was the shimmering barrier.

"Tianlong, Shenlong, Yinglong and Qiulong, we summon you to this world. You are needed!" Christik bellowed above the noise of the wind.

My heart was beating faster in my chest, a mix of nerves and excitement. Sensing what I was feeling, Lindaz placed her hand on the center of my shoulder, letting her calming power flow through me. I was too anxious to look at her to say thank you, but I knew she would be feeling my gratitude through her touch.

We waited and waited; the anticipation was palpable in the air. Then the shimmering barrier seemed to pulse with power, and a bright green scaled foot slipped through and landed on the ground. Its talons were long, sharp and deadly. The other front leg of the dragon slipped through and then its sleek green head. We watched as it looked around with fiery red eyes. Its tendrils on either side of its face moved around as if trying to get a sense of its new environment. I could see two large horns protruding from the top of its head, and it looked very fierce.

"Come forth Tian, we request your presence," Christik said firmly.

The dragon moved forward, allowing the rest of his body to come through the gate, and as it arrived, its whole body pulsed with energy while it grew in size before our eyes. As soon as it was through the star passage, it walked around us, lifting its head in the air as if it was taking in the scents in the air. Its body was long and almost snake-like, and its legs and the top of its body were a bright vivid green. Its underbelly was pale brown, and its dark brown horns stood out proudly against its brighter colors. When it reached Christik, it stopped and looked straight at her.

"Why am I here?" Tian asked in a dry masculine and gravelly voice.

Christik didn't appear to be intimidated whatsoever as she held his gaze.

"The Marilians are coming to try and destroy this planet, Tian. You have been summoned to fight with us," she told him respectfully.

Tian actually smiled at her words.

"I will fight with you, Christik. The Marilians have taken enough," he said forcefully.

The barrier began to pulse and shimmer again, and this time, it was a dark blue dragon leg that came through. As the sun hit its scales, they turned pearlescent with a mix of blues and greens. Another leg came through, and I noticed that its feet were a pale green, and it had gold metal bands around each ankle. Next, the head slid through the barrier, and it was stunning. It had huge white horns with gold bands around the tops of them and longer scales on its forehead, making the dragon look as if it was wearing a crown. The dragon also had longer deep blue tendrils from its nose as well as leather looking frills on the back of its legs down its head and neck.

Suddenly, the dragon raised its head, and it roared to the heavens. My whole body vibrated with the power of it. If its roar was any indication of what a powerful dragon it was, then the Marilians were going to get their arses kicked. The thought made me smile. As I watched, the dragon lowered its large head, and it slipped all the way through, again it grew in size as it emerged.

"Welcome, Shen," Christik said as she dipped her head.

The dragon lowered its head in a bow before striding gracefully towards Tian. When it reached the other dragon; it brushed itself affectionately against Tian as if it was in love. I was so busy watching Shen and Tian that I didn't notice that the third dragon was already coming through the star passage. The dragon was even more intimidating than the first two if that was possible. It was already three-quarters of the way out when I saw it and within seconds, its tail slipped through as its size doubled.

"Wow," I said in awe.

"That is Qiu, he is the most powerful out of all of the Long," Lindaz said with pride.

"I can understand why" I replied as I took in his long muscular body

All three of the dragons had long lizard type bodies, but Qiu's body was rippling with powerful muscles under blood-red scales. His dark brown, almost black horns were twice as big as the others' horns. His claws were gold and so was his nostrils and trim under his chin. Qiu's whole head was surrounded with large razor-sharp scales and at the tip of his long tail were the same golden scales. Tendrils stuck out from the backs of his ankles, and all down his head and neck was a trail of sharp steel-colored scales rising along his spine.

No sooner had Qiu's tail come through than the next and last dragon came through, although not as elegantly as the others. We suddenly saw a blur of golds and browns spilling and spinning from the star passage. Suddenly, massive wings spread out from the dragon's body, and they pierced the dry ground acting like anchors, stopping the dragon in its tracks.

It grew in size as it uncurled; its razor-sharp talons hit the ground and sank into the dry soil. Raising its head to the sky; it shook a long main of jet-black fur as a lion would do. The dragon turned to face all of us. It looked from one face to another with eyes that sparkled like stunning emeralds. Not only did this dragon have huge golden bat-like wings, but it also had a large singular horn like a twisted unicorn horn, which protruded from its forehead just above its green eyes.

I watched as the golden dragon gracefully made its way to the other waiting dragons. Christik began to rein in her power, closing the star passage and deactivating the Gate of the Gods. Once the barrier was gone and the pink stone was back, Christik turned to face me and glided in my direction.

"Come, Mel, I would like to introduce you to the Long or dragons as you call them," she said with a smile.

I was sure that Christik and all the angels, as well as her parents, could feel my excitement and nervousness. Christik reached out her hand for me to take, and without hesitation, I took her hand in mine, and I let her take me to the dragons. The Elders and angels followed closely behind.

I could sense how excited my baby was. She wanted to be close to them, and it felt like she was jumping on my bladder, treating it like a trampoline. I put my hand on my bump and thought to myself, '*You'll be able to meet them soon, baby girl.*'

As soon as Christik and I were standing in front of the dragons, they all lowered their heads in a bow.

"Thank you all for coming here, Longs," she told them, "We have brought you all here to fight for this planet and the human survivors. The Marilians are coming, and we can't let them win. Will you all fight with us?"

Qui stepped forward, so he was standing right in front of Christik, and he lowered his head, so they were literally eye to eye. Christik reached forward, and she placed her right hand gently on his face between his eyes and nose. I could see little sparks between them as they connected, and Qui closed his eyes.

"It is so good to see you, Qui," Christik told him affectionately.

Qui opened his eyes, and he raised his head.

"It is good to see you too, Christik," he told her, just as affectionately, "We will all fight for you and with you, my friend."

Christik gave the dragon a big smile, showing how pleased she was, and then she turned back to me and the elders.

"Mel, meet the mightiest of Longs from my world," she said.

I turned to Lindaz.

"You have many of them on your world?" I asked, surprised.

It was already a shock that they had four, and I still couldn't believe that they were actually stood in front of me, it just didn't seem real.

"Yes, we have many on our world, Mel. The others are coming through the other star passages our angels activated," Lindaz said. "Go and meet them," she added, pointing at the dragons with a big smile of her own.

I was full of nerves as I stepped towards Christik and the dragons; my pulse started to race as my body released its adrenaline. When I reached them, I stood next to Christik, and the dragons seemed a lot bigger and fiercer so close up. I could feel the heat of their breath coming from their nostrils, and it heated my already hot skin. Tian, Shen, Qui and Ying all began to move, and they lowered their heads so that their eyes were all level with mine.

"They are greeting you," Christik said gently.

She gave me a nod of her head, indicating for me to move forward more. With my pulse racing and my heart pounding in my ears, I walked up to Tian first, placing my hand onto his face just like Christik had done. He closed his eyes, and I felt his power through my hand as well as a connection that I didn't understand. When Tian opened his fiery red eyes, I removed my hand and moved on to Shen. When I placed my hand on Shen, I felt the same connection to her as Tian, and it was as if my soul was reaching to them. Being so close to her; I could tell she was female. Her face and body were sleeker with softer angles than Tian, and her hips were wider.

Ying was also a female dragon, and my connection to her when I touched her wasn't quite as strong. I felt a nervousness coming from her, and I wasn't sure if it was because of me. Lastly, I greeted Qui, placing my hand on his face. His brow was a lot more pronounced than the other dragons, making him look a lot more aggressive, but funnily enough, I felt the strongest connection to him out of all of them. My baby girl started to bounce on my bladder again, and I knew instantly that she felt the strong connection too. This time, there were sparks with the contact, and Christik gave a small gasp. I removed my hand

and took a few steps back, so I stood next to Christik again, and when I looked at her; she had a look of sheer surprise on her face.

Turning back to the dragons, I dipped my head low in respect before looking into their stunning eyes.

"Welcome, and thank you for coming," I told them sincerely.

"We will always come to the aid of our angels," Qui said with his rich masculine voice, "They saved my race when our own world was dying. We owe them everything," he added.

CHAPTER 19

A s I stood before the four dragons and absorbed Qiu's words, I realized why there was such a bond between them, Christik and the angels, and why they were so willing to fight with them. I felt so honored to be in their presence and also relieved that we had them on our side.

"Will you follow us back to our main craft?" Christik asked.

"We will," Qui answered for all of them.

Christik turned to the angels and the elders, and she started to lead the way to our small craft, and I followed. As she reached her parents, she gave them a nod of her head. Instead of her parents following us to the craft, they began to glide towards the dragons.

"Mel, if you could come with us please," Evest said with a smile, "I sense that you and Qui have a very strong connection."

I was so surprised by what Evest said that I looked at Christik with wide eyes.

Christik just smiled and nodded her head in the direction of the waiting dragons. I took in a deep breath and began to follow the elders. When we reached the dragons, I stopped and watched as Evest glided up to Shen. The dark blue dragon lowered the front of her body for the elder and Evest gracefully slid onto her back in one swift movement.

Lindaz walked up to Ying, and the gold and brown dragon lowered herself as Shen had. Even though Ying had wings; Lindaz was just as graceful mounting her. I looked from the elders to Qiu, and I wondered how the hell I was going to mount him. The raised steel colored scales all along his back looked as though they could cut me in two. Gingerly, I approached him, his massive muscles rippled underneath his blood-red shining scales. I looked into his fierce face.

"I don't know how to get on your back," I told him honestly and feeling very embarrassed, knowing that the elders were watching my every move.

"I will help you," Qui said in his very masculine drawl.

As I stood and watched him, his sharp silver scales on his back appeared, sinking into his spine before my eyes. '*Thank goodness for that*' I thought to myself. After all of Qiu's silver scales had vanished; he lowered himself as far as he could go, and he moved his front leg forward.

"Stand on my leg, young one, and I will help you up," he said.

I reached forward and placed both hands into the side of his lowered neck; his vivid red scales were cool and smooth against my fingertips. As soon as I stepped on into his leg, he began to raise it. I had to use my hands against his body to keep my balance, and within seconds, I was high enough to cock my leg over his thick muscular back.

Luckily for me, I was able to get on with the first attempt, and as I sat perched on his back, I suddenly felt very proud of myself. I was very aware of how excited my baby girl was at being so close to the dragon. She obviously felt the connection as strongly as I did.

"Are you ready, Mel?" Evest called over.

"Yes!" I answered.

Adrenaline began to flood my body again, and I wasn't quite sure what was going to happen. Only one of the dragons had wings, so I was assuming that the dragons were going to run, full steam ahead. I couldn't have been more wrong.

I felt Qiu's power building before I actually saw it. His power seemed to engulf us both, and I felt it flow through me in a huge wave. The moment it reached my head, both of us gave off a shimmering red aura. I looked over to Evest and Lindaz, and they were glowing the same colors as their dragons too.

"Hold on to my scales," Qui commanded.

I gingerly gripped two of his large scales just in time before he began to rise from the ground. It wasn't what I expected at all. I felt him curl his body, so his front legs touched his back, and his power seemed to build at the same time. Then boom, his power surged at the same time as he straightened his body, and we pelted forward as I held on for dear life. Qiu raised his head to the clear blue sky, and we were soaring upwards, the hot wind was blowing in my face.

Moments later, we were flying high, and I could see the small craft the angels were in just ahead of us. I held on tightly to Qiu's scales, and I looked behind me. The other dragons and the elders were easily keeping pace. They all looked so graceful flying through the air in a V formation, each giving the others room to maneuver.

The flight back to the main craft was amazing. I could see everything so clearly, unlike when I'd flown in a plane. I could see huge green areas where the angels had already healed the earth and also the brown areas that they hadn't reached yet. It was eerily quiet as we flew, there were no noises of planes or cars, no factories in operation, only the rush of the wind blowing past us. I'd never really paid attention before to the amount of noise we as a race made, and the contrast was startling.

Our journey back seemed to happen in a flash, and we were soon approaching the main craft. '*How on earth are the dragons going to get on board,*' I thought as I felt Qiu slow down. I watched as the small craft ahead of us entered the hanger through the side of the ship, vanishing from sight.

As Qiu and I got closer to the hanger entrance, I could suddenly feel the dragon shrinking beneath me. '*Oh God, please don't let me fall off now,*' I thought as my nervousness grew. Qiu dipped his head, making me lower my own body as I held tightly to his scales. I could feel my baby bump pressing against the dragon. I needn't have worried because Qiu gracefully swept into the hanger like an eagle, swooping inside before landing softly in between the small crafts.

I let out my breath, not realizing that I'd held it, and the relief that swept through me was intense. I stayed on him and watched with intrigue as the other dragons and the two elders entered and landed with the same elegance.

"I will help you down, Young one," Qiu said with his deep rumbling voice.

Qiu slowly lowered himself, making sure that I was still able to keep my balance, and then he raised his leg again for me. I held on tightly while swinging my leg over his back and reaching for his leg with my other foot. I knew I wasn't as graceful as the elders, but I didn't really care. I just didn't want to fall off and end up as a heap on the floor, looking like a beetle on its back. Luckily for me; my feet found the dragon's leg, and Qiu lowered me to the ground.

As I stood there in the hanger, I was acutely aware of how wobbly my legs were. They felt like jelly, but I wasn't surprised. I think I'd clenched my thighs against the dragon's body holding on for dear life the whole journey. However, what a ride! '*I can honestly say that I would happily do it again and again,*' I thought with a smile.

'*That is good to know, young one, as you will be riding me during the battle,*' I heard Qiu say in my mind.

"Damm it, another one who can read my thoughts," I said with a laugh, "I look forward to fighting with you, Qiu!" I told him honestly.

Qiu dipped his head at me just as Christik and the angels walked over to us.

"We have a large room for us all to use," Christik said politely, "Can you sense it?" She asked.

All four of the Dragons dipped their heads, and then they were gone; they disappeared in a split second.

"Come, Mel, we will meet them there," Christik said, and she glided towards the hanger exit.

We were soon arriving at a massive room, similar to the one where I'd spent time with the animals we'd rescued. When we walked in, all of the dragons were there, and they seemed very relaxed for the time being.

I walked over to Qiu, and as he lowered his head, I raised my hand, and we connected again.

"Thank you for helping us, Qiu," I told him softly.

I lowered my hand and, as he raised his head, his huge sparkling eyes locked with mine.

"You are welcome, young one," he replied.

"You all seem to have a strong connection with the angels," I said with a smile.

"Like your race, we were on the verge of annihilation, young one. The Marilians are an ancient race, who have destroyed many planets by taking all resources and races for their own," Qiu explained. "When they came to my planet centuries and centuries ago, they couldn't change us, but they did destroy our planet."

"So, the Angels took you to their planet?" I asked.

I could feel the heaviness in the great dragon's heart and the sadness from all of them as they listened to Qiu's words.

"Yes, when the angels arrived after the Marilians had gone, they knew it was too late to save our world. They refused to leave us behind, and they invited us to live with them," he told me.

"But how did they get you to their planet?" I asked.

Qiu appeared to smile at the memory.

"The angels built a star passage on our world so we could travel through it. When we arrived, they went out of their way to make us feel at home," Qiu said. "We will fight with them whenever they ask us too."

"I feel the same way about the angels too, Qui. I owe them everything," I told him sincerely, "My husband didn't want me to fight, but there's no way I can stand by and let my family and friends fight the Marilians without me, Qiu."

Qiu looked at me with understanding, and he smiled.

"Sometimes, the hardest fights are the battles against our loved ones' wishes. They need not worry for I will be fighting with you, and this time, I am not a hatchling," he said.

"We haven't got much time, Qiu. The other Longs have all arrived, so we need to get you all into position," Christik said with urgency in her voice.

"Exactly how many of you are there?" I said, totally surprised.

"There are hundreds of us now, thanks to the angels," Qiu replied with a smile.

I couldn't help but smile back at the dragon. I hoped that I would live long enough, so I could get to know about the dragons and get to know them.

"Let's get this show on the road!" Christik called out.

Christik walked up to Shen, and then she raised her hand, placing it onto the blue dragon's forehead.

"This is where I need you to be Shen, my angels are waiting for you," she said.

Next, she did the same to Ying, Tian and lastly to Qiu. The dragons dipped their heads, and I watched as the elders and Christik mounted the dragons.

"Come, young one, we have a battle to win," Qiu told me as his fiery eyes glowed brighter.

Not wanting to keep the others waiting, I mounted the fierce blood-red dragon, and then I looked to my angel friends.

"We can do this!" I told them, feeling my confidence build within me; "we can win this together."

The elders and Christik all looked at me with confident smiles. They all dipped their heads, and then they were gone. '*Are you ready,*' Qiu said in my mind, '*I was born ready,*' I told him.

In a split second, we also vanished from the room, and when we reappeared, we were on the ground next to the main craft. '*We are fighting from here?*' I asked Qiu with my thoughts. '*No, young one, like the angels, we can only travel like that within short distances. We will fly to our allotted location,* 'he answered.

Qiu's body began to rumble beneath me as his power grew, and he rose from the ground effortlessly. My whole body buzzed with power as he curled himself before raising his head and surging forward. I could just about see the elders and Christik high up in the sky, all flying in different directions on their dragons. We headed east, and Qiu soared in the darkening sky. The sun was setting, and the oranges, yellows and reds reflected off Qiu's red scales, making his already shimmering body look even more magical. The wind was trying to whip through my tied-up hair, making escaped wisps trail behind me.

'*Are we going to where my family are?*' I asked, feeling desperate to see my family. '*Yes, and we will be there soon, young one.*' Qiu replied in my mind again.

We flew for what felt like an eternity, but in truth, it was only a matter of minutes. I could feel us slowing down as we approached the town that we'd visited with Tracey, and I could still see people walking to their hiding places. My mind began to think of all the people who wouldn't be fighting. '*Christik, are the non-fighters safe in the underwater cities?* 'I reached out to ask. *'They are all safe, Mel, do not worry, concentrate on staying alive, please,* 'she said, and I could feel her genuine concern.

The buildings loomed as Qiu slowed right down, landing in the park area where hopefully, the Marilians would eventually land. As Qiu's feet touched down, I reached out to my husband. *'James, where are you right now?'* I asked.

Within seconds, he replied with confusion in his thoughts. *'We're at the library, baby, hang on, how the hell are you able to talk to me from Cubanaz?'*

There was a long pause, mainly because I knew he was going to go ballistic on me. *'I'm sorry, baby, I couldn't go and leave you all,'* I told him in a rush of words. *'I'm in the park area, but I have awesome backup.'* I could feel James' frustration, worry and upset flowing through the mental connection, and I could almost hear him take a deep breath as he resigned himself to the knowledge that I always put my family first.

'I'm coming to you, stay put,' he said curtly.

I stayed put on top of Qiu's back waiting for James, full of nerves and dreading the telling off I was about to receive.

Within minutes, James and our kids rounded the nearest building and approached the park. As soon as they saw Qiu and I, they stopped in their tracks.

"Fucking hellfire!" James blurted, as he took in the sight of his pregnant wife on top of a fierce and terrifying blood-red dragon.

I couldn't help smiling at his reaction and the looks of sheer shock and awe on my kids' faces.

"I want one! "Abigail said breathlessly.

"Oh, my god, I want one too," Anthony agreed.

As James and the kids started to walk towards us, I dismounted as gracefully as possible with the help of Qiu. The last thing I wanted was to land ungracefully straight on my ass.

James gathered me into his arms; his eyes never leaving the dragon, and the kids stood around us with their mouths agape, looking like they were all catching flies.

James released me, and he gave me the look normally reserved for the kids.

"You were supposed to go to Cubanaz, Mel," he said with disappointment.

"I know," I told him, "but when I was sitting on the craft, something told me that you guys would need me, so here I am."

James looked me over from my head to my toes, and a smile spread across his handsome, rugged face.

"Well, you certainly look the part, my lady, you hot little minx you," he said with a wink.

"Agghh, get a room," Harrison blurted out with a grin.

I walked back over to my new friend, and as I raised my hand, Qiu lowered his face to my palm.

"I would like you all to meet Qiu, the head of the Longs," I told my family.

"It is a great pleasure to meet you all," Qiu said, making the kids gasp.

They obviously weren't expecting the dragon to talk either. James moved over to Qiu with his shoulders back and his chest puffed out, trying to be brave in front of the kids, or maybe just me.

"The pleasure is ours, Qiu. I am very pleased to meet you," James said, as he gave the dragon a huge smile and then a dipped head in respect.

Qiu lowered his head and allowed James to place his hand on his scales. Next was Abigail, Harrison, Anthony and lastly April. All of my family greeted Qiu as a friend and with respect. Qiu happily let each of them touch his face and connect with him, and to be honest, I think he was enjoying the attention.

'The Marilians are passing through your atmosphere, get into your places everyone,' I heard Christik say in my thoughts. I knew straight away that she'd told everyone because I looked at James and the kids at the same moment that they looked at me.

"It's time, where do you want Qiu and me?" I asked my now worried husband.

As my husband looked at me, I could almost read his thoughts through his eyes; is it too late to send my wife away? Should I let her fight? Then I watched him take a long deep breath of defeat.

"Go and hide in the parking garage that Tracey showed us," James said with an urgency to his voice.

"Where is Tracey?" I asked, suddenly wondering why she wasn't with my family.

"Don't worry, she's with Akhenaten, now go baby," he said as he pointed in the direction of the large garage.

Not wanting my family out in the open, I swiftly took Qiu's waiting leg and slid myself onto his back. Qiu didn't wait for goodbyes but headed straight to the parking garage, and when I turned back to my family; they were already running back to the old library. As I watched them all running, I said a silent prayer, 'Please keep my family safe.'

I wasn't sure who exactly I was praying to, maybe anyone who was listening, even if it was just my dead parents. I hoped that they would be watching over us. *'We will fight and protect your family, young one,'* Qiu told me, *'they are stronger than you know!'*

Qiu and I got to the parking garage, and the solar lights had been turned off. It was pitch black, and I didn't know if anyone was already in there. The last thing we needed was for some scared humans to start attacking us. However, any humans should have an angel chaperone who would know about the dragons.

"Qiu, just to put my mind at ease, are there any humans in there?" I asked.

"No, young one, they are close but not inside this building."

"Ok," I said, feeling more relaxed.

As Qiu began to enter the dark garage, his body started to give off a powerful glow, letting us both see where everything was. There were still neatly piled guns and ammunition as well as grenades and other weapons I didn't recognize. Qiu moved all the way inside, and then he navigated his way to turn around. We were soon facing the entrance, and Qiu turned his glow off. Nobody would know we were there until it was too late.

It wasn't long before we heard the Marilians arriving in their ships. Part of me wanted to look up to the sky to see if the ships were exactly like my dream, but I knew that wasn't possible. We couldn't afford any mistakes. The Marilian ships sounded like thunder rolling through the sky, and I surmised that the Marilians didn't care about being quiet. They were such an evil force that they didn't care who knew they were coming.

While we waited for them to land, my pulse began to race, but it wasn't fear that was causing it, and it wasn't excitement for the coming battle. I was angry, correction, I was raging. Raging because the Marilians had the audacity to come to my planet to destroy it and to try and take my family and friends.

The noises from the crafts changed, and the muffled noises from their engines made it sound like they were landing, but I wanted to be sure. '*James, are you watching the fuckers?*' I asked, sounding more like Tracey than my usual self.

'*I'm watching them, baby; they're landing one of their ships on the park green now,*' James said, and I could hear his worry.

'*Let me know when it's time,*' I told him.

The longer I waited in the parking garage with Qiu; the more enraged I felt. The memory of the dream I had when they burned the animals was seared in my mind, and there was no way on earth I was going to let that happen.

'*They're starting to disembark, Mel, fuck me, they're massive,*' James exclaimed, and I could feel his surprise. '*Stay alive, baby! Now, let's go!*'

CHAPTER 20

I didn't have to tell Qiu it was time for the fight because he already knew. I could feel his power building beneath me like before, only this time, it was different. It was almost as if he was channeling my rage or maybe his own. The power I felt surging through me made me feel invincible. I was suddenly desperate to get into battle and teach the Marilians what an ass-kicking was like. Qiu began to glow a brilliant shimmering red as his power engulfed us both, and then he surged forward.

Qiu charged forward at speed, and I was sure that if anyone was to see us, they would definitely think twice about attacking. We charged through the streets heading for the park green, and as we came to the main road that ran through the town, we saw them in mass numbers. James was right, they were bigger than we thought and more vicious looking too, but that didn't dampen what I was feeling.

As we got close to the nearest Marilians, I pulled out the two handguns that were strapped to my outer thighs, knowing somehow that I wouldn't slip from Qiu's back. It was as if the dragon and I were one entity. My guns were already loaded and ready to go, I didn't even blink when I fired my first lot of rounds. The Marilian's skin was as tough as a Teflon vest, and what would have killed a human only just caused enough damage to slow the bastard down. It was going to take a lot of bullets for the fuckers to die.

Qiu roared as he saw what little damage my bullets were doing, and I felt him draw in a long deep breath. His power vibrated against me, and then he let loose. Fire shot from Qiu's mouth at such a speed that it knocked the nearest Marilians off their feet as they burned. There was no escape for them once they were hit, and there was no water for them to put themselves out. '*Try and control that fire, why don't you,*' I thought as I watched them panic.

Their roars of pain as their long dark hair and skin burned made my skin crawl, but I didn't and couldn't feel empathy for them. I wasn't a sadistic person, but the thought of the countless worlds they'd destroyed and the lives they had taken made me feel like we were doing the universe a great service.

When Qiu's fire stopped, I could feel the drain of power, and I knew it would be a while before he could do it again. I quickly looked around, and I finally spotted James and the kids not far away, just to the left of us, mingled with other humans and angels. All of them were battling against more Marilians. The scum bags were so bloody fast that my family was struggling to shoot them, but Anthony, who had opted to fight with a long blade, appeared to be fairing quite well. Our son was anticipating which way the Marilian was going to move, and then he was striking in that direction. His foe was getting cut deeply, long open slices visible along his thick arms and broad hairy chest, and I could see its hot back blood running down its body, dripping on the ground.

'*Qui, my family needs help,*' I thought. Instantly, Qiu turned, swiping at other Marilians as he neared them. His razor-sharp talons sliced through the monsters as if they were made of butter, cutting one of them nearly in half. Its shocked eyes widened as it raised its arms, trying to save itself from falling backwards. The top half of its hairy body tipped back while its legs gave way, thick black blood sprayed from its open torso, its knees smacking the ground and then its vile face. The rest of Qiu's victims dropped to the ground, all fatally wounded, liquid blackness pooling around their dead bodies. The other Marilians didn't care about their fallen ones; they only cared about finding humans.

A loud explosion rang across the sky, and I looked up just in time to see a burning Marilian craft plummeting to the ground as a fighter jet flew away, its engines creating a tremendous thunderclap. The burning Marilian ship crashed and exploded out of sight, sending plumes of black smoke into the air. Close to where the Marilian's ship had been was one of the angel's crafts, and I watched as it flew towards another of our enemies' ships, freezing it in the air. The fighter jet flew in a wide arc, coming back around in their direction. I didn't know what kind of weapons our pilot was using, but it was powerful. It shot from the jet at high speed and hit the enemy ship near the front, and as soon as it hit, the angels craft released it from its hold.

I forced myself to look away from what was happening above, and we headed towards my family and our fighting friends. As I watched my husband and kids fight and work together; pride filled my heart. April and Abigail were stood back to back, shooting round after round with handguns as we neared them. Abigail shot a Marilian straight in the left eye as it tried to rush her. Its large head flung back as the bullet burst its eyeball and penetrated its brain. Black blood and soft tissue oozed out of its now empty socket before it fell backwards, landing with a thud. Immediately, I knew that it was dead.

I quickly used the top of my hand to touch the com around my neck, trying to keep a hold of the gun, '*Christik tell everyone to aim for their eyes!*' I nearly shrieked to her. '*I understand, Mel*' she answered, as I sent her the mental images of what had just happened. It wasn't a pretty sight by any means, but it was the only way we would be able to put the Marilian fuckers down quickly, without sustaining massive losses. Acting quickly, I told the same thing to James and the kids through my com, and as soon as they heard me, they all began to aim for the Marilians' heads and eyes. My family was almost a blur of bullets and blades as they tried to dodge the Marilians' attacks with the help of their angel counterparts.

I thought we were doing well, until one of our foes reached out its hairy muscular arm, summoning the fire surrounding one of their burning fallen. The flames were drawn to its massive taloned hand as if its hand was a magnet, and the Marilian threw the flames straight for my family. I heard the scream before I actually realized it was me making the shrill, desperate sound.

"Nooooo…"

Before the raging flames could reach my family, more angels emerged from the surrounding buildings and their hiding places. The angels were still painted from their heads to their feet, and it was easy to still feel impressed. Barrels of water had been dotted along the streets as a precaution after what our prisoner had told us, and it was a blessing. The angels shot forward, raising their arms, and they pulsed a bright white with their power as they reached for the water. I knew it was all happening within seconds, but as I watched the scene; it was like slow motion.

The water rose from the containers, glowing from the angels' power, and it swirled as if they were mini whirlpools. The angels hurled the water at the Marilians and the flames that were about to engulf my family. Instantly, the air was full of smoke and glistening water vapor. The Marilians were suddenly confused, whipping their heads around to see where the water had come from. Then they spotted the painted angels.

I could see the Marilians' thick brows furrowing in their confusion as they looked at the decorated angels covered in brickwork, posters and door frames. I didn't know if it was because they were surprised that the angels were fighting with us, or because the angels were painted in all sorts of colors and patterns. Either way, I felt a shift in what they were feeling, and they weren't feeling as confident as they were before.

James, the kids and the others, took full advantage of the distraction and began to shoot again; aiming for the Marilians' blood-red eyes. I joined in the attack, reloading my guns just like I'd been shown, and I began to shoot. Between us, we must have taken down at least fifty of the bastards, and panic rose in the air. The remaining Marilians in the street started to run, and my god, they were fast.

We watched as they started to try the doors to the shops and empty businesses. Sometimes, they would come face to face with another angel, who would use their power to force them back into the street, and sometimes, they would encounter an ambush with our waiting friends, who now aimed straight away for their eyes. Every now and again, I would think about all the others who were fighting, in and around the area, praying that they were doing well in their fight.

The Marilians in our area soon started to realize that they were losing badly, the panic in the air felt desperate, and they started to run towards their ship on the green. We all began to give chase as fast as we could, but then we heard the rumbling of their ship. The angels carried on trying to help us by attempting to freeze the Marilians with their powers. However, the bastards were becoming very efficient at dodging the angels' beams. At first, I think we all thought that the Marilians were trying to retreat, but we couldn't have been more wrong.

As their ship rose into the air; huge mechanical cylinders emerged from the sides of it, and as the Marilians powered them up, we could see them begin to shine red. None of us knew what to expect at this stage. Abruptly, shots of fire started to rain down in all directions, and we all began to try and take cover as the fire hit buildings, humans and Marilians. The Marilians on board the ship obviously didn't care if they were hitting their own. Why would they? They must have thought that they could always make some more. I watched in horror as the fire hit again and again. Screams filled the air from our friends and our foe as their bodies burned.

When the initial shock of what the Marilians were doing wore off, the angels moved quickly back to our sides, trying to shield and deflect the fire shots and also put out of any flames that had hit our people. Some of our friends were burnt badly, layers of their skin burnt away, leaving raw red flesh. Others had big blisters forming on their arms from shielding their faces, and they were instantly flitted away, I assumed, back to the main craft. I knew they would be healed straight away, but I hated that they were suffering.

The Marilians saw that they had the sudden advantage; they turned back to the fight, and I was helpless when one of them grabbed Anthony. None of the angels had reached him in time, and he was completely alone. Our son managed to break loose from its hold. It was as if my nightmare was becoming a reality, as I watched Anthony fighting the Marilian fucker with his long blade, and the Marilian was desperately trying to slash at our son with its razor-sharp talons. I heard myself scream as the bastard's talons sliced through the air and then across Anthony's chest. The military vest that our son was wearing was no protection. Anthony might as well had worn a T-shirt for all the protection he had. Very quickly, blood began to run from the open wounds, trickling out from the large slashes. Anthony's eyes were wide with shock.

There were too many humans mingled with the Marilians for Qiu and I to run through the middle of, without hurting our friends or family in the process. I didn't have to tell Qiu that we needed to get to my boy; he'd already read my mind and had felt my pain. The dragon started to vibrate with his power, and as we began to rise in the air, I watched as the Marilian grabbed hold of Anthony by his shoulders. It pulled our son so close that they were literally nose to nose, it's snarling teeth an inch away from Anthony's face. Our son was in so much pain that the blade he was holding fell from his hand as shock kicked in.

Qiu was moving fast, but not fast enough, and I watched horrified as the Marilian snarled into Anthony' face with his burning eyes, and then it began to change my son. I screamed again as I felt Anthony's pain. Our son's blood was already starting to change from the wound inwards. I didn't know what to do, but as Qiu flew and swooped down to my son and the Marilian fucker, I flung myself at the monster with both of my guns blazing.

It took me many shots before I finally hit the Marilian in one of his red eyes. The look on its vicious face turned from a triumphant grimace to utter shock as its brain began to shut down. I watched with satisfaction as the bastard dropped to the ground with a thud. As soon as the Marilian was dead on the ground, I looked at Anthony. The fear and confusion on his young face were stabs to my heart. I wasn't paying any attention to the fighting around me at that point, or the fire that was raining down from the Marilian ship. Saving our son was my only focus.

I could feel my whole body starting to tremble with a rage and determination that I'd never felt before. It wasn't just coming from me; it was also coming from my baby girl. She knew her brother was hurt, and she was just as upset as I was. It was a stronger feeling than when I protected myself against Kay, when she had been turned. Dropping the handguns to the floor, I reached for Anthony, and I grabbed him by the shoulders just as his body started to slump. Anthony was turning, and his eyes were starting to change from green/blue to blood red. Coarse dark hairs were beginning to sprout from his skin, and his fingernails were starting to turn from nails to silver claws.

"No!" I shrieked, as I tried to hold onto him.

My feelings of rage and despair burst from me in a blue pulse of power. It vibrated through the very core of me as it released, surrounding my son and me. I watched in sudden amazement as the energy converted to the same blue fluid as before. It coated him and thickened as the energy flowed from me to him. Before long, Anthony was inside a blue fluid bubble capsule, and his body began to relax and slump even more in my hands, as his reddened eyes started to close. For some reason, I knew he would be safe now, protected in the bubble against the Marilians and the change that had begun. I released my son, letting the bubble touch the ground with Anthony floating inside it.

Now our son was safe; I turned my attention back to what was going on. I hadn't even noticed that Qiu was right behind me, using his own body to shield Anthony and I. Luckily, the fire from the Marilian ship didn't appear to hurt or damage the dragon, and I was very relieved.

"Are you ready, young one, we need to destroy their ship?" Qiu said urgently.

"Yes," I said, as my anger at what they were doing seemed to all but consume me.

I was so enraged that my body pulsed with the blue power that was still surrounding me and filling me inside. Qiu's own power was glowing a bright red, and as soon as I used his leg to leap unto his back, our energies collided and then blended together like we were one. I'd never felt more powerful as I did right at that moment. Qiu rose from the ground with me holding on to his large red scales. I looked down, and I could see the angels trying to freeze the Marilians with their power, as the rest of family and friends tried to shoot or slay them with their weapons. I was relieved at the sight because it appeared that we were winning.

Qiu and I headed for the Marilian ship as it repeatedly shot its fire at the people and angels below it, as well as the nearest buildings. There must have been Marilians independently controlling the fire weapons because, as soon as we started to get close, some of the weapons moved and began to aim right for us. However, the power that now surrounded Qiu and I deflected everything they had. Qiu was amazing, swooping this way and that, which made the Marilians turn more of their weapons our way, instead of everyone below. I didn't need to look down to know that my family was ok; I could feel that they were. The only negative thing that I did feel was their worry for Anthony.

I couldn't even feel the fire as it bounced off Qiu and I; I couldn't even feel a tickle. Qiu soared higher, flying above the ship, and I felt his power growing as his body started to expand. He swooped down towards the ship, and as we got close, he blasted the ship with his own powerful fire before swooping away. When I looked back at the ship, there wasn't a mark on it, and my heart sank. It wasn't because they had a shield or anything like that, it was because they were from a fiery and turbulent planet. Whatever their ship was made of, it was definitely fire resistant.

'*We need to try and knock it out of the sky,*' I told Qiu, '*the fighter jet is already busy trying to take down the smaller ships.*' I didn't have to say anymore. Qiu showed me with his mind what he was going to do, and the next thing I knew, we were soaring again, but this time, a lot higher. I was abruptly nervous because I knew what was coming. '*You will not get hurt, young one,*' Qiu said in my mind, trying to reassure me. We flew so high that we were among the clouds, and Qiu's power began to build again, only this time, it felt different.

For a moment, we seemed to stop in mid-flight before Qiu curled himself inwards, and I instinctively laid myself as flat as possible against his scales, holding on tightly as was humanly possible. Then, he shot us downwards as if we'd been shot from a cannon. The speed at which we were traveling was so fast that I could feel my cheeks vibrating with the G force. I kept my head down, trying to be as streamlined as possible while trying to breathe.

I looked up slightly just at the wrong time as the Marilian ship was looming towards us, and Qiu appeared to be aiming for the center of the ship. I knew what Qiu's plan was, but I honestly didn't know if it was possible, but I trusted the dragon. Lowering my head back down, so it was touching Qiu's scales, I waited for the impact. I felt us hit the ship as soon as Qiu's horns and head made contact. I could feel the force of the Marilian ship's metal as it tried to resist Qiu and the power he wielded, but there was no stopping us. Qiu's head and the rest of his huge body and me ploughed through the Marilian ship, leaving a massive gaping hole straight through its center, which filled with billowing black smoke and fire.

When we broke through to the underside of the ship, Qiu swooped beneath it, getting us away from the burning remains. As he soared up and away from it, I lifted myself to look at the burning craft. I knew as soon as I saw it that it was finished. The black smoke was coming out of the ship from every direction, and as we watched, it began to tilt as it started to lose power and control. I was filled with huge satisfaction while watching it fall from the sky while hoping anyone down below was getting out of the way. The ship started to fall from the sky sideways, and it fell so quickly that there was no escaping for the Marilians on board. It hit the buildings below it with such force that the ground shook beneath it, the buildings crumbled, the ruins filling with acrid black smoke.

We could hear everyone below us, cheering and rejoicing at our victory, but I knew we had a long way to go. When I looked down at the angels and people on the ground, I was thrilled to see the remaining Marilians all lying on the ground, and everyone was celebrating. Although I wanted so badly to celebrate with them, I knew in my gut that it was too soon. Qiu flew to the ground as close to James and the kids as he could, and I slipped off his back as soon as his taloned feet landed, not even waiting for him to lift his leg for me. Instantly, our power auras changed to their original colors of red and blue. I ran to James and the kids, wrapping them all in my arms and holding them tightly.

"It's not over by any means," I chided them, "we have friends still fighting, and we need to help them."

All of their faces dropped at my words, and I really didn't want to burst their bubbles, but we didn't have time to waste; we were needed elsewhere. James came up to me, and he cupped my face in his hands, kissing me on my lips.

"You are the most fearless and the most amazing woman I've ever known, do you know that," My husband declared.

I could feel myself blushing from the smoldering look he was giving me, and I could feel everything he was feeling, his awe, admiration and love for me.

"I love you," I whispered.

James' resounding smile said everything.

He removed his hands and took my hands in his.

"I love you, too baby, and you're right, we need to help the others," he said, suddenly very serious.

I turned to the nearest angel.

"Please take Anthony back to the main craft," I told them before turning to my family, friends and angels, "Let's go."

I knew the angels would take everyone where they were most needed, and as the angels flitted with my fellow humans, I mounted Qiu.

"Let's go to where we can help the most Qiu," I said, feeling the power between us connect once more.

Within minutes, we were soaring again, and below us, we could see the fighting raging. As we headed towards the nearest Marilian ship that was raining fire down, I had a feeling that we were going to do the same as we did before. Qiu began to fly upwards, but before we had the chance, something shot up from the ground right underneath the ship. It was a rocket, and it hit the Marilian ship on its left side, sending it into a sideways fiery descent, its weapons on the right continued to shoot fire bolts, right up until it hit trees and old buildings before exploding in plumes of black smoke and orange and red flames. When I looked to the ground, a man was looking up, he had a rocket launcher on his shoulder, and I think a huge grin on his face.

CHAPTER 21

I was so thrilled by what I'd just witnessed. It meant that all those fighting, who didn't have a dragon on their side, still had a chance of bringing down the Marilian ships. I took a moment to touch my com and reach out to Christik, Lindaz and Evest. '*I don't know where you are, but this is what's just happened,*' I told them as I sent them mental images of Qiu and I taking one ship down and images of the man taking down the other ship. '*Thank you, Mel,*' Christik said, '*We are at the fake holding structure, and we could use your help. Your family is already here.*' I was relieved to know that my family was with the most powerful of the angels, and the people below us seemed to be doing well against the remaining Marilians on the ground. '*We are on our way,*' I replied.

Qiu heard everything that was said between us, and the longer we were connected, the deeper our connection felt. '*I feel it too, young one,*' Qiu said in my mind as he began to soar to the clouds again. On the way to the fake holding structure, flying high on Qiu's back, I'd never felt so alive and free. We flew over more areas that the angels had already healed, and the sight lightened my heart. It also made me so much more determined to protect it against the monsters who wanted to ruin it all, just because they could.

Within a few minutes, I could see the large, white, fake holding structure in the distance with three of the Marilian ships above it. Two of the ships were striking bolts of fire in multiple directions, while the other was actively trying to take down Lindaz and Evest, who were trying to draw the ship away from the people and angels on the ground. *'We need to take down the ship that the elders are occupying, Qiu,'* I told the dragon, *'that way, the elders will be free to help us take down the other two.'*

Qiu reacted immediately, climbing even higher, and because we'd already taken down one of their ships, this time, I knew we weren't going to get hurt. I laid myself flat again as we climbed, but this time, I kept my head up, just enough so I could see everything. Qiu stopped in midair, coiling himself before shooting downwards straight for the ship. I should have been terrified as the ship loomed towards us, but I wasn't. Qiu's horns and head broke through the hull of the ship as if he was cracking an egg. The metal was nothing compared to Qiu's massive horns. I don't know if it was because I was watching this time, but it felt like slow motion as we ploughed our way through the various levels of the craft, leaving nothing but destruction behind us.

The moment we were free, Qiu swooped to the side, and we watched everyone else start to evacuate the area as quickly as they could. The ship burst into flames and began to fall from the sky at speed while moving in the direction of one of the other ships. My heart pounded in my chest as I wished and hoped they would crash together, and when the ship we'd just hit did indeed crash into the other; my heart rejoiced. Not being able to stop myself, I lifted myself and flung both of my arms in the air.

"Wooooo whooooo," I shrieked.

273

I'm sure I could feel Qiu smiling at my exuberant gesture. I spotted Lindaz and Ying flying towards the clouds, looking almost like a shooting star in a blaze of browns and golds. The sunlight bounced off Ying's golden scales, making the dragon look so magical that he was breathtaking. Ying's large gold horn pointed the way as Lindaz effortlessly sat on his back, with her shimmering hair streaming behind her, just like Ying's shock of ebony black hair was streaming behind him. As soon as they reached the clouds, Ying's massive wings spread out, stopping them for a moment as he curled himself inwards.

I held back onto Qiu's dark red scales as he flew in zig zags, and I held my breath, knowing what was coming next. Ying shot himself downwards like a golden arrow with Lindaz close to his back. They shot through the air at such speed that you could have easily mistaken them for a bolt of lightning. The impact noise rolled out across the sky like thunder. I felt the vibration through my whole body as I watched them crash straight through the Marilian ship. With the elders' power and the powerful dragon, they were a powerful force. As soon as they emerged from the underside of it, the ship broke into two. Fire and thick smoke began to rise from the two halves, and the ship fell hard onto the scattered buildings below.

There were no cheers from anyone on the ground this time. The fake holding structure had worked, better than we could have hoped for, and the Marilians were on the ground in force. I mentally chided myself for not acting quicker to help them. I was so focused on getting the ship down that I forgot that every minute counted. *'Let's kick some more Marilian ass,'* I said to Qiu.

I scanned the ground as Qiu descended, and I spotted a large group of Marilians fighting with some of our friends. Our friends didn't seem to be faring so well; all of them were covered in their own blood. '*I see them, young one,*' Qiu told me as we flew in their direction. Bodies were everywhere. We had lost so many people, and my heart broke at the burning and cut bodies strewn on the ground. Some were charred beyond recognition, others had fatal wounds from the Marilians' talons, laying in their own blood. The angels were doing their best, but there were too many Marilians and not enough of us. '*We need to see your talons in action,*' I thought to Qiu, Tian, Shen and Ying. The resounding dragon roars that rang through the air told me that they'd heard me.

Qiu and I didn't stop and wait for them. As Qiu swooped down and landed on the ground, I scanned the area, spotting some of our friends who were already turning. There was nothing I could do for the people who had already changed or who were dead, but I was determined to try and save the ones who weren't lost yet. As soon as I slid off Qiu's back, he began slashing at the closest Marilians, his talons shredding their tough skin and thick hair as I ran to the nearest changing human. Thick black blood began to spray in all directions.

The woman I approached first was wearing combat gear just like myself; her body was strapped with empty knife sheaths and gun holsters. She'd obviously been fighting with everything she'd had. Blood was streaming from a deep gash in her neck, and when she looked up as I approached her, her eyes were burning the fiery red of the Marilians. The woman's once smooth black skin was now beginning to sprout coarse dark hair like the Marilians too, and I wasn't going to let her change any further.

The woman snarled at me as soon as I reached for her. She bared her teeth as though she wanted to rip my throat out, but I could already feel the power within me reaching for her. The moment my hands touched her face; it was as if I'd given her a massive sedative. I felt the power flowing out of me, and I watched as it started to coat her from her face, head and downwards to the rest of her body. Just like Anthony, she began to slump to the ground as the blue bubble capsule formed around her.

The battle raged on around us, and I could hear the cries from the Marilians as they met with the talons of the four dragons. They didn't stand a chance with the elders' power, freezing them on the spot. I could only imagine what the other dragons were doing around the world, and I hoped that they were just as effective as ours. Once the woman was secure and safe, I quickly ran to the next changing person, letting my power cover them and halt their turning. Again and again, I stopped another person changing, dodging Marilians as I moved from one place to another. It didn't even occur to me at the time that we had to deal with the people afterwards.

Just as I was helping a teenage girl, who wasn't much older than Abigail, I heard a massive rumble rolling across the sky. '*Holy shit*,' it was another ship, and it was bigger than the others we had already taken down. It was heading straight for us. There wasn't enough time for the dragons to take to the air and get into position, and I could feel my panic and worry start to build immediately. I looked around wildly, wondering what the hell we could do to protect everyone.

"Take cover!" I shouted as I sprinted towards my dragon.

It was as if Qiu and I were one, both of us began running to each other. I quickly flung myself onto Qiu's back, trusting him to raise his leg for me. Christik and the elders quickly ran to their dragons too, gracefully leaping up onto their backs and starting to take flight immediately. The Marilian ship kept coming, and the moment it reached us, something opened beneath it. I was expecting fire to rain down like the other ships had done, but instead; something black shot out from the ship like black lightning, and it shot straight into the ground. There was no telling what it was, and as soon as it was released, the opening underneath the ship closed. '*What the hell was that*?' I asked the elders. '*We do not know, Mel*' came the short reply.

Suddenly and out of nowhere, two missiles shot into the sky, coming from opposite directions, a blaze of orange and white trailing behind them. We all watched as the two missiles headed straight for the massive Marilian ship, praying that they weren't going to miss. We didn't need to worry. The first one hit the ship on the left side; piercing it effortlessly and exploding in a spectacular fashion. Explosions rapidly burst from the hull in the missile's wake, just as the second one hit. The second missile came from the right, it hit the ship exactly where the black lighting was shot from. We watched in awe as the ship seemed to implode on itself, before a massive shockwave burst from it, knocking everyone off their feet, including the Marilians.

The sheer force of the blast knocked me off Qiu's back, and there was nothing I could do to stop myself. I fell through the air with my arms and legs flailing wildly, and then instinct took charge. I tried to curl into a tight ball to protect my baby, and my whole body braced myself for the impact that was coming. When the impact didn't come, and I couldn't feel anything, I slowly raised my head, wondering what the hell was going on.

I was glowing the bright blue, and I was inside a shimmering power bubble of my own. Straightening myself to an upright standing position; I let my feet touch the floor, and my hand went to my swollen baby bump, '*You really are amazing, baby girl*,' I cooed to my daughter as I felt her move and kick, as if in answer. The crash of the Marilian ship hitting the buildings and the ground made the earth roll like an earthquake, and I swayed inside the bubble.

I quickly looked around, watching everyone trying to keep their balance, and I was instantly relieved to see that so many people were unharmed from the blast. The angels had acted quickly by shielding as many of our friends as possible who had been closest to the blast, and the Marilians appeared to be in momentary shock themselves. Many of them stood back up, looking to where their main ship had just been destroyed, before turning back to us all with their red eyes blazing. Their anger was palpable in the air, and that only made them more dangerous.

The Marilians attacked, all rushing at the same time to the nearest human with their teeth bared and their razor talons raised as they surged forward. The moment I tried to walk forward, the bubble began to absorb back into my body, allowing me to get back into the action. We were adrenaline-pumped already, and luckily, we were quick to react. Marilians and humans charged at each other as the angels tried to freeze the monsters. Our friends and I reached for the weapons that were still on our bodies or that were within reach. I charged at the nearest Marilian with handguns in both hands, grateful that I'd strapped so many weapons to my body.

I didn't wait until the Marilian reached me, aiming shots at its face as we ran towards each other, hoping that one of the bullets would hit a bright red eye. The slime ball rushed at me, swiping its talons at my chest as it neared, and as soon as it opened its mouth to roar, I took another shot, not realizing that I was aiming at its snarling mouth. As soon as the bullet passed between its bared teeth, hitting the back of its throat and exiting from the back of its head; its shocked eyes looked at me in disbelief before it fell backwards onto the ground. I didn't stick around to watch its black blood pool on the floor.

As I started to run towards the next Marilian bastard, suddenly Tracey appeared in front of me with Akhenaten holding her hand. Both of them quickly let go of each other, Akhenaten's hands instantly glowed with the bright white light of his power, and Tracey reached for her weapons that were strapped to her waist. They were quite the team. Akhenaten blasted his power at the Marilians to freeze them, and Tracey started shooting the fuckers in any orifice that she could find. They were the definition of a power couple as Marilians dropped one after the other around them.

"Did you like our missiles?" Tracey shouted as she shot dead yet another Marilian.

"That was you two?" I shouted back as I aimed, shot, and missed another Marilian rushing at me.

"Hell, yeah, it was us," she shouted proudly.

Suddenly, there was someone reaching over my right shoulder with a huge handgun in his large hand. The gun fired at the rushing Marilian, hitting it right in its left eye, the Marilian's head flung back with the impact, before the monster dropped heavily with a thud. I knew the hand belonged to James instantly, without even seeing him.

"Where are the kids?" I asked quickly before the next Marilian set its sights on us.

"Don't worry, they're behind us kicking ass," he said as he took a shot at another Marilian.

I turned quickly, knowing that my husband literally had my back. I wanted to see with my own eyes that the rest of my kids were really ok. Not that I didn't believe my husband, but I really needed to see them whole. My kids were ploughing through the Marilians like a force of nature. Abigail and April were back to back, shooting at any Marilians who dared to challenge them. Every time they ran out of bullets, they'd grab another magazine from their bodies as if they'd been trained by the world's best military. Harrison was just as fierce as he protected both of the girls. His face showed that he meant business, and he wasn't interested in taking prisoners. Holly and Nalik were fighting not far from them, looking just as organized as Tracey and Akhenaten, although Nalik did seem to have a more concerned look on his angelic face than the older angel.

"Ok, the kids do seem to be holding their own," I admitted to James, as I aimed and shot at another one.

Just as I was about to take another shot, the ground began to quake beneath our feet. James instinctively grabbed my arm as the quaking turned into violent shaking. Buildings and trees around us started to sway, windows began shattering in their frames as we all struggled to keep our balance.

"What the fuck! Earthquake?" I asked James as he desperately tried to hold on to me.

"I don't know, it sure feels like it," he said, as he tried to look at our kids.

We'd both felt many earthquakes in our lives, having both lived in California our whole lives, unlike my English parents, but something about this one felt different. As the ground began to settle again, a sense of dread washed over me from my head to my toes, as if I'd dived into an icy lake.

"Something doesn't feel right, James," I said, as I wildly looked around for Christik and the elders. I spotted them, and they were standing in the middle of the road, looking at each other in confusion.

THE MARILIANS

The Marilians that were left looked just as worried as I felt inside, and they were no longer trying to fight. I could feel a panic rising among them, and I couldn't understand why. I didn't think it was because they thought they were losing. There was something else going on; I just didn't know what. I touched my com, reaching out to Christik. *'Was that an earthquake, Christik?'* I asked. *'We are not on top of your planet's fault lines, Mel; there should be no earthquakes here,'* she said, sounding just as confused as I was.

One of the Marilians raised its muscular arms in the air, its talons catching the rays of the sun, and it roared a blood-curdling noise. *'What the hell?'* The bastards all looked at the roaring Marilian in surprise, and I could see some of them were scowling at the sound. I didn't have a clue what it meant, and I was completely stunned when one by one, the Marilians turned and started to sprint away. Something told me that it wasn't a good sign.

"What the fuck is going on?" I asked no one in particular, as an icy chill ran down my back, making me shiver.

The Marilians were all running in different directions, sprinting around the side's old buildings and through the streets. They were so fast that there was no way any of us humans were quick enough to chase after them. We were all watching them in total confusion.

"I don't understand what the hell is going on here!" Tracey shouted over.

Akhenaten had a worried look on his face too. Christik, the elders and all four of the dragons were stood watching the fleeing Marilians. After the last Marilian dashed out of sight, we all began to walk towards each other. Everyone who was still standing began to walk towards us and the fake holding structure, helping and carrying

281

those who needed help. As we gathered together, we all had similar expressions of surprise and unease.

"What is happening here?" I asked Christik as she approached with her parents and the four dragons following behind.

Before she had a chance to reply, Lindaz took a knee, and she placed a hand on the ground, closing her peacock colored eyes. After a few moments, she looked up abruptly; her eyes were swirling like silver whirlpools. I watched her eyes gradually turn back to their normal colors, and the sense of dread washed over me again as Lindaz stood back up.

"What is it, my own?" Christik asked.

"The Marilian ship has unleashed a terrible weapon into the heart of this planet," Lindaz said, as she shook her head in sorrow. "It is something that we cannot heal, my own."

I couldn't believe what I was hearing. After everything we'd already been through, our planet was going to fricking die anyway.

"You can't do anything to save our planet?" I asked, desperately.

"No, Mel," she said, with so much sadness that I could feel my heart breaking.

"What do we do now?" James asked as he looked from Lindaz to Evest to Christik.

Everyone who was within earshot was looking helplessly at each other, and those who couldn't hear were frantically asking what was happening.

"We will all go back to our main craft to organize an evacuation," Evest replied with confidence. "Christik, please tell the viziers what is happening."

THE MARILIANS

We were all so stunned by Lindaz' words to say anything more. None of it seemed real, and all I wanted to do was to get back on board the angels' main craft and hug my husband, kids and check on Anthony. The angels moved quickly, taking the nearest humans by the hand or arm, flitting everyone back to the main craft. As soon as I saw the kids, James and Nalik leave; I walked back towards Qiu and climbed unto his back. The elders and Christik mounted the other three dragons, and after the last of our friends left, the four of us took to the sky.

At this point, I didn't care about the Marilians that were now running loose on our planet. I knew that by now, the other angels were taking everyone to the angels' crafts, and the humans who didn't fight were all still safe in the underwater cities. If our planet was truly dying, then the Marilians were going to die with it. Qiu flew us high in the darkening sky, and the stars were starting to appear. Everything was running through my mind as I sat on Qiu's back, and I could feel a lump in my throat form as my heart broke. '*I am sorry, young one,*' Qiu empathized, '*the angels will do everything they can to save you all, and all of your creatures.*'

I knew what Qiu was saying was true, but I loved everything about our planet, from the oceans to the stars in the sky, and the thought of not seeing any of that again felt like too much to handle. Especially because I knew I wouldn't be able to share any of it with our new daughter. Tears began to stream down my face as I started to sob, and I let them fall freely.

CHAPTER 22

I cried all the way back to the main craft with Qiu trying to comfort me, saying things like, '*There is always hope, young one, all things happen for a reason, we don't understand as yet.*' Did anything he said make me feel any better? Did it hell! Every time we flew over another healed area, my tears would fall harder. It was comforting to know that Qui understood the feeling of loss and grief.

As we approached the large hanger on the main craft and Qiu began slow down; I wiped my eyes. I knew my face was probably blotchy and puffy, but I didn't care. Qiu began to shrink in size, and he swooped gracefully into the hanger alongside Ying and the other dragons. I could see Christik and the elders waiting for me with somber faces. I slid off the dragon's back with his help, and when my feet touched the ground, I nearly crumpled in a heap. My legs felt like jelly, and all of a sudden, my hands were shaking uncontrollably; I felt as if I was going to pass out.

Christik rushed forward, catching me before I had time to hit the floor, and instantly, I could feel her power flowing through her touch on my arms.

"What the hell?" I murmured.

"Give yourself a moment, Mel," Christik said, as I looked at her in utter confusion, "You have just been in battle, and you have used nearly all of your energy, trying to stop others from changing."

I let her hold me up, and I lowered my head, trying to take in long deep breaths to stop me from passing out. It took quite a few minutes of Christik sharing her power, for not only my energy to recharge but also for my emotions to be back on an even keel. I was grateful again to have such an amazing friend.

"Where are my family and all the others?" I asked, feeling more like myself again.

"They are in the large meeting room. Would you like to walk there or flit?" Christik asked with a soft smile.

"I think I'd like to flit this time," I told her with a smile of my own, "I don't think we have time to waste, do we?"

"No, we do not," was her short reply.

Christik looked at her parents, giving them both a nod before we both disappeared from the hanger.

Within a split second, we were stood inside the large meeting room next to the angels' control room. My family was there waiting, and so were our friends; angels and humans. The room was filled with a total mix of emotions. Relief that everyone was here, apart from Anthony, of course, and heartbreak because we had lost so many precious people, we had only recently got to know. I wanted desperately to be with my son and heal him, but at least I knew he was safe for the time being.

James and the kids all rushed towards me as soon as they saw me, taking me in their arms. It was the best group hug that I'd had in a while, and I could have stayed there all day, even though at one point,

I could barely breathe. The elders and Christik all took seats at the large wooden table, and everyone else followed suit. I sat myself next to James, the kids and Nalik, wanting to be close to them all. My eyes scanned my family as they took their seats, making sure that they were ok. I knew that the angels would have healed them straight away if they had been hurt, but I desperately needed the reassurance.

Everyone was exhausted, and I could see from everyone's postures that a lot of sleep was needed. Even Christik and the elders looked totally drained. Christik looked at her mother with a very sad look on her beautiful face.

"What exactly did you feel when you touched the earth?" She asked Lindaz somberly.

Lindaz's eyes seemed to lose some of their sparkle as she held her daughter's steady gaze.

"I do not know or understand what the Marilians weapon was, but I do know it shot down to the Earth's inner core," she said with a sadness echoing in her words. "The dark energy is solidifying the outer molten core, and it has started a chain reaction that we cannot stop. If we had time to understand what the weapon was, we would have a chance of saving this planet, but time is not on our side."

Every word was like a stab to the heart, and I think we were all reeling from the reality of the situation.

"I don't fucking believe this!" Tracey almost shouted.

Everyone turned to look at her.

"First, our planet was dying because of us, and now it's fucking dying because of the fucking Marilians!"

We all felt as frustrated and upset as Tracey was, and most of us nodded in agreement.

"How much time do you think we have, my own?" Akhenaten asked as he took Tracey's hand, trying to comfort her.

Lindaz and Evest both looked ashen as they looked at everyone at the table.

"We have only hours before the planet becomes dangerously violent. So, we need to act fast, to get everyone on our crafts. It would take too long to go through the star passages," she explained.

"But where will we go once we're away from here?" I asked, desperately.

Everyone looked at the elders expectantly.

"We will take you all to our planet until we can find you a new home," Evest said calmly.

What about all the animals?" Mimi asked with wide eyes.

"We can take them all with us, Mimi. Do not worry," Evest told her as he rose from his seat.

Lindaz and Christik both stood from their seats too.

"We need to evacuate the underwater cities and get everyone on board. My angels will meet us down there," Christik said.

Without another word, the angels all moved to the closest human friend, flitting us all to the hanger again. We boarded the small crafts in silence and exhaustion, and no sooner had the last butt made contact with the last seat, we were already on our way to the underwater city Cubanaz. Within minutes of leaving the main craft and with my head resting against James' shoulder, I fell asleep out of total exhaustion, with the last bit of Christik's shared energy depleted.

I woke to James gently stroking my face. For a moment, I dared to hope that it had all been a terrible, terrible dream, but as I looked around at the angels and my family; my hope turned to dust, and my heart sank again. Their distraught faces made it clear that this was our living nightmare. There was nowhere to moor the crafts when we arrived at Cubanaz. Small crafts were already moored at every available entry. Christik stopped the craft with ease, so we were floating close to where we moored the last time we were there, and she disconnected herself. The moment the seats released us, the angels and elders flitted us all inside the underwater city.

When we arrived in the big hall where Holly had recently got married all shivering like idiots, everyone seemed to be nervously talking, obviously worried about what was happening above them on land. As soon as everyone started to see us all standing there, a silence swept the room like a wave. Within a couple of minutes, the whole room was deathly quiet with all eyes on us. Christik glided forward to address everyone while the rest of us stayed where we were. It was as if everyone in the hall could sense that something bad had happened. Christik cut straight to the chase.

"I am afraid we all have to leave Earth," she said, with a voice that made it clear she was serious.

Murmurs of confusion swept the room in another wave.

"We defeated the Marilians; however, they released a weapon into the heart of your planet, and it is now being destroyed from the inside out," she explained.

Suddenly, the room erupted with loud voices full of questions and concerns. Christik held up her hands, and gradually, the hall fell silent once more.

"We do not have time too," she began to say.

The ground beneath our feet began to tremble, and I could feel the strong vibrations in my feet. I quickly reached out my hand, grabbing James' shoulder for support as he grabbed for Abigail and April. Both girls looked around wildly as the tremor become stronger, and people were being knocked from their seats. The hall was suddenly in chaos as everyone was trying to either keep themselves upright or pick themselves off the floor. The angels were as always, cool, calm and collected, reminding me that they'd probably been through things like that many times. Christik raised a hand to her throat, making it glow.

"Everyone, stay calm and wait for this to pass," her voice bellowed over the noise of everyone's panic and screams.

Everyone was trying to grab their loved ones, especially their younger loved ones. You could see the sheer panic in their faces and hear everyone's panic as they called out names or screamed. As I watched the chaos unfold, the tremor rolled through the great hall. The beautiful glass windows and ceiling began to crack, and water started to break through, only adding to everyone's panic and terror. Christik and the elders looked at each other with a determined look on their faces.

"Everyone, make your way to your nearest craft, my angels are waiting for you!" Christik bellowed.

No one needed to be asked twice. The angel's words seemed to give everyone some focus, even if it was telling them to leave. Everyone seemed to get their asses in gear, herding their loved ones to the exits that they could see. James, the kids and I moved out of the way to let everyone leave. We knew that we weren't going to be left behind, and we all wanted to make sure that everyone was safe before we left. Icy cold seawater was rushing in quickly, and before long, people needed to wade through the knee-high seawater to get to the crafts. The angels guided the people to the crafts and like a well-oiled machine; quickly getting everyone boarded.

"They will all wait for us at our main craft," Christik said as if she had read my mind.

I swear that was exactly what I was thinking, and I was relieved to know that we'd all be leaving Earth together.

"What about the Dragons?" I asked, suddenly worried about Qiu and the others.

"Do not worry, Mel, they would have gone home through the star Passage by now, and my angels are closing the gates behind them," she assured me with a small smile.

We waded through the water to watch the last of our friends board the final craft with the last of the angels. As the craft left and the barrier appeared, Christik, the elders and our angel friends flitted us back to our own craft.

As soon as we were on board, Holly looked to Nalik.

"I would like to see out there," Holly told Nalik, pointing towards the underwater city we'd just left.

Nalik nodded to his new bride, and as we all took our seats and Christik connected with the craft, Nalik placed a glowing hand onto the side of the ship, making it see-through. None of us could help ourselves; all of us twisting in our seats to see what was happening to Cubanaz below. It was a heartbreaking sight. All of the angel's hard work was being destroyed before our eyes. The beautiful pearlescent glass was shattering with the strengthening tremors and falling through the water. The gold and silver vines were twisting out of shape, and huge chunks of the buildings were breaking off and either landing on the sand or helping the city's demise. I could only imagine what was happening on land. There were no signs of any sea life this time, so I knew that the angels had already rescued them.

As soon as Christik was one with the ship, we began to move. The craft moved swiftly through the deep water as she steered towards the surface. When we broke through the surface, it was as if our Earth was saying goodbye with the most spectacular sky. Reds, oranges and pink hues splashed the sky, and it was spectacular. I tried to take in every single detail, knowing it was the last, and I knew even before James wiped my tears that they were flowing freely down my face. We were soon flying with the beautiful colors behind us, and as we flew to the main crafts; all of us were holding or touching another for comfort.

When we arrived back to the main craft, there were no other crafts in sight, and as we flew into the large hanger, we could see all the smaller crafts lined up. Everyone was disembarking and being led away by the angels in small groups. Christik landed our craft, and none of us spoke as the door opened, and we all stepped onto the deck. I don't think any of us knew what to do or how to feel at that point. When Christik and the elders disembarked the craft, they all began to glide towards the exit and, like a herd of sheep, we all followed.

The angels led us down the long pearlescent corridor behind all the people who were being shown to their new quarters. Everyone was going to have to share living quarters, but it was probably a good thing. We needed each other more than ever now. The further down the corridor we got, the fewer people there were, and before long, we were nearing the main control center, and there was only our group left.

When we entered the control room, we could feel that the angels were all on high alert. Here and there, red flashing lights appeared, and every time they did, an image would appear on the large shimmering glass window in front of all the consoles. Images of earthquake tremors and the carnage they caused were being shown as if we were watching a movie. Once bustling cities were now crumbled, smoking ruins with huge cracks ripping through them. The healed trees and shrubs were all uprooted, and our only condolence was that there were no animals still on land. Christik led us all through the middle of the consoles to the huge glass window.

"All of your people have been evacuated; it is time to leave," she stated.

It was as if my heart sunk all the way down to my toes.

"What about the Marilians who are still down there?" James asked her.

"I know that they caused this, James," Christik said, and she waved at the carnage on the huge glass window, "However, we have already picked the survivors up. It is not in our nature to leave the helpless, even if they are to blame."

James didn't say another word, only nodding in agreement. As much as I hated what the Marilians had done, I didn't feel any hate towards them either at that moment, even though we should, and I think it was because we knew that most Marilians actually started out as another race before they were changed. Most Marilians hadn't had a choice about being who they were.

"Maybe Mel can try and heal the Marilians when you are all settled. I am sure that many of them would appreciate being turned back to their own kind and being sent to their home worlds," Christik said softly.

It was a lovely thought, and I was abruptly hopeful that I could save them.

THE MARILIANS

"Christik, we need to go now," an angel called from his lit-up console.

The glass wall cleared to show the scene from below the main craft, and it was scary as hell. Obviously, we couldn't feel the earthquakes that were happening below, but we could suddenly feel pressure in the air and also a vibration again. All of us had our eyes glued to the images. It was as if the rocks and the earth beneath the surface were bursting up through the surface of the Earth's crust. Red hot lava exploded up out of the large cracks that were forming, creating geysers of fire. If it wasn't happening to our planet, then I think we all would have been in awe, but it was happening to our planet, and it was dying before our eyes.

"Head for home now!" Christik commanded as another fiery geyser exploded far too close for comfort.

Abruptly, all the angels around us began to push their buttons and move their dials. Suddenly, we were moving fast; the main craft shot forward and upwards towards the sky. It felt bizarre that the ground was now a reflection of the fiery colors of the sky. My heart sank again as we flew away, and I felt James' strong arms wrap around me, pulling me close to his chest.

"We're going to be, ok, baby," he said gently next to my ear.

As the angels' main craft sped away from our dying planet, it felt like a piece of my heart was dying with it, and I wasn't the only one who felt that way either. The sadness and feeling of defeat in the main control room were heavy in the air, from the humans and the angels. As the craft flew higher, we could feel the shock waves of every eruption from the surface of our beloved planet as it was in its death throes. The angels' craft started to tilt and sway with the force, making us all hold on to the nearest consoles, next to the large glass window we were standing next too. The angels had to use their power to steady themselves too.

When I looked up to the huge window, I noticed that the sky was no longer variations of just reds and oranges, it was full of shades of blacks and greys from all the smoke that was now billowing from every direction too. Everything was burning from the fire and lava that was being forced up from the center of our planet, burning at such hot temperatures that everything wasn't just burning, but it was all being incinerated.

The higher and further away we flew; the less we could feel the strength of the destruction below. The craft wasn't swaying and tilting like before, and my eyes were just starting to see stars as we headed towards Earth's atmosphere. Within minutes, we were bursting from our planet's ozone layer and were in Earth's orbit. Through the massive glass window in front of us, I could see all the other main crafts coming from different directions to fall in line next to us. It was wonderful to see so many that had been all over our world.

"All crafts have been accounted for!" One of the female angels at the front consoles called out to Christik.

"That is good to hear," Christik said with a soft smile.

We stood next to the glass window, still glued to the changing images and clinging to each other. We watched in shock as our whole world became a mass of explosions, fracturing all over before finally exploding in one massive burst. The shockwave washed over the angels' crafts, shooting us forward even faster. As hard as we tried to steady ourselves, we couldn't keep our footing, and we were flown towards the nearest consoles. The closest angels acted quickly, catching us with their power before we crashed into their workstations.

When the craft began to steady to normal speed, the angels released us, allowing us to get back to our feet.

"Take us home," Christik told her angels with a dip of her head.

The angel then turned to us.

"Come, you all need to eat and drink something before you sleep," she urged.

We were all like walking zombies as we followed her, the elders and the angels back to the meeting room. As we took our seats at the table, not caring who sat next to whom, angels quickly flitted in with trays of food and drinks. Seeing the steaming hot coffee and honey did raise my spirits a little, and I hoped that it would warm my soul. None of us really felt like eating, but we knew that we needed to get our strength back up. Thinking of my baby girl, who'd been quiet for quite a while, I forced myself to eat some food as well as the coffee and juice.

I must admit, I did feel better once I started to eat, and my family and friends began to follow suit. There wasn't much conversation between us as we sat around the table. We didn't know what to say or how to feel.

"I know you have broken hearts, and you feel the loss of your friends and planet, but the universe always has a reason for the things that happen," Evest said softly.

More than one person looked at Evest as if to say, '*are you fricking kidding me*. The elder looked on them with compassion and kindness in his eyes.

"The Longs went through what you are experiencing right now. They will also help you get through this," he assured us. There are more planets than you can possibly imagine. We will help you find a new home."

"I can't even imagine living on a new planet," Trudy said quietly, "I've never been interested in astronomy, so I haven't got a clue."

Evest gave Trudy a warm smile as he stood from his seat at the end of the table.

"Let me show you," he told her warmly.

CHAPTER 23

Like we'd seen before, the elder raised his hands, and both of his palms started to glow. There, in the center of the large wooden table, images began to form. At first, I thought we were looking at our Milky Way, but as more planets and billions of stars appeared, it started to look like a whole universe.

"The universe is limitless," Lindaz said, as her husband began to zoom in one direction to another.

The solar systems were all various sizes and colors, with more stars than I thought was possible. Every so often, Evest would zoom in on a planet to show us. Some looked hostile like the Marilian's planet they'd shown us, while others looked beautiful and inviting. With our slightly renewed energy levels, we began to be more with it and started to Ooo and Ahh at the planets that were being shown to us, making the angels smile.

"I don't see any water on these planets or any suns near them," James said as he watched.

"Not all water is the same color as Earth's, James," Evest replied, "and not all suns are yellow. Every planet, sun and star are unique as they have all been through individual changes.

297

"I suppose that makes sense," James admitted; "It's hard to imagine grass being red or oceans being orange," he added with a smile.

"When we find a planet that you can all thrive on, you will adjust to your new home. Just as the Longs adjusted and thrived on our planet," Christik told us.

Evest showed us so many different planets and solar systems that I was beginning to see stars, even when I blinked my tired eyes. I was ready for my bed, and I still wanted to see our son. I wanted him out of the blue bubble capsule and back to normal as quickly as possible. I don't know if Evest picked up on what I was thinking.

"I believe that you have probably all seen enough for now. You all need to sleep and recover," Evest said gently as the images disappeared, and his palms began to dim.

"Thank you for showing us," Trudy told him, everyone else agreed and rose from their seats.

As everyone started to leave, Lindaz glided towards James and me.

"Can you stay a moment, please?" She asked quietly.

The kids all turned to look, and their poor faces were drained.

"Go back to our rooms, darlings; we'll be there soon," I assured them.

They were so tired that not one of them tried to argue. They left quietly following Nalik and Holly. After everyone else had gone, Evest and Christik glided over to the three of us. Lindaz reached forward, and she took my hand.

THE MARILIANS

"I know how desperate you are to have your son back. I also know how exhausted you are, so we are going to help you," she said as she held my surprised gaze.

My heart suddenly felt lighter, and I smiled in gratitude. Without any warning, Lindaz flitted us to a large holding room. There were many people, men and women who were contained inside the blue bubble capsules. I hadn't realized how many I'd tried to help. I scanned the room, but it was hard to see clearly from a distance. I couldn't feel anything from any of the people inside their bubbles. Christik glided across the room, stopping at a slighter longer capsule. I should have realized that it was Anthony when I was looking because he was so tall, but I still wasn't really thinking straight.

We walked over to them both, and I peered inside the blue fluid. Just like what happened to Kay, the capsule had halted Anthony's change. My heart began to pump harder in my chest as my emotions became stronger. Lindaz and Evest glided either side of me, both of them placing a hand on my shoulder, while Christik placed both of her hands on my shoulder blades. Immediately, I felt their power seeping into my body, and our daughter began to turn and kick.

I trusted my baby, the angels and myself, raising my hands out to our son. The power within me was immense, supercharged by the angels, and I released it on Anthony. It burst free from my hands, connecting with the blue bubble, and the chain reaction began as before. Ripples began to appear, rapidly changing into waves, and I stared at Anthony, watching as the change was reversed. I couldn't see his eyes changing back as they were closed, but his fingernails started to turn from the silver metal back to human, and the dark coarse hair seemed to absorb back into his body. Before long, the waves were so turbulent that I couldn't see anything anymore.

As soon as his change back to fully human was complete, the feeling of the power changed inside me. The fluid reached for me, and I allowed it to flow back into my body with ease. Anthony began to slowly sink to the ground as the bubble thinned, and within minutes, he was lying motionless on the floor still covered in blood. The gashes across his chest had started to bleed again the moment he was free from his containment. I'd never seen our son looking so beaten and cut up.

The elders and Christik acted quickly, gliding forward and kneeling around his body. James and I watched with racing pulses as the angels released their power into our boy. He looked completely lifeless, but we soon realized that the angels were healing him. First, the bleeding appeared to slow down and then stop altogether. Then we could see the cuts all over his face, arms and hands begin to close as his bruising faded.

Anthony's fingers were beginning to twitch, and my heart started to match my pulse when he opened his eyes. Slowly and surely, our son was being put back together, inside and out. Christik must have known as soon as he was conscious.

"Be still Anthony, we are healing you," she told him softly.

Our son began to move his head as he tried to look around.

"Mom, Dad, Christine?" He called out in a croaky voice.

'*Holy hell, Christine!*' I thought. I'd been so busy worrying about my family that I'd forgotten that Christine had been with her dad fighting. '*Shit!*'

"We are here, son, let the angels heal you, ok," James told him as he turned to me.

James shrugged his shoulders, indicating that he didn't know if Christine was alright either. My hand went straight to the com on my chest. '*Christine, are you ok, darling?*' I asked, hoping and praying that I would get an answer. '*Christine, are you ok?*' I reached out again with a little more force.

'*I'm ok,*' she said quietly, '*my dad is gone, and I didn't even get to tell him goodbye.*'

My heart was breaking for her as she said the words. '*Are you with anyone right now?*' I asked gently.

'*Yes, Shawn and Luiza are with me, and Livik.*'

I was so relieved that she was ok, devastated, but ok. I was also relieved that she hadn't been alone '*Would you like to stay with them for now, or would you like to be with Anthony?*' I asked.

There was no reply for a moment as she thought about what she wanted. '*I need Anthony, please.*' It was the response that I was expecting.

'*Christik and her parents are just about finished healing him, my darling*' I told her, '*Why don't you ask Livik to bring you here, and then you can stay with us. Would that be ok?*'

There was no delay in her answer this time. '*Yes and thank you, Mel.*'

I felt the connection break, and within a few minutes, Livik appeared with Christine on her arm, shivering from the flit. The moment Christine saw Anthony on the floor being healed by the angels, she rushed over to our son, dropping to her knees.

"OMG, Antony, are you ok?" she asked with worry in her voice.

Anthony's head turned as soon as he heard his girlfriend's voice.

"I'm ok now, honey," he told her with a stronger voice. "I was cut quite bad and partly changed, but my mom healed me."

301

Her face took a look of sheer horror.

"You started to change into one of them?" She involuntarily shrieked.

"Do not worry, Christine, we cannot feel anything of the Marilians anymore. Your one is close to being fully healed," Christik told her as she continued to let her power heal our boy.

"Thank you," she told the angel, before turning to face Anthony again, "Anthony, my dad, he's gone."

Her voice broke with the words that were full of pain and loss. It was horrible to see the pain in her young face. I would have given anything to have been able to bring her dad back to her. I'm sure our son felt the same way. I could tell by his expression that he shared her pain, and I knew that he'd really liked her dad.

"What happened?" Anthony asked her gently.

Christine began to tremble as she began to relive the recent memory. Without saying a word, Lindaz placed one of her hands-on Christine's thigh, helping her through her internal anguish.

"When the big ship came and shot the black thing out, me and my dad got trapped down a side street with Livik. There were four Marilians fighting us, and Livik did her best to protect us, but my dad got slashed across the neck. Livik couldn't heal him without putting me in danger," Christine whimpered, "It wasn't Livik's fault. My dad bled out within seconds, and as soon as Livik knew he was gone, she flitted me out of there."

Anthony squeezed her hand gently.

"I'm so, so sorry, honey," he told her softly.

By then, all four of us had tears streaming down our faces. Livik came along side me, and when I looked at her, her guilt was evident.

"You did the right thing," I told her, "Her dad would have wanted you to protect her at all costs."

Livik dipped her head and then turned back to look at Christine, Anthony and the angels.

It was a few hours later that we arrived back at our rooms with Anthony and Christine. Our son was fully healed, and we were all relieved but totally exhausted. There wasn't any sound from the kids, and I knew that they wouldn't be waking anytime soon, especially now we all knew that the Marilian threat was now over. Before we could even think about climbing into bed, we all needed to shower and get cleaned up.

James opened the barrier between our rooms, so Anthony and Christine could use the kids' bathroom and get ready for bed. My sweet husband led me to our own bathroom, carefully removing the empty holsters from my torso and my thighs. I was so drained that I was beyond grateful he was helping me. I wasn't hurt, but I felt bruised all over, and I'd used muscles in the battle that I didn't know I had.

"If I wasn't so dead tired, I think I could be very turned on right now," James said, as he removed the large knife and sheath that I hadn't used from around my ankle.

"Trust you to think about sex right now," I chuckled.

My husband gave me his sexy smirk as he pulled off the combat top I was wearing. I'd never felt so dirty and grimy. Everything I had on was covered with dirt and blood, human and Marilian. Within minutes, I was completely naked, and when I looked down at my body, my skin was just as dirty as the combat gear I'd been wearing.

James quickly stripped off, too, and I didn't have the energy to help him. He led me to the shower, and when the fresh water hit my skin; it was heavenly. We both stood under the water for a few minutes, savoring the feeling of the water washing away the battle and the monsters we'd fought.

"Turn around, baby," James said softly.

I didn't argue. I turned around with my back to my husband, and I let him gently massage and wash everything away. By the time he'd finished and washed himself, I was totally spent.

When we got back to the main room, fresh but tired, Anthony was at the table with Christine huddled next to him.

"I know you probably don't feel like it, but you both need to eat and drink something," I told them with a small smile.

I was pleased when they both began to reach for some food as James and I sat down to join them.

"Christine, you can stay with us for as long as you like, ok. You're part of our family too," I told her as she popped some strawberries into her mouth.

"Thank you," she replied after she swallowed her mouthful.

We ate and drank the rest of the spread in silence, just content to be in each other's company. After Anthony and Christine closed the barrier to the kids' room, James and I collapsed onto our bed. It had never felt so good. Within seconds of James wrapping his arms around me, I fell into the deepest sleep I think I'd ever had.

When I finally woke up, I felt stiff and still sore. My muscles ached as if I'd been in a triathlon. James was no longer in the bed, and when I looked around for him, I saw him in one of the comfy seats by the small table, already eating breakfast.

"Hi, badass wife of mine," he said with a grin.

"Hi, Rambo," I said with a smile, "Is it still morning? I feel like I've slept for a week."

"I've got no clue, baby, there's no way to tell," James said as he pointed to the circular window in our room.

There was no sign of the kids as I slid out of our bed and made my way to the window. As I walked past my husband, I kissed him on his neck, and he handed me a much-needed coffee. There was no light coming from the thick glass window, and all I could see were billions of stars. It was mind-blowing.

"I can't believe that we're in space. It just doesn't seem real," I said breathlessly.

James rose from his seat to join me at the window, wrapping his strong arms around my bump. Our daughter began to kick against his open palms.

"It doesn't feel real to me either. I stood next to that window for ages when I first woke up too," he said. It's certainly going to be a new adventure, isn't it."

We stood there for ages, watching the stars pass us by, not really believing what we were seeing. It was quite a while before the kids all started to wake and make their way out of their room for breakfast. By the time Anthony and Christine got up, the rest of us were showered, dressed and fed.

Holly and Nalik arrived as Anthony and Christine went off to get their showers, and they took seats at the table to join us. After asking how they were feeling and how they'd slept, James asked the most difficult question.

By Beth Worsdell

"How many people did we lose, Nalik?"

The angel lowered his head in sadness, not wanting to say as he knew how upset we'd be. When he finally looked up to James, his sadness was clear to see in his eyes.

"I am afraid that we lost eighteen percent of your population, James," he said quietly.

It didn't sound like a large amount, but when you considered how few of us were left, it was a large chunk of our population. It also meant that there were going to be many children without parents and many more single parents than before.

"We are going to have to make sure that there are no children left alone. There will be many children and adults, who are going to need a lot of love and support from everyone," I told the angel.

Nalik nodded his head in agreement.

"Christik and the elders would like you to join them, after you have all been thoroughly checked over, in the medical room," he told us.

Once Anthony and Christine were dressed and ready to go, we made our way to the medical room together.

When we arrived, there was a steady flow of people coming out, men and women of all ages, and they looked surprisingly good. We saw a seating area with people waiting, and we took the empty seats that were available. It certainly felt more like a doctor's waiting room this time. There were rows and rows of beds, occupied by other survivors, all being treated by blue-haired and winged healer angels. We watched patiently as the angels used their power to scan their patients for injuries and healed them.

It wasn't long before it was our turn, and we were led to some empty beds. I really felt like I needed a crane to lift me into the bed. Not only was my bump beginning to be cumbersome, but my muscles were so sore that I really didn't want to use them. As I struggled to get on the bed, another angel came over to help. When I looked up, I was pleased to see that it was Zanika.

"You know that you should not have been in the battle, do you not," Zanika said with a smile.

I raised an eyebrow at her words of gently scolding.

"Do you really think I would have let my family fight without me, Zanika?" I asked.

"I think it would have taken more than the Marilians to stop you being in battle with your family, Mel," she replied with a smirk. "Lay back please."

I laid myself on the bed using my elbows, and it felt good to be able to relax my muscles again. The first angel glided away, leaving me in Zanika's capable and glowing hands. Starting at the top of my head, Zanika slowly moved her glowing hands over my body, checking and healing me. I felt the tension and soreness melt away as her power flowed into my body, and it was heavenly. All the tightness in my neck and shoulders released, and the relief was huge.

When she got to my bump, she took her time, making sure that my daughter was ok. While she continued down my body, I looked either side of me to see what was happening with my family. One by one, they were finished and were making their way towards the exit to wait for me and James. My husband was done by the time Zanika was finishing at my feet, and he walked over to join us.

"How are my ladies doing, Zanika?" He asked with a smile.

"Your wife is healed from her brushing James, and your daughter is perfect," she replied, "Would you like to see?" She asked.

James nodded with wide eyes before calling the kids over to join us. Zanika used her power to raise the top of my bed, not wanting me to miss out on seeing my new daughter. Once I was sat more upright, she moved one of her hands over the top of my bump, while holding out her other hand with her palm facing up towards the ceiling.

We watched with anticipation as both of her hands began to glow, and the image of our new baby appeared before us. We were all amazed at the clear image in front of us and the details we could see. Our baby had tight, dark blonde curls all over her head, just like our other children had had when they were born, and her eyelashes were pale and long. Her skin was still covered in the waxy vernix that protected her, and she had the cutest little nose and mouth.

As we watched her, it was as if she knew, and she kicked a little leg out, and a smile appeared on her small, round angelic face. The kids were all full of ahhhs as they watched their new sibling.

"Look at her wings, they are beautiful," Holly said in awe.

Our new daughter did have beautiful wings, and they were neatly folded behind her back. We could make out her small feathers, all neatly lined against each other, the tips of the feathers floating in the fluid.

"I wonder if our baby will look like my new sister, "Holly said quietly.

"What, I'm going to be a grandpa?" James squealed.

"We're going to be grandparents?" I asked, with a huge smile on my face.

Holly was grinning from ear to ear, with her suddenly glowing angel husband at her side.

"Apparently so," Holly said, still grinning, "We've just been told by the angel who checked me over."

"OMG, we're going to be aunts and uncles too," Abigail said, as she cheered and clapped her hands.

My heart felt uplifted, and it was just the sort of news that was going to help us all heal from our loss.

"Our child could be the first human to be born on our planet, depending on how quickly it takes us to find you a new home," Nalik said.

"We are so happy for you both," I told them.

I had to speak for James because although he was still grinning like an idiot, he was in shock. It suddenly became very real for him that his baby girl was going to be a mother. James nodded at my words. Zanika's hands began to dim as the image of our daughter disappeared. I wasn't disappointed as I knew we'd be able to hold her in our arms soon.

"We will be able to see your baby soon enough," Zanika told Holly and Nalik.

"I will be able to check on our child, anytime that Holly wants," Nalik said proudly.

"Ok family, help me off this bed, so I can hug my daughter, please," I asked.

I wasn't feeling stiff or sore anymore, but it was still a challenge with my bump getting bigger. James and the boys helped me off the bed, and the moment my feet hit the floor, I reached for my daughter. I hugged Holly so tightly, and within seconds, we were all having another family group hug.

"Ok, I need to breathe, family," Holly giggled.

All our children and Christine congratulated Holly and Nalik. The angel glowed the whole time, especially every time the word baby was said.

We all felt a lot more lighthearted and positive as we walked to the large meeting room. When we bumped into Tracey and Akhenaten on our way, Nalik couldn't wait to share their happy news. We were still talking about babies when we arrived.

There were many people in the meeting room, and it was basically our original group, minus John of course. Many of our angel friends were there too. Christik was at the head of the table, and after we took our seats, she rose from her chair.

"Thank you all for coming this afternoon. We are very pleased to see you all here and that you are all healed," she said warmly. "We lost many lives during the battle, and I am sorry that you have lost more friends and family. My angels collected as many of the dead as possible, so we can give them appropriate burials."

Christine gasped and place a hand over her mouth, fighting to control the sobs that were now trying to escape her. Anthony quickly held her in his arms to comfort her.

"I believe your father is one of them, Christine," the angel told her gently. "It will be up to you and the others whether they are buried on our planet or on your new home. You will have time to decide."

Christine couldn't speak, but she nodded her head at Christik's words.

"What are we going to do about the children who've lost their parents and the no single parents, or the adults who are alone now?" I asked the angel.

"Please do not worry, Mel. My angels are already actively trying to place children with new adopted parents. They are also encouraging single mothers or fathers to pair up with other parents who are in the same situation. The same is being done for people who are now alone."

"I can vouch for that," Tracey added. "Akhenaten and I are adopting three kids from the same family who have lost their mom in the battle. We're collecting them after the meeting."

I could feel Tracey's happiness at the thought of being a mom again, with sadness that they'd lost their one and only parent. The kids were going to be very lucky to have such amazing new parents.

"Our plan now is simple," Christik continued, "we will take you all to our own planet, while we try and locate a new world for your race. While en route, Mel will help us heal the survivors she contained and hopefully change back the Marilians we captured. If that is ok," she added as she looked at me with a smile.

"Sounds like a plan to me," I answered enthusiastically.

"What are we going to do with the Marilians once they've been changed back into whatever they were before?" Harrison asked politely.

Murmurs went around the room, and everyone began to wonder what the Marilians could really be.

"It will be tricky," Lindaz said, adding to the conversation. "The Marilians we have captured could be from anywhere in the universe. There will be no telling what kind of planet they could be from."

"We will have to put them in Mel's capsules until we know if they can survive on this craft. We do not want to lose any more lives," Evest added.

"Ok, let's get this show on the road," I said with a grin.

Thank you for reading. I can't wait to read your Amazon and Goodreads reviews. You can leave your reviews here-
Amazon
Goodreads

"A New World" book three in the Earth's Angels trilogy is coming soon…...

ABOUT BETH WORSDELL

Beth Worsdell is an English born author, who has lived in America since 2011 with her husband and four children. Beth loves to spend time with her family and their two golden doodles.

Writing is something Beth has always had a passion for. Beth began to write poetry as a child into adulthood, which turned into songwriting in 2007 when Beth was writing a poem, and the melody began to form in her mind.

Beth has written many songs over the years, writing about love, life and all the shenanigans in between. However, for the last couple of years, her focus has been on completing the Earth's Angels Trilogy.

By Beth Worsdell

Don't forget to follow Beth on her author pages, social media pages and join her angels on her website www.bethworsdellauthor.com Beth has regular giveaways, so keep updated.

Want to get featured on Beth's website? Send Beth a photo of yourself with your copy of her book, eBook or paperback, and send it to her via her social media or website.

Don't forget to tag Beth in your Earth's Angels, The Marilians or A New World posts, as it makes her smile, and she loves to share.

Leave your Earth's Angels and The Marilians book reviews on Amazon and Goodreads today. Let other bookworms read your feedback.

#BeAnEarthAngel

LINKS

https://www.bethworsdellauthor.com/
https://www.facebook.com/BethWorsdellAuthorFantasyFiction/
https://www.facebook.com/EarthsAngelsTrilogy/
https://twitter.com/bethworsdell
https://twitter.com/EarthsAngelsNo1
https://www.instagram.com/bethworsdell/
https://www.instagram.com/earthsangelsbookno1/
https://www.youtube.com/channel/UCspTifrWrB3jsieleiN3-bw

Author Pages

https://www.amazon.com/Beth-Worsdell/e/B07JG9RYGN

https://www.goodreads.com/author/show/18523294.Beth_Worsdell

https://allauthor.com/author/bethworsdell/

https://booksprout.co/author/7141/beth-worsdell

https://www.bookbub.com/authors/beth-worsdell

By Beth Worsdell

THE MARILIANS

Printed in Great Britain
by Amazon